THE COREY FORD SPORTING TREASURY

"The past never changes. You leave it and go on to the present, but it is still there, waiting for you to come back to it."

Corey Ford — *The Road to Tinkhamtown*

THE

Corey Ford Sporting Treasury

Minutes of the "Lower Forty" and Other Treasured Stories Written by Corey Ford

Compiled and edited by Chuck Petrie

With an introduction by
James W. "Doc" Hall, III, M.D.

WILLOW CREEK PRESS

Minocqua, Wisconsin

The contents of this volume have been previously published in YOU CAN ALWAYS TELL A
FISHERMAN, UNCLE PERK'S JUG and THE BEST OF COREY FORD. Except as noted the
pieces first appeared in *Field & Stream*. Copyright 1953, 1954,
© 1955, 1956, 1957,1958 by Henry Holt & Co. Copyright © 1961, 1962, 1963, 1964, 1965,1966,
1967 by Holt, Rinehart & Winston, Inc. Copyright renewed 1981, 1982, 1983, 1984, 1985, 1986
by S. John Stebbins and Hugh Grey.
"Just A Dog," copyright 1941 by Corey Ford.
"A Dialogue for Autumn," originally published as "If They Could Only Talk" by Corey Ford and
Sidney Hayward; copyright 1952 by Corey Ford and Sidney Hayward; copyright renewed 1980
by S. John Stebbins and Hugh Grey. "The Road to Tinkhamtown," copyright © 1970 by Holt,
Rinehart & Winston, Inc.
"You Can Always Tell A Fisherman" appeared in *The Saturday Evening Post* under the title "The
World's Fussiest Sport;" copyright © 1958 by The Curtis Publishing Company; copyright renewed
1986 by S. John Stebbins and Hugh Grey. "How To Guess Your Age" reprinted from *Collier's*,
copyright, 1949, by Corey Ford; copyright renewed 1976 by S. John Stebbins and Hugh Grey.
The foreword from HAS ANYBODY SEEN ME LATELY? is copyright © 1958 by Corey Ford;
copyright renewed 1986 by S. John Stebbins and Hugh Grey. "The Time of Laughter," from the
book of the same title, is copyright © 1967 by Corey Ford

Printed in the U.S.A

ISBN# 1-57223-002-9
(Previous ISBN# 0-932558-37-2)

Published by   Willow Creek Press
               Outlook Publishing
               PO Box 881
               Minocqua, WI 54548

Cataloging-in-Publication Data

Ford, Corey, 1902-1969
  The Corey Ford Sporting Treasury

  1. Hunting stories, American. 2. Fishing stories,
American. I. Petrie, Chuck. II. Title.
PS3511.03935C6 1987
813'.54   87-2202

CONTENTS

FOREWORD

Millions of readers of *Field & Stream* magazine remember the late Corey Ford's monthly column, "The Minutes of the Lower Forty." Two generations of readers were treated to the diabolical antics of the members of the Lower Forty Shooting, Angling and Inside Straight Club, who held their meetings in — and usually centered their activities around — the fictional yet not-so-imaginary rural town of Hardscrabble, USA.

The club members — Doc Hall, Judge Parker, Angus McNab, Colonel Cobb, Cousin Sidney, Dexter Smeed and a few select others — were then and are now personifications of fellow anglers and hunters known to all sportsmen. Meeting at fellow member Uncle Perk's hardware and dry goods store (Jno. Perkins, Prop., Guns & Fshng Tckle Bot Sold & Swopt) the organization hatched many a plot to advance its own aims — mainly to enhance the hunting and fishing opportunities of its members.

The club's archenemy, Deacon Godfrey; the local game warden, "Owl Eyes" Osborn; farmer Aldo Libbey — whose lower forty alder patch the club members often hunted (and from which the club derived its name) — Mink Brook; Moose Mountain . . . are names of people and places endeared to those who followed Corey Ford's "Lower Forty" column.

And now the town of Hardscrabble, USA, and its cast of lovable characters are back where they belong — in the hands of

Corey Ford fans. The major portion of *The Corey Ford Sporting Treasury*, Part I, is a collection of some of the author's best "Lower Forty" stories. It is preceded by an introduction by Doctor James W. Hall, a close friend who Ford characterized as Harscrabble's "Doc Hall."

Part II of the volume contains some of Ford's other well-known articles, some of which originally appeared in *Field & Stream*, *Colliers*, and *The Saturday Evening Post*. They are included in this volume because they are *not* "Lower Forty" stories — the stories with which most sportsmen connect Ford — but relate to the reader the author's skills as a serious writer as well as a humorist.

The third and final part of this book contains only one story: "The Road to Tinkhamtown." This short story is heralded by some as one of the finest pieces of outdoor literature ever written, and, once read, it is one that the reader will probably never forget.

Chuck Petrie

INTRODUCTION

I met Corey Ford upon entering Dartmouth College in the fall of 1951. I was introduced to him by Sidney Hayward, secretary of the college and the man who provided the inspiration for Corey's character "Cousin Sid" of the Lower Forty.

On the day of that memorable meeting, Hayward and I had driven east from Hanover — along a sparsely traveled highway flanked by flaming hardwoods, evergreens, and the imposing granite walls of New Hampshire's White Mountains — on our way to Corey's rugged timber-and-stone home at Freedom. There, Corey met us at the door in a tweed jacket and rumpled gray flannels, quizzically grinning around his pipe, his right eyebrow uniquely cocked, and with his English setter, Cider, at heel. He gripped my arm warmly, his gaze keenly locked into mine, and drew us to the massive fireplace in his den.

Thus began our friendship of eighteen years: surrounded by ceiling-high bookshelves and hunting trophies, listening to Corey's characteristically warm and penetrating conversation and hearing his infectious laugh, which trailed off into a giggle. Over those years our friendship was enriched by our hunting and fishing experiences; travel to Alaska and the Far East; and my living with him in Hanover while I attended the Dartmouth Medical School and assisted with research for his writing, all the while growing and pleasuring in his world of humor, knowledge, and widely varied friendships. Along the way, I acquired my nickname, "Doc Hall," assigned by him, also, to a character in "The Lower Forty Shooting, Angling and Inside Straight Club" columns he wrote for *Field & Stream*. Together, in 1952, we cooked up the idea for the Lower Forty while at the Red Dog Saloon, in Juneau, Alaska.

Corey Ford began his professional writing at Columbia University when he became editor of the humor magazine *The Jester*. This began his career of over forty years as a published author of screen writing, thirty books, and approximately 500 stories and articles in the major magazines of his time, including *The New Yorker*, *Saturday Evening Post*, *Colliers'*, *This Week*, *Vanity Fair*, *Reader's Digest*, and *Field & Stream*.

Corey based himself in New York at the Algonquin Hotel in the early twenties. During this period of explosive flowering of American literature, he associated with editor Harold Ross, E.B. White, Dorothy Parker, W.C. Fields (a close friend), Robert Benchley, Frank Sullivan (his roommate), Ogden Nash, F. Scott Fitzgerald, Edna Ferber, Ring Lardner and many other celebrated writers. His essay "The Time of Laughter" vividly chronicles this period. These formative years shared with his friends at "21," the Dutch Truth Club, Moriarty's, and other celebrity hangouts influenced Corey's literary growth, in the judgement of many critics, to become the preeminent voice of parody and satire in American journalism. John Riddle was the pen name he used for many of his early works.

Humor was Corey's original and sustaining genius. I remember him pointing out to me that the basis of all humor is really pain or misfortune — someone has to slip on the banana peel. However, his artistry with this was always unique and kindly. His skill was such that he never needed to resort to profanity or smuttiness for laughter in his writing, and this was typical of his conversation as well. Corey's perception of human foibles and hurtles was acute, and woe to persons or organizations exemplifying egotism, hypocrisy, greed, or pomposity when they were dissected and exposed by his scalpel-like pen!

Corey's scope broadened profoundly throughout his career, eventually encompassing history — World War II books (*Short Cut to Tokyo, War Below Zero,* and others) — the American Revolution (*A Peculiar Service*); biography (*Daughter of the Gold Rush*); outdoors (five books and hundreds of stories and articles); environmental concerns and nature (*The Biggest Bear On Earth, The Plunderers*, and many more); and man and dogs (*Every Dog Should Have A Man*). He knew these topics well and cared passionately for them.

Corey was an expert on Alaska. I accompanied him on some of his trips there, and once we flew with Clarence Rhodes, then chief of the territory's U.S. Fish and Wildlife Service, from southeastern Alaska to the Aleutians in his Grumman Goose, and were guests of Governor Greening and other central figures in Alaskan development. Frank Dufrense, the first game commissioner of the Alaska Territory, who worked by dog sled from Nome to Anchorage, and who later became a noted writer, was one of Corey's intimate friends.

As a student living with him in his 19th century colonial home in Hanover, I can clearly remember Corey's working. After we'd finished breakfast he would climb the stairs to his study and write all morning — with hard pencil and yellow legal pad, in his precise script. Returning after lunch, he then revised and edited all afternoon. Some of the time this would flow very smoothly, and at other times he might labor for weeks to get it just right. He loved the English language and was a perfectionist; the entire manuscript of his last novel received only one correction from his editor. I think his was the most completely personal and self-reliant type of work I have ever observed.

As author in residence at Dartmouth, Corey was surrounded by English majors and launched the humor magazine *The Jack-O-Lantern*. Corey lived in a man's world. He adopted Dartmouth students as his family, the college then being all male. He sponsored the rugby club and founded the boxing club, helping to train our pugilists in the gym at his home. His closest friends were writers, bird hunters, fly fishermen, outdoor photographers, dog trainers, conservationists, and men of travel and adventure. He deeply committed himself to his friendships, and his friends responded with deep attachment to him.

Conversations between Corey and his friends were stimulating, comfortable, and satisfying. He would listen carefully and perceptively to others' ideas, often bantering playfully with words, using his pipe as a baton to orchestrate the flow. He loved practical jokes and puns, and he often spiced our talk by inventing the first line of a limerick, requiring that we complete the rhyming.

Corey was a very private man outside his circle of close friends. He disliked public speaking and shunned personal publicity. He took a dim view of winter, skiing, baseball, "meat" hunters, television, large parties, mechanical gadgets, cats, and most politicians.

He had rigorous vitality. As a minor vanity, he wrote age "50" on his hunting licenses each fall. He was exceedingly generous, giving his professional advice to writers and financial support to his major interests. He anonymously donated his entire officer's salary (he was a colonel in the U.S. Army Air Corps from 1942 to 1945) to the Air Corps Relief Fund, primarily directed to widows of fallen pilots. We labeled his home "The Ford Foundation."

I always think of Corey as being the quintessential American sportsman: a self-reliant Yankee who loved the flex of a fine fly rod, the thrust of his 20-gauge Parker, and the flash of his English setter. Corey's beloved dog Cider, so named because he "worked in the fall," reflected his master's personality. Cider took a gentlemanly approach to hunting. He would archly survey the covers and independently work those that he chose at his own pace, savoring the whole experience of the hunt over the independent acts of pointing and retrieving.

Corey never cared much about the weight of his game pocket. To him it was the fine country, the *pursuit* of the bird or the trout, and the companionship of understanding friends that counted most. He loved and understood his quarry far more than he cared to make a kill, with a sensitivity that marked him a truly complete sportsman. Although he was equally at home in the literary world of New York or Hollywood, I knew he much preferred to be in the field.

Corey Ford profoundly enhanced my life, and he continues to do so when I reread his works. I wish you the stimulating experience of knowing him, also. So, join me in reliving his time. Let's slip into our game vests and case the shotguns. We'll drive past abandoned farms and stone walls and cross an old covered bridge up toward Moose Mountain, to a secret cover. Corey has cried "Hi on!" to the setter, tamped his pipe and begun a new limerick, "There was a young girl from Juneau . . . " Let's follow him toward the tag alders along Mink Brook.

James W. Hall, III, M.D.
December, 1986
Medford, Oregon

PART I

CONSTITUATION OF THE LOWER FOURTY

The annual election meeting of the Lower Forty Shooting, Angling and Inside Straight Club was held in the rear of Perkins' Sporting Goods Store, because that was where the members happened to be gathered when Judge Parker brought up the question of new candidates for the Club. His suggestion presented some rather unexpected problems. In the first place, the members discovered, there wasn't any Nominating Committee to propose the candidates for membership. In the second place, the Club's Constitution didn't provide any rules for electing them even if they were nominated, because in the third place, as it turned out, there wasn't any Constitution.

"This is a very serious situation," the Judge informed his fellow members, scowling over his spectacles in his best judicial manner. "How are we ever going to take any more members into the Lower Forty?"

"What do we want any more members for?" asked Doc Hall, who was still smouldering because Judge Parker had not only snagged a two-pound squaretail right out from under his nose in

Mink Brook yesterday, but also because the Judge had taken it on a spinner. "As far as I'm concerned," he remarked, leaning against the counter and directing a baleful glance at his partner, "we've got more members than we need right now."

"We've got to do something," Cousin Sid insisted. "Let's draw up an official set of rules and bylaws, and everybody can follow them."

"Why not let each member make his own rules," Colonel Cobb suggested, "and follow them himself?"

Judge Parker rapped for attention on Uncle Perk's glass showcase. "In view of my own not inconsiderable legal experience and training," he offered modestly, "I'll be glad to serve as chairman of the Rules Committee." He beamed at his fellow members. "Now, then, does anybody have some good rules to suggest?"

"I pr-r-ropose," said Mister MacNab promptly, "that we abolish all dues."

"There aren't any dues," Cousin Sid reminded him.

Mister MacNab's face fell. "In that case," he countered, "I pr-r-ropose having dues, so then we can abolish them and save all that money."

"Any other suggestions?" Judge Parker asked.

Doc Hall gave a dark look at the Judge. "I'd like to propose a rule against using spinners in Mink Brook."

"If we pass a rule like that," Judge Parker replied, bristling, "I'd like to propose another rule against putting a chunk of grasshopper on the barb of a dry-fly hook."

"I just happened accidentally to snag a grasshopper on my first cast," Doc retorted hotly, "and what's more, if you're going to get personal, how about a rule against sneaking down at night with a pitchfork to Farmer Libbey's manure pile and—"

"Now, then, boys," Uncle Perk interrupted hastily, pulling out his lower desk drawer and pouring a jug of Old Stump Blower on the troubled waters, "let's forget about rules for the time being, and git on to somethin' else."

"Personally I think we ought to have an official Club emblem," Cousin Sid offered enthusiastically. "We could get Walt Dower to design us a coat of arms, for instance, like a ten-pound rainbow rampant on a broken rod, with one hand on a Bible and the other hand upraised. Then maybe if we could think of an appropriate Latin motto about fishing—"

"How about *carpe diem?*" Dexter Smeed suggested.

Judge Parker shook his head as the suggestion was thrown out, followed by Dexter Smeed. "The first thing we need around here," commented the Judge, "is somebody to call this meeting to order." He cleared his throat. "In choosing the president of the Lower Forty," he began, "we must look to a man who is obviously the outstanding sportsman among the members, a man who possesses a thorough knowledge of firearms and ballistics as well as a mastery of the bamboo rod, a man who not only can take the biggest trout of the season in Mink Brook—" He paused patiently until Doc's strangled protests had subsided "—but whose uncanny skill with a shotgun can score a double in grouse while one of his fellow members is still fumbling to put the shells in his barrels—" He glanced over his spectacles at Colonel Cobb, who reddened slightly "—and who in addition is so expert with a rifle that he can shoot from the hip at two hundred yards, and drop a running deer which another one of his fellow members has just missed cold—" He cast a significant glance at Cousin Sid "—a man, in short, whose sterling qualities of character and leadership—"

"If you're going to be president of this Club," Doc broke in, leaping to his feet, "I'm resigning from the Lower Forty right now."

"You can have my resignation as well," said Colonel Cobb, descending from his perch on Uncle Perk's counter with a heavy thud. "I'm against all these rules and regulations. Nobody's going to tell me what to do, even if I want to do it."

"As a matter of fact, I resign, too," added Cousin Sid. "I'm tired of cleaning all the fish that everybody else catches, let alone cooking them and then washing the dishes afterwards."

"I shouldna wish to be the only member," Mister MacNab sighed, reaching for his hat. "There'd be nobody around to fur-r-rnish free refreshments."

"Wait a minute, boys," Uncle Perk pleaded, "before we fly off the handle." He waved the jug of Old Stump Blower to lure the indignant members back. "Why don't we work out a simple Constitution that we can all agree on? Mebbe somethin' like this."

He set an ancient typewriter on his desk, inserted a piece of brown wrapping paper, and began to tap the keys one by one with a stubby forefinger. The members watched over his shoulder as he wrote:

CONSTITUATION OF THE LOWER FOURTY

Artickle One: Rules.

They ain't no rules.

Artickle Two: President.

Everybody's President.

Artickle Three: Membership.

If ennybody else wants to join this Club, go ahead, but don't bother us about it. We've went fishing.

Uncle Perk pulled the sheet from the typewriter triumphantly.

"I hereby move that this here Constitution be filed away someplace where nobody can remember where we put it," he said. "Meantime I seen an old lunker under the Hardscrabble Bridge this morning, and any you fellers that want to are welcome to come along and watch me catch it."

The election meeting of the Lower Forty promptly adjourned *sine die*.

FLY TYING
MADE EASY

The regular February meeting of the Lower Forty Shooting, Angling and Inside Straight Club was given over to tying trout flies, because, after all, next month would be March and then it would be April and after that May would be here; so it really wasn't any too soon to get a few flies ready for Opening Day. The meeting was held at Cousin Sid's home, so the other members wouldn't get their own houses all littered up.

Judge Parker opened the session by reading a few excerpts from a manual entitled "Fly Tying Made Easy," which the Judge's wife had given him for Christmas. "The basic principle of fashioning a trout fly," he began, holding the book at arm's length in order to make out the fine print, "is to create a likeness of the natural insect on the water. Trout feed on a varied diet including winged insects, grasshoppers, small crustaceans, hellgrammites, larvae, and nymphs, and the angler must imitate these as closely as possible."

"Anybody can imitate a nymph," Colonel Cobb shrugged, pouring himself a highball of Cousin Sid's best bourbon. "All he needs is five or six yards of cheesecloth, a pair of silver slippers, and a wand with a star on the end."

Judge Parker ignored the interruption. "Before attempting to tie a fly," he continued reading, "the angler should make a careful study of the living organisms in the stream he plans to fish. For this purpose, we recommend a long-handled dip net with a fine wire-mesh bag, which may be dragged along the bottom of the pool in order to collect a few specimens of the insect life in the water."

"Maybe he could collect a few trout while he's at it," Doc Hall suggested, lighting one of Cousin Sid's choice cigars, "and save himself all the trouble of tying a fly to catch them."

Judge Parker gave him a severe glance. "All the amateur requires are the essential tools such as a vise, magnifying glass, mirror, embroidery scissors, forceps, lance, buttonhook, fly-tying wax, cement, shellac, varnish, thread-clips, bobbin, bodkin—"

"What's a bodkin?" asked Dexter Smeed.

"It's a female bobbin," the judge said firmly, and resumed reading. "—as well as an assortment of various colored silk threads, worsted, hurl, wing feathers, and hackles." He inserted his forefinger in the book for a moment. "Personally I make it a point to visit the poultry show every spring," he confided to the Club. "You'd be surprised how you can improve your collection of hackles by strolling along past the wire pens and pilfering a few choice neck feathers when nobody is looking."

"I always buy my wife a new hat for Easter," Doc Hall recommended. "I pick it out for her myself, because I know just what feathers I need."

"I steal baby's bonnets," Colonel Cobb confessed, rubbing his hands and cackling, "and unravel them to get the worsted."

It was moved and seconded that the Club should borrow Cousin Sid's assortment of hackles for today's lesson, since it just so happened that none of the members had remembered to bring his own fly-tying materials along. Judge Parker volunteered to give a personal demonstration, since he had had considerable experience in the art. "After all," the Judge reminded them, "I am a fly fisherman of long standing."

"Sometimes he's stood for-r-r as long as two hours," Mister MacNab nodded to the club, "waiting to sneak into somebody else's pool."

"We'll follow the instructions carefully," Judge Parker began, setting the open manual on the table in front of him and backing off a couple of feet to see it better. "The first step is to place the hook in the vise, like this." He scowled at the diagram in the book. "On second thought, I guess it's the other end of the hook that goes in the vise. *There* we are." He adjusted his spectacles, and peered at the directions. "Now tighten the vise securely, and tie off the head of the hook with a whip-finish knot, as follows: Hold the end of the thread in place with the thumb of the right hand (A), spread a loop with the second and third fingers of the left hand (B), pass the spool of thread through the loop with the fourth and fifth fingers of the right hand (C), and pull it tight with the sixth finger of the third hand (D). Now, then, has anybody seen that spool of thread?"

"Here it is under the table," said Doc Hall.

"Thank you very much," Judge Parker said, mopping his forehead. "All you have to do is finish the knot by cutting off the end with a sharp knife like this. Well, I seem to have cut the wrong thread, but maybe if I sort of wind it around the hook a couple of times it will hold all right." He licked the perspiration from his lips. "The next step is to select a good hackle for the legs of the fly."

He opened the lid of the box, just as a gust of wind swept across the room, filling the air with feathers like a pillow fight in the nursery. Judge Parker glared at Dexter Smeed.

"I'm sorry," Dexter apologized, shutting the window again hastily, "it was getting kind of close in here."

Judge Parker snatched a feather that floated past him, and scowled at the directions. "Grasp the tip of the hackle firmly, and spread it by pulling the fibers against the grain back to the butt. Well, I must have pulled a little too hard that time, but I guess there's enough of it left to wind around the hook once or twice." He shook his head. "I don't understand why it keeps coming unwound again, but I'll just fix it with some of this cement here if I could . . . get this confounded . . . bottle open . . ." He held the bottle upside down and shook it. "The cork seems to be stuck or something."

"There isn't any cork," Doc Hall said.

"What? Oh. I guess you're right," Judge Parker murmured, gazing down ruefully at the puddle in his lap. "That's all right, I was planning to send this suit to the cleaners, anyway. Let's see, now, has anybody seen that hackle? That's funny, it must be somewhere. I had it right here a minute ago."

"What's that stuck to the seat of your pants?" asked Cousin Sid.

Judge Parker cleared his throat. "Well, actually the wings are the most important part of a dry fly," he said quickly, glancing again at the manual. "Select a good stout tail feather, yank out a couple of hunks of webbing, and arrange them side by side on the shank of the hook, holding them in place with the forefinger while tying them securely with a loop of thread." He gazed at the Club triumphantly. "Are there any questions?"

"How are you going to get your forefinger out again?" asked

Colonel Cobb.

It was unanimously resolved to adjourn the meeting to Uncle Perk's Sporting Goods Store, and pick out a few good trout flies for Opening Day. Cousin Sid promised to join the other members in a couple of hours, as soon as he got the mess in his living room straightened up again.

SHADRACH'S
STUFFED TROUT

At the next meeting of the Lower Forty Shooting, Angling and Inside Straight Club, it was announced that henceforth their regular sessions would be held in Perkins' Sporting Goods Store, inasmuch as Cousin Sid's wife had put her foot down and declared that there'd be no more Club get-togethers in her front parlor.

"I don't mind their stealing all the food out of the icebox," she had announced to Cousin Sid after the last all-night meeting. "I don't object to their spilling beer on the carpet, or burning cigarette holes in the davenport, or leaving muddy prints where they propped their boots on the sofa cushions. But when they pull all the colored yarn out of my Great-Aunt Hattie's knitted sampler to use for tying flies," she stated flatly, "it's time to call a halt."

Uncle Perk accepted the news with equanimity. "Don't guess it'll make much difference nohow," he shrugged, "seein' as how you're allus hangin' around here anyways." He pulled down the shades, bolted the front door, and hung a "Closed for Inventory" sign in the window. "Worst part of runnin' a store," he grumbled, taking a jug of Old Lightnin' Rod out of the lower left-hand drawer of his desk, "is the goldurn customers that keep droppin' in and interferin' with business."

Uncle Perk's store ("Guns & Fshng. Tckle., Bot Sold & Swopt") was in its usual state of comfortable disarray. Bamboo rods and shotguns were stacked along the walls, the counters were littered with shotgun shells and tangled bass plugs, and the room had a nostalgic smell of gun solvent and oiled leather and ripe pipe tobacco. Uncle Perk leaned back in his swivel chair, crossing a pair of high-top hunting rubbers on his cluttered desk, and fondled a .22 revolver, sighting it absently at a duck calendar on the opposite wall. "Man's got to keep his shootin' eye in," he murmured, "with gunnin' season only a few more months away."

Doc Hall tilted the dusty jug to his lips, and his eyes encountered the glassy eyes of a huge stuffed trout hanging above the desk. "Quite a fish you got there, Uncle Perk," he admired.

"Corker, ain't it," Uncle Perk nodded. "Went six 'n' three-quarters pounds, that's the biggest squaretail ever come out of Mink Brook. Reckon it's just about a record for these parts."

"What did you take it on?" Judge Parker asked.

"Oh, I didn't take that trout," Uncle Perk said. "I wisht I had. No, it was Shadrach Savery took it," he said, lowering his voice, "only don't let on I told you. Shad don't want nobody to know."

"I'd never quit bragging if I got a trout like that," Colonel Cobb said in surprise. "He can't be much of a fisherman."

"That's the sad part of it," Uncle Perk sighed. "Poor ole Shad, he's about the fishin'est fellow I ever see. He used to be out on the stream morning to night, an' he'd allus bring back his limit and one in his boot, but of course that was before he married Angie." He shook his head. "I never knew what possessed Shad to get married, unless it was one time he got kicked in the head by a horse. Sometimes getting kicked in the head by a horse is apt to make a man foolish. Seems Shad used to have a pet skunk, and one winter it died, and I guess he must have been lonely, because next spring he come into the store and told me he'd married Angie instead.

" 'Where are you going for your honeymoon?' I ast him.

" 'Wal, I thought of spending a couple of weeks fishing down to Maine,' he said, 'but Angie she wanted to go to Boston and see some shows, so we compromised,' he said. 'We're going to Boston.'

"I didn't see Shad around the store any more after that, but I began to hear a lot of rumors. Somebody said that Angie made him get rid of all his tackle and busted his rod and even give away all his fishing clothes, because she claimed that fishing was a waste of time. I couldn't believe it myself till I seen him. He was walking down the street with Angie, carrying an armload of groceries, and as he come past the store he turned his head and glanced at some trout flies I had in the window, and Angie said: 'Shadrach,' That's all she said. 'Shadrach.' Did you ever get a hornet down your waders? That's how Shad jumped, and he kep' on walking, and I broke out a jug of cider and we all had a drink to poor ole Shad, he was a nice feller when we knew him.

"It was about a month later that Shad come into the store. I don't mean he come right in, he hesitated outside and looked up and down the street both ways and then he sort of sidled through the door and scuttled over here where I'm setting now, and I could see he was so excited he was shaking all over. 'Perk,' he says to me, 'you know what happened?'

" 'Did Angie run off with a tonic salesman?' I ast him.

" 'No, it's better than that,' he says, 'I just seen the biggest honest-to-God old walloper of a trout I ever see in my life,' he

[15]

says, 'it must have drifted down out of the lake, and it's lying in the pool just below the bridge right now, and I wondered if I could borrow a rod because something seems to have happened to mine.'

" 'What will Angie say?' I ast him.

" 'She's to the Ladies' Aid meeting,' he says quickly, 'she won't be home till dark.'

"So I lent him an outfit, and he took off, and I waited till dark but he didn't come back. I was just getting ready to lock up for the night when he showed up. He was carrying something wrapped up in his coat, and he laid it on the counter, and I tell you, mister, I couldn't hardly believe it. 'It finally come to a Number-Twelve Fanwing Coachman,' Shad says proudly. 'All my life I been waiting to get a trout like that.'

" 'Congratulations, Shad,' I says, 'you'll have your pitcher in all the papers tomorrow.'

"His face went white. 'Don't ever let on to anybody I caught it,' he said, 'or it'll get back to Angie.' He reached in his pocket and took out the spending money that Angie let him keep out of his salary. 'Just have it mounted and keep it for me, will you, Perk?'

"So that's how I happen to have it hanging here. Now and then whenever he can sneak away from Angie, Shad likes to come into the store and admire it for awhile. He don't say nothin', just sets and looks up at it with a sort of a sad smile, and then he gets up and goes out again. I noticed a funny thing the last time he was in here. Him and that glass-eyed trout are getting to look like each other. I guess it's the kind of a look you get when you've been hooked."

Uncle Perk leaned back in his swivel chair, leveled the .22 revolver, and squeezed off a couple of rounds at the duck calendar on the wall. The bullets dug a hole in the plaster a few inches to one side.

"Never can remember to lead a duck enough," he grumbled. "Last year's calendar was a pheasant, and I could hit it every time."

THE ALIBI CUP

The regular October meeting of the Lower Forty Shooting, Angling and Inside Straight Club was held in Cousin Sid's hunting camp at Pleasant Lake. A vote of thanks was extended to Cousin Sid for coming back from the hunt early to get supper, and as a token of appreciation it was moved and seconded that he could do the dishes, too.

The first order of business was a report by the Admissions Committee, who said they'd been thinking of making Dexter Smeed a regular member of the Club. It was the feeling of the Committee that they might as well take him in because he came to all the meetings anyhow. Judge Parker admitted he didn't see much else they could do. "Besides, he's my wife's nephew," the Judge added morosely.

Cousin Sid objected because he claimed Dexter didn't know one end of a shotgun from the other. "The other day he asked me what bullets it took," he said, "and he thinks ballistics is a form of aesthetic dancing, and as far as being an outdoorsman is concerned, he doesn't know enough to come in out of the rain."

"Where's Dexter now?" asked Colonel Cobb.

"Out in the rain," said Cousin Sid.

"He's a dub," Doc Hall agreed. "Why, he doesn't even know how to bring a gun to his cheek, or mark the line, or swing with the bird, or follow through. He couldn't hit a backhouse door if he was standing inside."

"By the way," Colonel Cobb inquired, "how many birds did you get today?"

"That's aside from the point," said Doc. "The only reason I didn't get any birds was because they kept on flying after they were obviously stone dead. For instance, this grouse got up right in front of me and took off across an open field, and I figured out the wind direction and trajectory and rate of climb, and I used my modified barrel with Number Eight chilled which throws a pattern of 29.3 square inches at fifty-five yards, and the only explanation is that the bird didn't know enough to fall."

"That's like what happened to me today," Judge Parker said. "I was just stooping over to pick up an apple, and I wasn't really used to my new gun, so I didn't know how to work the safety fast enough, and there was steam on my glasses, and I was afraid to fire because I didn't know who was in front of me, and anyway, how do you expect to hit a grouse if it deliberately ducks behind a hemlock?"

"Grouse fly faster than they used to," said Cousin Sid. "Either that or the shells they make nowadays are slower, or else the guns weigh more when you try to hold them. Another thing, it's farther back home after the hunt is over, and they've put a little hill in front of the camp that I never noticed before. That's why I never touched a feather."

Colonel Cobb put down his glass, and rapped for order.

"Gentlemen," he began, "I think the time has come to award the Alibi Cup for 1958."

He lifted a handsome silver loving cup from the mantel.

"As you all know," he said, "this impressive trophy is presented by the Club each year to the member who brings home the best alibi. The lucky winner is required to fill the cup every time the other members want a drink. I won it myself last year, as a result of missing a ten-point buck in broad daylight at twenty yards because a birch tree jumped right in front of the barrel."

He beamed at the other members.

"After what I've just heard," he began, "I hereby suggest the names of Doc Hall and Judge Parker and Cousin Sid—"

The door opened and Dexter Smeed entered. He was wearing a golf cap and a business suit and low shoes, filled with water, and he carried his gun over one shoulder by the barrel. "Boy, these grouse are sure hard to hit," he began. "I was climbing over a stone wall, and I had a grapevine twisted around one ankle, and a strand of barbed wire was caught in my crotch, and my hat was down over my eyes—"

"And you'd laid down your gun for just a moment," Doc Hall suggested, winking at the others.

"That's right," said Dexter, "and I had the shells in my pocket, and the bird flew right at me instead of going away—"

"And the sun was in your eyes," Judge Parker suggested.

"I couldn't see a thing," Dexter nodded. "I just lifted up my gun and pulled both triggers."

"My boy," said Colonel Cobb, "let me congratulate you. You are definitely the leading candidate for the Alibi Cup. That's the best excuse I've heard today for missing a grouse."

"That's just the trouble," Dexter said. "I didn't miss it."

He reached into his coat pocket, and laid four grouse on the table.

"Every time I fired at them," he sighed, "they fell down. I don't understand it."

Judge Parker and Doc Hall and Cousin Sid looked at each

other in silence. The Colonel cleared his throat.

"Gentlemen," he said, "I hereby propose the name of Dexter Smeed for membership in the Lower Forty."

The election was unanimously approved, and the meeting adjourned after it was resolved that Cousin Sid should clean the birds, as usual.

DOGS ARE ALMOST HUMAN

The monthly meeting of the Lower Forty Shooting, Angling and Inside Straight Club was over a little sooner than usual, owing to a slight altercation between Judge Parker and Doc Hall over their respective bird dogs. As Colonel Cobb said later, you can argue with a man about religion or politics or even women, but you can't argue with him about his dog.

The whole thing started when Judge Parker's pointer growled at Doc Hall's setter. They didn't exactly fight, but they walked sort of stiff-legged around each other and the hair stood up on the backs of their necks, and the Judge said "Shut up, Timmy" and Doc said "Toby, I'm ashamed of you, quarreling like that." They pulled the two dogs apart. "I never saw Timberdoodle act that way before," Judge Parker apologized to the Club, "but I guess he isn't used to seeing another dog racing around, upsetting things and ruining the furniture."

"I don't know what you mean by that," Doc Hall bristled, "just because October likes to get up in a chair. He sleeps in the same room with me, and he's very well behaved."

"Personally I don't believe in spoiling a dog," Judge Parker said, "not if you want to make a good hunting dog out of him."

"Then what's your dog doing right now," Doc demanded,

"lying on the sofa?"

"He's lying on top of my hunting coat," the Judge said, "waiting for me to take him out. Pointers are very intelligent."

"Toby wouldn't lie around and wait," Doc Hall said, "he'd pick up the coat and bring it over to me. That's the difference between pointers and setters."

"I suppose you're going to tell me that a setter has more brains," the Judge said indignantly.

"Of course he has," Doc retorted, his voice rising. "A pointer is just a machine. A setter *thinks*."

"Reminds me of a very intelligent bird dog I had once," Colonel Cobb interrupted, filling the glasses from Uncle Perk's jug. "I was leading him down the main street of Boston, and he came to a solid point on a total stranger. I knew my dog never made a mistake, so I asked the stranger if he was carrying a bird in his pocket, and the stranger said he wasn't. So I asked him if by any chance he'd been handling a grouse lately, because I never knew my dog to be wrong before, but he said no, he never saw a grouse and he wasn't even a hunter. So I had to apologize for my dog, and I shook hands and said 'I'm sorry, sir, my name is Cobb. 'Pleased to meet you, the stranger said. 'My name's Partridge.' "

Judge Parker and Doc Hall emptied their glasses in unison. "But to get back to what we were saying," the Judge resumed, "a setter just tags at your feet. I'll take a pointer if I want a day's hunt."

"Most of the day," Doc said, "you hunt for the dog."

The Judge glowered. "At least, a pointer's steady. He'll bang into a point and hold it all afternoon."

"A setter knows better than that," Doc Hall said triumphantly. "Toby'll back off a point and come and get me, and lead me back to where the bird is. A setter's more dependable—"

"A pointer don't bump birds—"

"Like that dog of mine I was telling you about," Colonel Cobb broke in quickly, filling their glasses again, "I was hunting him late one fall, and he disappeared and I couldn't find him. I looked all night, and all the next day, and then it came on to snow and I had to give up. Well, sir, next spring after the snow melted I happened to be walking through that same cover, and there was the skeleton of my dog, still solid on his point, and right in front of him was the skeleton of the grouse he'd been holding." He sighed. "That's what I call staunch."

Judge Parker and Doc Hall gave him a cold glance. "As I was about to point out," Doc said, glaring at the Judge, "a setter will figure out the cover, and the directon of the wind, and he'll find more birds in an hour than a pointer could find in a week, because he's got sense. He's almost human."

Judge Parker swallowed his drink in a gulp. "I s'pose you think your dog's more human 'n' my dog," he shouted indignantly. "Why, you take Timmy—"

"I wouldn't take Timmy," Doc taunted, "if he was a gif'."

" 'F you'd like to step ou'side," said the Judge, rising unsteadily and peeling off his coat, "I'll show you which dog is more human or not."

"Okay 'th me," said Doc belligerently, taking off his glasses, "we'll settle this thing righ' now."

"Wait a minute," Colonel Cobb said, pulling them apart. "Why don't you settle it right? We'll take both dogs out to the White Church cover tomorrow, and turn 'em loose, and see which one finds the most birds. The winner gets a jug of Old Stump Blower."

"I'd like to enter that contest, too," said Dexter Smeed. "I got a little dog out in the car, name of Fluffy."

"Who ever heard of a bird dog named Fluffy?" said the Judge sullenly.

"I got it from some friends that found it," Dexter said, "it's not exactly a setter or a pointer either, it's got a short tail and one ear flops down and its coat looks like a moldy piece of bread, but it can hunt because it got into a skunk the other night, so I thought I'd bring it along and see what it could do."

"I tell you what, Dexter," the Colonel said, "you better leave Fluffy in the car tomorrow. The other two dogs might get discouraged."

The Club got an early start the next morning, and all the members went along on the hunt except Dexter, who decided he'd better stay in his own car and keep Fluffy company. Doc's setter and the Judge's pointer each got a bird on the first cast, and then they moved on into the big alder cover beside the brook and disappeared. "Toby's solid on a point somewhere," Doc said, "if we could find him."

"We better find Timmy," the Judge said, "Toby's probably backing him."

They hunted a couple of hours, and Doc started blowing his whistle, and the Judge shouted himself hoarse, and they both fired their guns, but there was no sign of the dogs. The only sound was the steady honking of Dexter's horn. At last they turned back and headed for the road. Dexter's car was parked by the church, and the pointer and the setter were jumping up and down beside it and whining and panting to get inside.

"Call your dogs off," Dexter shouted, rolling down the window a crack, "before they scratch all my paint."

The Judge and Doc didn't even look at each other. They broke their guns, and ran to the dogs, and grabbed them by their collars. "I never saw Timmy quit a hunt before," Judge Parker admitted sheepishly.

"I wish I knew," Doc muttered, "what got into Toby."

"Maybe I should have mentioned," Dexter said, "that Fluffy's in season."

There was a moment's silence. Colonel Cobb picked up the jug of Old Stump Blower and presented it to Dexter Smeed. He gazed at the two dogs thoughtfully.

"It only goes to show," he murmured, "that dogs are almost human."

MISTER MacNAB'S HAIRSE

It was Mister MacNab, the association's self-made treasurer, who personally called an emergency meeting of the Lower Forty Shooting, Angling and Inside Straight Club. It seems that Mister MacNab has just acquired a combination hearse and ambulance in good condition, complete with genuine chrome trim, purple curtains and tassels (which could of course be removed if it were functioning as an ambulance) and a flashing beehive red light (which could be covered up if it were serving as a hearse); and it was his suggestion that the members of the Lower Forty should chip in together and purchase this vehicle as a community property. The members were a little puzzled by his proposal.

"In the first place," Judge Parker said frankly, "I can't figure how you ever got hold of a contraption like this."

"Well, 'tis a sad story," Mister MacNab replied, "and I shall be only too glad to relate the unhappy details if ye'll set ye doon and partake of some of Uncle Pairk's refreshments which I am sure that ginnerous soul will be only too glad to pr-r-rovide."

Mister MacNab himself opened the meeting with a swallow of Old Stump Blower, and began his tale. Not long ago, he explained, a distant uncle named Angus MacNab, an undertaker in East Orange, had passed away unexpectedly; and since Mister

MacNab was his sole heir, he had hurried down to New Jersey to attend the services and, more important, to hear the reading of the will. The services were quite successful, Mister MacNab said, but the will was a total failure. Uncle Angus, it was disclosed when the estate was appraised, had so little cash on hand at the moment of his demise that by the time he was given a fitting burial — a matter which had to be taken care of by a local competitor, since the late lamented was unable to conduct his own funeral — the only legacy which his nephew inherited was the hearse.

"For-r-rtunately I was able to defray part of the cost of the return trip," Mister MacNab reported, "by renting the hairse to transport the remains of a deceased Democratic politician from Bridgeport, Connecticut, who had departed this life rather hastily following a disagreement with the Jairsey City organization. After delivering the body to his bereaved widow in Bridgeport, I chanced to come upon a lovely accident on the Merritt Parkway, and carried the victims to the New Haven Hospital. There I picked up an alcoholic case which I drove to Boston, and from Boston I moved an illegal shipment of lottery tickets as far as Portland, Maine, where I took on a barrel of fresh lobsters for local sale to help to reimburse me still further." He glanced at some penciled figures in a small pocket ledger. "So all I wish to be remunerated for," he concluded, "is my hotel expenses in New Jairsey for three days, plus the flowers for poor Uncle Angus's funeral, plus the rental of a dark suit for the sad occasion, not to mention gray gloves and spats, plus the sum of four dollars that I was forced to expend for taxi fare when I got lost on the bus system in the Oranges and was late for the sairvices, plus the fee for a local attorney I hired later to probate the will, which comes to the gr-r-and total of eighty-three, ninety-five, or sixteen dollars and ninety-seven cents per member."

Judge Parker shook his head. "What could the Lower Forty do with a hearse?"

"We could paint it red," Dexter Smeed suggested.

"Why could we paint it red?" asked the Judge.

"Then it would be a hearse of a different color," Dexter replied, laughing heartily.

Judge Parker waited until his wife's nephew had been ejected bodily from the meeting, and order was restored. "As I was saying," he repeated, "what possible use would it be to this club?"

" 'Tis a sterling piece of equipment, gentlemen," Mister MacNab pointed out quickly, "with removable iron cot, stretcher-hangers to keep it from sliding, and a folding seat for the attendant, as well as a built-in medicine cabinet, clip for the oxygen bottle, two small glass vases with ostrich plumes, and a siren."

"We're not in the undertaking or ambulance business," Doc Hall shrugged.

"Think of all the advantages," Mister MacNab argued. "It's big enough to transport the entire membership at once, and we could carry our fishing rods on top and use the oxygen-bottle clip to hold our rifles, and in case of rain we could all sleep inside." He was aware that his arguments were falling on deaf ears. "I'll tell ye what I'll do," he offered shrewdly. "I'll supply this vehicle when we go deer hunting tomorrow, and you can detect its remar-r-rkable possibilities for yourselves."

The Club's annual deer hunt the following day turned out very successfully, at least as far as Judge Parker was concerned. He had taken his stand at the end of a small ravine, through which the rest of the members were driving, and toward the end of the afternoon he nailed a good-sized buck. The others hurried toward him at the sound of his shot, and discovered the Judge standing beside a high wire fence, scratching his head. "I knocked the critter down," he said, "but it got up again and jumped the fence into Deacon Godfrey's land. I drilled it through the shoulders, so it can't go far."

His fellow members surveyed the No Hunting or Trespassing signs dubiously. "What are you going to do?" Cousin Sid asked. "You know the Deacon will have the law on you if he catches you on his property."

"I'm going after my deer," the Judge insisted, crawling through the barbed wire. "The rest of you can drive down the back road, and meet me on the other side of old Godfrey's woodlot."

It was almost dusk when Judge Parker emerged from the woods, hauling his trophy behind him, and they helped him load it hastily into the rear of the waiting vehicle. So intent were they on this task that no one heard the sound of approaching footsteps. Their first warning was Deacon Godfrey's triumphant shout: "Arrest that man, Sheriff! He's been huntin' on my land."

Woolboot Jackson, the local sheriff, stepped out of the shadows and shone his flashlight on the hearse. His jaw dropped in astonishment. "Wait a minute, Deacon," he murmured. "There must be some mistake. This here's a funeral."

Deacon Godfrey looked a trifle bewildered. "I thought I heard a shot."

" 'Twas merely a backfire," Mister MacNab assured him from the dark interior of the hearse, "as we were hurrying to transport the body of the deceased to its final resting place." His voice quavered with emotion. "The poor dear," he sighed.

Deacon Godfrey and the sheriff peered at the dim form on the stretcher, completely covered with a sheet. They removed their hats respectfully.

"And now if ye'll both kindly stond to one side," Mister Mac-Nab added, signaling Judge Parker to step on the starter, "we must be on our way to conclude our mour-r-rnful duty."

As the hearse rolled rapidly down the road, Mister MacNab switched on the overhead light, and made some hasty computations in his pocket ledger. "Estimating the probable fine for tr-r-respassing at one hundred dollars," he said at last, "I figure that the saving to the Club exactly equals my investment in the hairse, or twenty dollars per member."

"You said yesterday your total expenses were only Eighty-three, ninety-five," Doc Hall objected, reaching for his wallet. "What's the added amount for?"

Mister MacNab replaced the ledger in his pocket. " 'Tis my fee for professional sairvices," he explained. "It's what poor Uncle Angus always char-r-rged."

COON DOGS
FOR SALE

The members of the Lower Forty Shooting, Angling and Inside Straight Club had gathered in Uncle Perk's store, waiting to start out on a coon hunt as soon as it was dark. Beneath the familiar weatherbeaten sign over the front door — "Guns & Fshng. Tckle., Bot Sold & Swopt" — was a new slogan in crude letters: "Coon Dogs 4 Sale or Rent." Uncle Perk gestured proudly toward a litter of squirming black-and-tan puppies in a flat box behind the potbellied stove. "Corkers, ain't they?"

"Isn't it a little early to start advertising them yet, Uncle Perk?" Doc Hall asked. "After all, they're only six weeks old."

"They're mighty precocious pups," Uncle Perk insisted. "Before they even had their eyes open, a customer come into the store wearin' a coonskin hat, and danged if every last pup didn't start pawin' the air and hollerin'. Take right after their mother."

"Is Belle coming with us tonight?" Colonel Cobb inquired, fondling the long floppy ear of Uncle Perk's particular pride and joy.

"Reckon them pups'll have to give their maw a night off," Uncle Perk nodded. "It wouldn't be a hunt without old Belle." He gazed at her affectionately. "She can track a coon so good she knows where it's been before it gets there."

[35]

"I guess all coon dogs are pretty smart," Judge Parker suggested.

Uncle Perk settled back in the battered swivel chair behind his desk and hung a leg over the side, swinging his hunting boot negligently. "Wal, now, I wouldn't go so far's to say that," he reflected. "I known some coon dogs that wasn't all they might have been. Like for instance you take that dog old Eb Millet used to have, the one we all called Solo on account of he was the only dog like him. Solo couldn't follow a coon if it was carrying a lantern. Only of course you couldn't never tell that to old Eb."

Uncle Perk took a dust-covered jug from his bottom desk drawer, tilted it to his mouth for a moment, and passed it to the assembled membership. He ran a checkered shirt sleeve across his lips.

"This Solo wa'n't a bad-looking dog," he recalled, "if you don't mind a spaniel that's been bred to a shorthair pointer that's a cross between an Aireyodale and a Great Dane. His legs was splayed, and he had a lower lip like a camel, and his tail was coiled so tight it lifted his whole rear end off the ground, but of course a thing like looks don't matter if a dog'll bark on coon. The trouble with Solo, he barked on everything *except* coon. He might have been a good squirrel dog if he stuck to squirrels, or else if he'd been satisfied with rabbits he might have made a rabbit dog, but Solo chased 'em all. He'd bark on possum or deer or skunk or a plain house cat, and if there wasn't anything else to bark at, he'd chase himself in circles all night till he caught up with himself and found out who he was.

"But, as I say, it didn't do no good to tell old Eb. He kep' insisting he had the best coon dog in town, and he'd as leave take a swing at anybody who didn't agree with him. He was just plumb foolish about that dog of his'n. I remember one night we all set out on a hunt together, and old Eb tagged along with his Solo dog trotting at his heels, snuffing at the ground and now and then letting out a yip whenever he smelt a chipmunk or maybe a garter snake. We was hunting along the bottom of Farmer Libbey's pasture, and Aldo Libbey got his gun and come along with us that night, because somebody'd been getting into his henyard lately, and Aldo was hoping he could catch him. Old Aldo was pretty burned about somebody stealing his chickens. 'I'd give a hundred dollars in cash,' he said, 'if anybody nabs that no-good thief.'

"Well, we was starting back up the hill toward the farm again, and all of a sudden I noticed Solo wasn't trotting behind us any more. I knew he couldn't of run home, because he was too scared to go back alone unless somebody was with him. I started to say something to Eb, and just then we heard the gol-durndest catouse going on somewhere ahead of us, near Farmer Libbey's chicken yard, and above all the commotion we made out a dog barking. Eb grabbed his gun and started on a dead run. 'That's him!' he shouted to us. 'That's Solo. He's treed a coon!'

"Eb was already to the tree when we caught up with him, and Solo was barking at the foot of it, and Eb was trying to climb the trunk and keep Solo from pulling him back down in his excitement. I shone my light up into the tree, and sure enough see a pair of eyes way up above me. Eb lifted his shotgun.

" 'Hold your light steady on that coon, Perk,' he said to me, 'while I shoot it down.'

" 'Don' shoot, mister,' the coon hollered back. 'I'll come down if you'll just call off that damn dog.'

"We all held our guns on him, and he climbed down, shaking

like a leaf, and it was the same thief all right that had been steal-ing Farmer Libbey's chickens. Aldo Libbey, he was so pleased that he took out his wallet and handed a roll of bills to Eb.

"Eb he looked at them for a minute. 'What's that for?' he asked slowly.

" 'It's your reward,' Aldo Libbey said, 'for catching this chicken thief your dog just treed.'

"Old Eb shook his head, and his lower lip stuck out just like Solo's. 'Keep your money,' he said, grabbing his dog by the collar and starting away. 'My dog wouldn't tree no man.'

" 'Eb, you dang old obstinate fool,' I yelled after him, 'that's a hundred dollars in cash you're passing up.'

" 'Solo,' Old Eb insisted over his shoulder, 'he's a coon dog . . .' "

Uncle Perk sighed, took his old shotgun from the wall, and beckoned to Belle.

"Come on, let's get started," he said to the members, "before some dang customer comes in to bother us."

THE LOWER FORTY EATS CROWS

The regular meeting of the Lower Forty Shooting, Angling and Inside Straight Club was something of an emergency session, owing to the fact that Farmer Libbey needed a dead crow. It seems the crows were pulling all his young corn, and Aldo called up and asked if the Club would please shoot one to hang on a pole in his field. The Lower Forty is a very charitable organization, devoted to public service, and the members did not hesitate to drop everything else they were doing at once in order to rally to the aid of a neighbor in distress.

"No sacrifice is too great," Judge Parker insisted, hastily calling off an important court case he was scheduled to conduct that afternoon, "when duty calls."

"Especially when a few crows are calling at the same time," Doc Hall agreed, phoning his patients to announce he was canceling all his appointments for the rest of the day.

"Too bad we haven't got an articulated owl," sighed Colonel Cobb, as he left the afternoon edition of the *Gazette* halfway through its run, and raced out of his editorial office to join the carful of fellow members honking impatiently at the curb. "There's nothing like a stuffed owl to bring the crows in fighting mad, peeling off their coats and handing somebody their glasses to hold."

"Personally I always prefer a live tomcat in a bird cage," said Cousin Sid, tiptoeing out the rear door of the local high school with his shotgun. "You hoist the cage into a tree, and start it swinging back and forth, and you'll have every crow in the neighborhood swarming around it in no time." He stowed a handful of No. 6 shells in the pockets of his vest. "Then another advantage is that when you're all through shooting the crows, you can wind up with the cat."

"Decoys are all very well," Judge Parker scoffed, "but the most important thing in crow shooting is strategy. A crow is just about the smartest thing in feathers, and it takes an expert to fool them." He tapped the brakes on the car, and a flock of crows feeding in an adjoining field took wing instantly and flew out of range. "See what I mean? They recognized the numbers on my license plate."

"They sure got sharp eyes," Uncle Perk agreed. "They'll spot a shotgun a mile away. Only way to git near 'em is to fasten a row of tines to the end of your barrel, and carry it over your shoulder like a rake."

"It's all a matter of str-r-rategy," Mister MacNab insisted. "Pairsonally when I want to sneak up on a bunch of cr-r-rows, I put on a nursemaid's cap and apron, and wheel a per-r-rambulator down the road. Then when I'm full abreast of the beggars, I yank the blanket back, and pull out my ten-gauge Magnum, and start fir-r-ring. Fools 'em every time," he nodded.

Judge Parker halted the car at Farmer Libbey's gate, and the

[40]

members loaded their shotguns. "I'll make a little side bet with you, Doc," Judge Parker challenged, as they started across the pasture. "If I don't get the first crow today, by God, I'll eat it."

"I'll take you up on that," retorted Doc Hall.

They crept across the pasture cautiously, making their way toward a stand of small spruces growing at the top of the hill. The sun was warm, there was no wind stirring, and they could hear some crows cawing contentedly in the distance. The members concealed themselves in the shelter of the young trees, and Judge Parker took out his wooden crow call.

"Maybe the rest of you'd better let me do the calling," he suggested tactfully. "It's quite an art to call crow, and they'll detect the least false note. The best procedure," he explained, "is to start off with a little friendly chitchat, sort of like this." He placed the call to his lips. "Joe! Joe! How are you, Joe? Nice day, ain't it, Joe!" He listened carefully for a moment, frowned, and tried again. "Hey, Joe! Where the hell are you, Joe?" His face grew purple. "Joe, you blankety-blank black blank—"

"You've got to make it sound more inviting," Doc Hall criticised. "Offer them something enticing, like this." He mouthed his own call. "Joe, Joe, look what I found! A dead horse! Hurry up and bring the neighbors!"

"How about a fighting call?" suggested Colonel Cobb. "You know, make 'em mad." He took a deep breath. "Over here, Joe! Get the gang! I've cornered that flat-faced son of an owl that raided the roost last night!"

"Maybe if we all started calling together," said Cousin Sid, "it would sound like a family argument. Not even a crow can resist getting in on a family argument."

The members crouched in their respective stands, and at a signal from Judge Parker they began calling in unison, setting up a raucous clamor. From the other side of the knoll, where Dexter Smead was hidden, came a high piercing caw. Judge Parker scowled.

"Shut up, Dexter," he called. "You'll scare them away with a noise like that."

"That's not me," Dexter replied. "That's a real one."

A lone crow swooped over the crest of the hill, wheeled in midair, and circled back above the small spruces. There was a single deafening blast, and the bird folded its wings and plummeted to the ground, landing with a thud. Judge Parker ejected a smoking shell from his gun, and strolled toward it with a satisfied smile.

"If I do say so myself," he beamed, "that was a very good shot."

"What do you mean?" Doc Hall objected, popping an empty shell from his own gun. "I fired at the same time. This happens to be my bird."

The spruces parted behind them and Farmer Libbey emerged, lugging an ancient muzzle-loader. "Heard all the commotion goin' on," he explained, "so I come over here to help you fellows out." He picked up the dead crow, and examined it. "Yep, I see I hit it right dead center."

Uncle Perk glanced at Judge Parker and Doc Hall, and cleared his throat. "By the way, Aldo," he asked, "you happen to know how to cook a crow?"

"Seems to me I read a recipe someplace," Aldo Libbey recalled. "First you parboil it for three or four hours, and then you dig a deep hole, and make a bed of embers, and then you put the crow on the embers, and cover up the hole again. They say it

[42]

tastes just like roast chicken."

It was unanimously resolved to leave the crow with Farmer Libbey, and adjourn to Pete's Diner for some roast chicken, because, after all, you couldn't tell the difference.

AWL HANDS — DIP!

The spring meeting of the Lower Forty Shooting, Angling and Inside Straight Club was held on the bank of Mink Brook, where the smelt were said to be running. The members had been a little skeptical when Uncle Perk first suggested a night of smelting, but he had assured them it was the height of sport. "Beats horn poutin' or even diggin' clams," he insisted. "And when it comes to eatin', they ain't nawthin' like a mess of first-run smelt in the spring."

"Do they rise to a dry fly?" asked Doc Hall.

"Wal, no, not exactly," Uncle Perk admitted. "All you need is a pair of rubber boots, a smelt net, some warm clothes to change to when you fall in the brook, a pair of pants with a canvas seat to turn barbed wire, a pail to put your smelt in, and a jug. The jug," he explained, "is in case you don't get any smelt to put in the pail."

"Sounds good to me," Judge Parker said. "When do we start?"

"Usually smeltin' begins along about sundown," Uncle Perk explained, "and quits any time after sunup the following morning. If you see a man walking down the street next day with blood-shot eyes and staggerin' a little, and all to once't he walks smack into a telephone pole and falls down flat and lies there and goes to sleep, then you have seed a smelt fisherman."

The Club gathered at dusk in Uncle Perk's store, and he led

them to his favorite smelt hole, where Mink Brook runs through Farmer Libbey's lower pasture. The March air had a sharp edge, and they built a bonfire on the bank and huddled around it to keep warm. Other watch fires began to glow up and down the length of the brook, and now and then a group of rival fishermen trudged past them in the darkness, giving them sour looks. "Smelt fishermen ain't exactly sociable," Uncle Perk whispered. He hailed an ancient character with his head wrapped in a wool muffler: "Hi."

"Any luck last night, Elmer?" asked Uncle Perk.

"Didn't see nawthin'," Elmer grumbled. "This brook ain't what it used to be," he complained, "and what's more it never was."

Uncle Perk shook his head as Elmer disappeared into the shadows. "Hope they start runnin' tonight on the full moon," he sighed. "Ain't no sight I know of that's sadder than a fisherman comin' home along about dawn, lugging a big pail in his hand, with three cats following him up the walk yowlin' and lickin' their chops, and his kids are waitin' on the porch, and his old lady's got the frying pan hot and the corn meal and salt pork laid out, and he turns his pail upside down into the sink, and one small smelt slides out. When you come right down to it, the smallest thing in the world is a smelt surrounded by three starving tomcats, a rugged man, a hungry woman, and bunch of drooling kids all set to eat it."

"By the way," asked Cousin Sid, "who was Elmer?"

"He's the head he-hooper," Uncle Perk said with a note of respect in his voice. "Elmer's the oldest smelt fisherman on Mink Brook, he's dipped here ever since he was knee high to a snake's shoelaces, and nobody else ever starts dippin' till Elmer gives the word: 'Up and at 'em boys!' "

The night air was getting colder, a dank mist rose off the water, and the steady tinkle of spring peepers in the swamp around them suggested winter sleighbells. Judge Parker started to shiver, and Uncle Perk uncorked the jug of homemade Old Power Saw, and the Judge took a healthy swig. Colonel Cobb borrowed the jug for a moment and then passed it to Cousin Sid, who handed it to Doc Hall, who give it in turn to Dexter Smeed. Suddenly, around a bend in the brook, Elmer's high-pitched hail shattered the silence.

"Here they come, boys. Awl hands — *dip!*"

Up and down the length of Mink Brook, the air was filled with flailing nets and splashing boots and swinging pails, punctured by an occasional exchange of strong and vigorous language as a fisherman trespassed into a neighbor's waters. In and out through the crowd Owl Eyes Osborn, the conservation officer, moved like a weasel in a henhouse, making sure that nobody took more than his legal right. The splashing upstream grew louder, and a crouching figure approached them, working his way down the current into Uncle Perk's pool. There was a sudden swish as Perk's smelt net came whistling down through the air and landed on the intruder's head, followed by a resounding kerplunk as Uncle Perk yanked the net and the culprit landed sitting down in the stream. "Teach you to dip where I'm dippin'," Uncle Perk threatened. "Git back and dip where you're supposed to dip."

The members trudged back and forth across the stream, stumbling over boulders, sliding across sunken automobile tires, and occasionally catching their clothes on the strands of barbed wire which Farmer Libbey had strung across the brook to keep his cattle in. Their boots leaked and their arms ached from dipping, but nary a smelt showed up in their nets. One by one they crawled back to the welcome fire on the bank, and warded off the chill by swigging Uncle Perk's bottomless jug.

"Guess they ain't really started runnin' yet," Uncle Perk sighed at last. "We might's well wait till the full moon's up." He peered through the darkness at a lone figure, still flailing the stream with his net. "Come on back, Dexter," he called, "and git warm."

Dexter turned to head back to the bank, the rubber soles of his wading boots skidded off a submerged log, and he did a neat back-flip and sank out of sight in the water. He rose spluttering and wallowed toward shore, icicles forming on him as he climbed the bank. His teeth chattered like castanets as he sat beside the fire and tugged off his right boot, and held it upside down. A torrent of water poured onto the grass. Suddenly Judge Parker made a dive toward a silver object flapping in the firelight.

"Dexter," he yelled, "take off your other boot quick!"

The members gazed happily at the solitary smelt. "Nice going, Dex," said Colonel Cobb. "Let's cook it right here."

"Not on your life," Dexter protested, grabbing his trophy. "I'm going to have this mounted."

From the distance came a high-pitched yell: "Here they come again. Awl hands — *dip!*"

"What are we waiting for?" Uncle Perk shouted, racing toward the brook. "Git to dippin'!"

Dawn was breaking as the members staggered back to the bank, and emptied their brimming pails into a burlap sack. Cousin Sid swung the bag over his shoulder and they started back to the car triumphantly. "I tell you what we'll do," said Uncle Perk. "Tonight you come around to the store, and I'll cook 'em over the stove in the back room, and we'll have a real old smelt fry."

Unfortunately the proposed meeting of the Lower Forty failed to take place. Judge Parker's wife phoned that afternoon and said the Judge was sick in bed with a bad cold. Doc Hall's wife reported the Doc had a chill and was sitting with his feet in a mustard bath. Cousin Sid's wife explained that Sid was so stiff he couldn't move, Dexter Smeed called up to say he was going to stay home and sleep for a week, and Colonel Cobb's secretary announced that the Colonel was suffering from a severe hangover and couldn't leave the house. Uncle Perk shook his head as he rolled the smelt in corn meal and dropped them one by one into a sizzling frying pan.

"Too bad the rest o' the members couldn't be here to enjoy this feast," he chuckled to himself. "I always say, they ain't nawthin' like a mess of first-run smelt in the spring."

THE DREAM HOUSE

You could have knocked over the members of the Lower Forty Shooting, Angling and Inside Straight Club with a jungle-cock feather when they picked up the weekly copy of the local *Gazette* and discovered that Colonel Cobb was engaged to be married. Judge Parker read the social item aloud to his fellow members, and they stared at one another in stunned silence. "I'd say the *Gazette* must have made a mistake," he murmured incredulously, "except for the fact that the Colonel himself runs the paper."

"What I can't figure," Doc Hall sighed, "is how a dyed-in-the-wool old bachelor like he is ever decided to forsake the joys of single blessedness."

Uncle Perk shooed a mouse from the slab of store cheese on the counter, cut off a wedge, and munched it dourly. "I'll tell ye how it happened," he grunted. "That Millie Floss decided for him. She's been tryin' for years to hook anybody in these here parts that wears a pair of pants, but they all married away from her, till Colonel Cobb was the most likely batchelder left." He shrugged. "It ain't a bad catch for a designing she-female like Millie, seein's how the Colonel owns a newspaper an' a prosperous printin' business an' half the real estate in taown."

"Aye, I can compr-r-rehend the r-r-romance better," Mister MacNab nodded sagely, "now you bring in the element of har-r-rd cash—"

The conversation halted abruptly as the strap of sleigh bells inside the front door jangled, and the bridegroom-to-be sidled a trifle sheepishly into Uncle Perk's store, exuding an unfamiliar odor of after-shave lotion. His battered fishing hat had been exchanged for a brand-new gray fedora, the customary growth of stubble had been scraped clean from his chin, and in place of his usual canvas jacket and red bandanna he wore a neat double-breasted business suit. Judge Parker took one look at these devastating results of Cupid's dart, and reached hastily for Uncle Perk's jug. The Colonel faced his fellow members in obvious embarrassment.

"Just wanted to explain that I won't be able to make the Club meeting at Beaver Meadow this coming Saturday," he apologized. "Millie, she don't go in much for hunting and fishing." He lowered his eyes. "She—she's going to teach me golf."

Judge Parker choked violently on his drink, and had to be patted on the back until he could catch his breath.

"By the way," Cousin Sid asked, to relieve the tension, "are you and the bride going to live in your old apartment over the *Gazette*?"

"Hmm? No," Colonel Cobb replied with something very like a sigh. "No, Millie's decided to build a dream house up on Hardscrabble Hill. An architect friend of hers in New York has just drawn up the plans." He indicated a roll of blueprints under his arm. "I'm on my way to go over them with her now."

Uncle Perk darted a significant glance at the other members. "Mind if we have a peek at 'em first," he asked mildly.

"Why, no, not at all," Colonel Cobb said, spreading out the blueprints on the counter and weighing them down with the

[52]

cheese knife. "This first one is the front elevation," he explained. "Millie decided she wanted a ranch-type house, with a sweeping L wing and garage attached—"

"That garage is much too low," Doc Hall objected. "You need enough room overhead for chain hoists, so you can raise and lower an aluminum canoe onto the top of your car. It ought to be at least six feet higher."

"Wouldn't that sort of spoil the roofline?" Colonel Cobb hesitated. "I mean, if the garage stuck up higher than the rest of the house?"

"Doesn't make any difference," Doc insisted, making the necessary changes on the blueprint with a black crayon. "You've got to have storage space for your tent poles and dog trailer and a couple of outboard motors."

"I guess you're right," Colonel Cobb nodded. He flipped over another blueprint. "Here's the cellar plan," he continued. "The center part is Millie's rumpus room, and over here is her laundry, and the rest of it is a storeroom to keep her flower pots and gardening tools and spare tropical fish tanks—"

"Where's your indoor rifle and pistol range?" demanded Cousin Sid. "You need at least fifty-three feet of open space for target practice, with a firing platform at one end and a sheet-metal stop at the other." He reached for the black crayon. "Cut out the rumpus room, and get rid of the laundry, and move the storeroom into this little space behind the furnace. That'll give you a nice big workshop where you can load ammo, and varnish rods, and dry trout lines, and hang up your waders for the winter."

"Sounds like a good idea," Colonel Cobb said. "I always needed a good workbench for making rods and tying flies and all." He turned another page of the blueprints. "This is the up-stairs floor plan," he went on. "Millie wanted a big picture win-dow in the living room—"

"Picture window!" Judge Parker snorted, X-ing it out promptly with the crayon. "You need a couple of old-fashioned sliding sashes, so you can lift them in a hurry in case a woodchuck happens to show up outside—"

"With separate clips in each window sill to hold a varmint rifle and a deer rifle," Cousin Sid suggested enthusiastically. "That way you can lay down anything that comes across the lawn."

Doc Hall scowled at the blueprint. "Wotinell's this room here?"

"That—that's Millie's music conservatory."

"No, it isn't," Doc said firmly, correcting the blueprint. "It's a nice paneled den, with trophy heads and stuffed fish and a bear rug on the floor." His crayon moved back and forth as he talked. "We'll use this whole wall of the living room for built-in gun cabinets with sliding glass doors and indirect lighting."

"But Millie was planning to hang some oil paintings—"

"What you want is a few Remingtons and Charlie Russells," Doc advised, "and some old ammo calendars, and autographed targets, and here over the fireplace you can have a concealed pro-jector and screen to show colored hunting and fishing slides—"

"And a target on the opposite wall where these bookcases are," Judge Parker added, grabbing the crayon, "so you can sit beside the fire after supper and practice with your air rifle—"

"And a beer cooler beside your easy chair," Mister MacNab urged, "with a tr-r-rap-door in the living-room floor to drop empty beer cans down into the cellar. Think of the time ye'll save for added dr-r-rinking."

Uncle Perk was shaking his head over the kitchen plans. "You got to get rid o' this electric stove," he frowned, "an' git yourself an ole-fashioned woodstove which a litter of pups could sleep behind, and I'd forget about this dishwasher because you'll need all the space under the sink to store sacks of dog food, and nach'ally you'll have to cut a dog hole in this here door, with a two-way swingin' panel lined with felt so's the dog won't catch its tail." He turned over a final blueprint of the landscaping. "Is this your kennels?"

"That's Millie's outdoor patio," said Colonel Cobb faintly.

Uncle Perk drew a thick black line across the blueprint. "The kennels've got to go here in front of the house," he decided, "so's you can have a fly-castin' pool in back where her sunken garden was supposed to been." He peered through his spectacles at the result. "Naow, then," he asked, "ain't that more like it?"

"It's a real dream house," Colonel Cobb nodded, his eyes shining. The glow in his eyes faded. "I bet Millie likes it, too," he said without conviction. "I tell you, I'm the luckiest fellow in the world . . . "

That Saturday the members of the Lower Forty gathered in Uncle Perk's store and assembled their gear for the Club's fishing expedition to Beaver Meadow. Cousin Sid gazed around him sadly. "It's going to seem funny," he began, "making the trip without Colonel Cobb—"

The sleigh bells jangled as the front door opened, and Colonel Cobb sauntered in. He was wearing a battered fishing hat, and he had on his old canvas jacket and red bandanna, stained with fly-dope. "See I got here just in time," he observed casually, placing his fly rod beside the others on the counter.

"What about Millie?" Judge Parker asked in surprise.

[55]

"Millie?" The Colonel thought a moment. "Oh, you mean Millie. Well, we had a little disagreement the other day over those changes in the blueprints, and she ran off and eloped with that architect friend of hers in New York." He took a swig from Uncle Perk's jug, and wiped his stubbled chin with the back of his hand. "I told you," he grinned, "that I was the luckiest fellow in the world."

HOW TO CATCH
A HORN POUT

The July gathering of the Lower Forty Shooting, Angling and Inside Straight Club marked the first, if not last, of the club's new series of educational lectures. The membership had voted to enliven their meetings with a few talks by local experts on "Little Known Facts of Lesser Known Sports," and Uncle Perk, as the least-known sportsman anybody could think of, had been asked to start the program off with some advice on "How to Catch a Horn Pout." His advice, in brief, was: "Don't."

"Poutin'," Uncle Perk began, leaning back in his swivel chair and peering over his spectacles at the members of the Lower Forty gathered in the rear of the store, "is such a lesser-known sport that there is a serious question whether it's a sport at all. It more or less falls in the same class with froggin' or dippin', except when you go poutin' you get pout, and froggin' you get frogs, and dippin' you get smelt, but all of them you wind up gettin' wet. Wives generally claim that horn poutin' is immoral and leads to drinkin'," he said, "which is nonsense, of course, because nobody ever goes poutin' till he's had three or four drinks already, so it is just as true to say that drinkin' leads to poutin'."

He pulled open the lower right-hand drawer of his desk, lifted out his familiar jug of Old Stump Blower, and took a thoughtful swig. He wiped his moustache with the back of a hand, and passed the jug across the desk to the other members.

"Tell me, Uncle Perk," Doc Hall asked, taking a swallow and handing the loving cup to Judge Parker, "just what is a horn pout?"

"Wal, now, that's a question," Uncle Perk admitted, shoving a pile of unpaid bills onto the floor and crossing a pair of hunting rubbers on his desk blotter. "Some folks say it is a bullhead that's really a catfish, which I don't mind insulting cats but I do hate to associate a fine fambly like the fish fambly with anything as ornery as a pout. Sideways it looks like a kind of a pollywog, but head on it has a face like this Rossian feller Khrushchev just after somebody's proposed a toast to Comrade Stalin. Its main feature is five long whiskers with spikes in the end, and when your boat fills with water and them little dears start swimmin' around the bottom, and suddenly your foot slips and your rear end lands unexpectedly onto one of them, it's like getting into a bathtub and sitting on the bath brush."

"What do you use to catch them with?" the Judge inquired.

Uncle Perk rummaged in a pocket for his pipe. "Experts say the best bait is the gill of a horn pout," he said, blowing through the stem with a gargling sound, "but that means you got to catch a second horn pout before you catch the first one, so most folks prefer doughballs, or else a piece of pickled tripe, but a real old-timer like Hoop, for instance, he'd never use nawthin' but good old garden hackle."

"Who's Hoop?" Dexter Smeed prompted, as Uncle Perk paused to pack his pipe with crumbled shag.

"Real name was Hosmer Murch," Uncle Perk explained, striking a match across his rump, "but everybody called him Hoop on account of he used to be the old He-Hooper Horn Pouter of Purdy Pond." He sucked the flame into the charred bowl, and tamped the coals with a calloused thumb. "Until he quit," he added ominously.

"What did he quit for?" Colonel Cobb urged.

"Wal, it's a long story," Uncle Perk said, "so mebbe you better bolt the front door and hang out that 'Closed for Inventory' sign." He called to Cousin Sid: "Pull down the shades, too, or else some pesky customer might see a light and start yammerin' to get in."

He exhaled a pungent cloud of blue smoke, and locked his hands behind his head.

"The trouble with Hooper Murch," he recalled sadly, "his wife didn't approve of poutin'. She couldn't understand why a man would sit in a leaky boat all night and fight mosquitoes, and she mistrusted it was probably just an excuse to get out on the lake and romance one of them summer widows, and Hoop wanted to know how anybody could get romantic in six inches of water with his hands all slime, but his wife kep' asking him: 'Well, then, what else would you want to go horn pouting for?'

" 'To catch horn pout,' Hoop told her.

" 'In that case,' she ast, 'why don't you ever bring any home like Eben does?'

"Wal, that hit ole Hoop in a sensitive spot, because he was a very devoted pouter but not exactly what you'd call a lucky one, and him and his brother Eben Murch had been going out to Purdy Pond together for years, and Eben would always catch a bucketful, but all Hoop ever caught was his death of cold. So he decided the only way he could convince his wife was to get a horn pout to prove that was what he went for, and that afternoon he sneaked down to Purdy Pond and rowed out to Brother Eben's horn pout hole pole. Horn Pout fishermen all have their favorite holes, which they mark with a long pole so they can find them in the dark, and Brother Eben had a hole that was a corker. Hooper looked at it a long time, and then he glanced around to make sure nobody was watching, and then he moved Brother Eben's pole twenty yards or so to a mudflat. He marked where the hole really was by sighting on a pair of birches on the bank and counting thirty-six strokes of the oars back to shore, and then he went home and changed to his best clothes, and told his wife he needed the car that night to go to a lodge meeting, and he got a jug of hard cider and headed back to Purdy Pond just at sunset, which is when the pout always bite best, not to mention the mosquitoes.

"Brother Eben's boat was already anchored over the mud flat, and Hoop waved to him cordially, and sighted on the birches and rowed thirty-six strokes, and let his anchor down. Right off he begun haulin' up horn pout as fast as he could take a swig from his jug. He was so busy filling his bucket that he didn't even wonder why it was getting dark so quick, and he lit his lantrun and kep' on fishing. All to once't a flash of lightning made all the trees stand out on top of Moose Mountain, and there was a clap of thunder, and suddenly it come on to rain. Hoop grabbed the oars and started rowing for shore so hard he kicked over the lantrun, and he had to steer by the flashes of lightning. To make matters worse, somebody had deliberatey moved the shore, and instead of heading for a nice skidway of logs where he always hauled up his boat, he got turned around and run onto a flat rock about two inches under the surface, which he tried to shove himself off with an oar and the next thing he knew he was up to his neck in Purdy Pond, watching his bucket slowly filling with water and sinking and all his horn pout swimming out. He made a grab for the last one, spines and all, and crawled up onto the bank on his elbows, and it was hard to tell which was wetter, him or the pout.

"Wal, Hooper figured his wife wouldn't appreciate it if he come in the front door and dripped all over her livingroom carpet, so when he got home he snuk around to the kitchen door and tiptoed inside. He poured out his boots into the sink, and then he peeled off his wet clothes right down to his bare skin and hung them behind the stove, and then he looked around for something to dry himself. He see his wife's best silver platter on the kitchen table, with a napkin over it, and when he took off the napkin there was a lot of little triangular sandwiches on the platter, which he figgered was real thoughtful of his wife to leave for him. So while he was drying himself with the napkin he ate the sandwiches, and when the napkin give out he blotted himself with a pile of embroidered tea doilies that was on the table, and he finished rubbing down with a lace tablecloth. By this time he was feeling a nice rosy glow, and he put his pout on the empty platter and started for the living room, humming happily.

"'Look, darling,' he called to his wife, 'surprise!'

"He opened the door and stood there, clad in nothing but a horn pout on a silver platter, and his wife give a sort of a strangled squeal, and so did all the other ladies of the Wuncaweek Bridge Club that she was entertaining, and that," concluded Uncle Perk, "is why Hooper never went horn poutin' again." He opened the lower left hand drawer on the desk, and took out a fresh jug. "Last I heard he'd reformed, and was going around denouncing poutin' as a sin, which he says it is just an excuse to have a drink."

[61]

"That's r-ridiculous," Mister macNab snorted, reaching for the jug. "Since when did a mon ever-r need an excuse for that?"

THE
GUN AUCTION

It was about eight-thirty of a sultry August evening when the Lower Forty convened on the steps of Uncle Perk's store. You could tell it was getting on in the summer season, for all the young reptiles from the boys' and girls' camps at the Lake had paired off and were twosoming in and out of the village soda shop across the square, hand in hand. Unfortunately the general romantic mood failed to warm the members of the Club. They sat on the granite doorstep without speaking, their necks all craned up the street in the same direction, like a flock of suspicious geese watching for an approaching hunter.

Cousin Sid glanced at his watch for the tenth time in as many minutes, and sighed. "I only hope there hasn't been an accident."

"While the mon has our pr-r-roperty in his sacred trust," Mister MacNab added with a muffled groan.

To quiet his nerves, Uncle Perk trod into his store, took a gulp from a jug cached beneath the counter, and slipped a snap clothespin onto the tail of the store cat which was purring atop the cheese. He ambled back to his place on the front steps, feeling a little better.

"We never should have let him go alone," Doc Hall muttered

as another quarter-hour dragged by. "You know how the Judge is when he gets involved in one of these gun auctions. Probably we'll never see him again—"

He checked himself abruptly as screaming tires gangbusted around the corner, and Judge Parker broadsided his station wagon to a violent stop before the store. He took the steps in one leap, groped under the counter, and revived himself with a swig from Uncle Perk's jug. The members hovered in the doorway.

"What did you do?" Doc Hall asked uneasily.

"Two hundred," replied the Judge, swallowing and shuddering violently, "miles in four hours. Had to drive very carefully with all that plunder on board." He took a second gulp from the jug to overcome the effects of the first one, and helped himself to a slab of cheese. "Didn't even stop for any supper," he added in a self-righteous voice, striding back to the car.

They watched in silence as he removed a long blanketed bundle from the rear of the station wagon and mounted the steps again, humming to himself. He placed it on the counter, elevated his spectacles to the bridge of his nose, and thumbed a notebook.

"Let's see, now," he began. "Mister MacNab gave me one Model 1866 Winchester carbine, condition excellent. Caliber .44-28-200, rim fire, flat-nose bullet. Forty-six rounds of Winchester ammunition, head-stamped H, after old Tyler Henry, in original box. His grandfather's deer rifle. Four cartridges, four deer. Right?" He glanced at Mister MacNab, who nodded impatiently. "Also one Model 1873 Winchester, caliber .38-40, fancy grade, condition excellent, which his father acquired from a late lamented who shot himself with it after issuing some bad checks, contrary to the statute in such case made and provided and against the peace and dignity of the State, wherefore—"

"It was to pay for the casket that my feyther took it off the widow," Mister MacNab corrected with simple dignity.

"So I put these two rifles into the Maine Firearms Auction, just as I put everything else you fellows gave me," reported the Judge. "It seems there were four big Winchester collectors there, and they got to fighting, and as a result the rifles brought—" Judge Parker glanced at his notes, "—two hundred and thirty-seven dollars, less fifteen percent auction commission, which comes to—"

"Exactly two hundred and one dollars and forty-five cents net," Mister MacNab said promptly. "Mon, ye done wonder-r-r-ful. Where's the cash?"

The Judge lowered his spectacles, borrowed the cheese knife, and cut his wife's brand-new clothesline which he had used to bind the blanketed roll.

"You forget that each and every one of you told me to auction off your old guns and use the proceeds to get something I thought you might like. Right?"

Mister MacNab licked the perspiration that had suddenly gathered on his upper lip.

"Well, just look at this." Judge Parker held up a superb old Holland and Holland .303 double with twenty-six-inch barrels, fine engraving, clean-cut checking, three leaf rear sight, and complete set of cleaning tools. "Nothing like her anywhere in these parts. A hunter's dream. Handles just like a light woodcock gun, and still has the smash of a .303. Luckily there wasn't anybody bidding except a few rich New York summer complaints, and I stole her for two hundred and a quarter." He beamed at Mister MacNab. "So if you'll just give me your check for twenty-three dollars and fifty-five cents to balance accounts, we'll be square."

Mister MacNab fainted and was laid behind the counter where no one could step on him. The Judge waited patiently until business could be resumed.

"Doc Hall here," he went on, "gave me a .44 Remington Army cap and ball, engraved, with ivory grips, ninety percent original finish, which his great-uncle won from a Rebel cavalry officer at a poker game in a Richmond house of ill fame about a week after Lee's surrender. A Boston and a Philadelphia collector started scrapping over it together, and it returned an even three hundred, which comes to just two-fifty net. With the proceeds—"

He paused dramatically, flipped the blanket, and produced a gleaming Ithaca ten-bore magnum with double recoil pads, single trigger, ventilated rib, and one-power Weaver scope. Doc Hall's eyes had the gleam of a Marine lieutenant, just back from a year in Korea, watching his wife step out of her shower.

"—I secured this brand-new Ithaca for a flat two hundred," concluded the Judge, "which means that I owe Doc fifty-five bucks, minus five as his share of my traveling expenses, which I deem reasonable and fair."

The member's faces lit up one by one as Judge Parker revealed the rest of his loot. It developed that Colonel Cobb had traded a rusty-bored .58 Model 1863 Civil War Springfield for a fine .257 featherweight Mauser. Uncle Perk had exchanged a Model 1876 full-magazine Winchester .45-75, popularly known as the Centennial Model and as heavy as two crowbars, for a good used Ithaca twelve pump with ventilated Polychoke. Cousin Sid had converted a pair of Remington .41 rim-fire derringers, that he had found in the town vault while serving as selectman last year, into a long .357 Smith and Wesson Magnum. The Judge himself had swapped a 12-bore semi-auto, which several reliable gunsmiths had failed to cure of jamming every third round, into a reliable .222 Remington he'd coveted for years.

"It just goes to show," he said with a smug smiles, "you've got to be a real honest gun trader to outsmart these ruthless pirates you meet at an annual firearms auction."

Judge Parker was still smiling the following afternoon as he wound up his court session by reprimanding a local reprobate who had been taking short trout, and confiscating his four-ounce fly rod to replace the Judge's own battered pole. Mister MacNab was waiting outside the courthouse as he emerged. He handed the Judge a check for $23.55, and a five-dollar bill.

"Just to balance my account for the wee rifle, and also my share of your expense money," he said, "though I do think ye travel awful dear."

The Judge pocketed the money. "Glad you like that Holland and Holland," he said in relief. "Frankly at first I was just the least bit afraid—"

"Now, then, dinna ever worry about the few extra dollars ye may put in a fine old Holland and Holland," said Mister MacNab contentedly. "This morning I traded it off to Deacon Godfrey for his original Stanley Steamer, which he has nae run since 1920 and which he has kept hidden ever since under a hay-stack cover in his back barn. I wired for bids, and so far up to now the highest offer—" Mister MacNab squinted at a sheaf of telegrams, "—is twelve hundred and fifty dollars." He beamed at the Judge. "To show my gr-r-ratitude, old mon, ye can hae the hay-stack cover for a bonus."

YOU CAN
ARGUE ALL DAY

It was a lowery fall afternoon, and the members of the Lower Forty Shooting, Angling and Inside Straight Club had huddled around the stove in Uncle Perk's store at the end of a cold day's hunt. Their wet boots were steaming on the floor behind the stove, and the members in their stockinged feet sprawled along the counter and on upended cracker barrels, enjoying the warm nostalgic country-store smell of coffee and kerosene and salt pork and cheddar cheese, and browsing through the magazines on the display rack. "Here's quite a spread in the latest *Field and Stream*," Judge Parker remarked, flipping the pages with interest, "all about the different kinds of upland game. Each writer seems to have his favorite bird."

"The way I look at it," Uncle Perk observed, leaning back in his swivel chair and tamping tobacco into the charred bowl of his corncob pipe, "they ain't but one favorite bird, and that's the pa'tridge. Now I'm gen'ally conceded to be pretty near the best danged wingshot anywheres around Hardscrabble, an' I can send a handful of chilled seven-and-a-halfs after a pa'tridge as quick's anybody, but I admit it's quite a trick to aim right where it is." He rasped a match across the desk top. "I could explain the trick," he suggested, drawing on the flame of the match, "if somebody was to ask me how."

"How?" asked Cousin Sid.

"What you got to do in pa'tridge gunnin'," Uncle Perk informed the membership, jabbing the stem of his pipe for emphasis, "is to figger out ahead of time just what a pa'tridge is gonna do when he gits up. That's all there is to it. Like f'rinstance you can be pretty sure he'll either fly from left to right, or else he'll fly from right to left, or else he'll fly at an angle this way an' climb, or else he'll fly at an angle that way an' dive, or else he'll go straight up in the air, or else he'll run along the ground a little ways, or else maybe he'll come toward you, or go away from you, or fly off to either side of you, it all depends. But if you just remember that he's bound to do one thing or the other, you're pretty apt to get your bird, provided of course you didn't forgit to take the safety off your gun, or put in a new shell, or the pa'tridge didn't git up just as you was halfway acrost a bobwire fence with three, four spikes caught in the crotch of your pants, one boot jammed between a couple of rocks, a length of grapevine tangled around your gun barrel, and a good solid eighteen-inch pine tree between where you are and where your bird went. Otherwise," Uncle Perk concluded mildly, exhaling a cloud of rank smoke, "they ain't really nothin' to pa'tridge gunnin' at all."

"Grouse hunting is all very well," Doc Hall shrugged, "but I hold that the sportiest thing in feathers is the woodcock. Sits tight for a dog, doesn't run, lights again nearby so you can get a second point, and there's nothing to beat a timberdoodle spinning and twisting and zigging when you expect it to zag. The only way to hit it is to work out the problem mathematically." Doc cut himself a slab of cheese from the wedge on the counter, and spread it on a cracker as he talked. "If a charge of shot is traveling from twelve to fourteen hundred feet per second, and a doodle at, say, forty yards, is moving at thirty miles an hour, that means it should be led by 4.4 feet—"

"And by the time you've got all that worked out," Judge Parker interrupted, "and your eye has telegraphed the information to your brain, and your brain has sent word to your trigger finger, and your finger has released the trigger, and the trigger has released the hammer, and the hammer has slammed onto the firing pin, and the firing pin has ignited the primer, and the primer has fired the powder, and the powder has blown the shot out through the muzzle of the gun, your woodcock has disappeared somewhere into the next county, and there you are, apologizing to your bird dog again." He shook his head. "I claim if you want real shooting and plenty of it, there's nothing like doves. There's just about the fastest thing that flies. You aim at the first one coming past you, and if you lead it enough, you'll maybe hit the last one in the line. That's the upland game bird for the real purist."

"A purist," said Colonel Cobb, "is a man who goes to a lot of pains to deprive himself of a little pleasure." He reached for Uncle Perk's jug. "For a real smart upland game bird, I'll string along with the wild turkey every time. It has better eyes than a fox, better scent than a bear, and better hearing than a sheep." He took a long swig, and his eyes glazed nostalgically. "You get out there on a turkey ridge before dawn, and along about first light, just when you can count the eyelets in your boots, you see Mister Gobbler come feeding down the ridge toward you, and your heart gets pumping so hard it shakes the tree you're resting up against. It's like they used to say in Alabama when I was hunting with Chet Noble down around Clarke County: 'Effen a man has a boy baby and shoots him a turkey gobbler, then he's a man.' "

"The grouse may be exciting, and the woodcock tricky, and the dove fast," Cousin Sid said, "but I wouldn't trade them all together for a covey of bobwhite quail exploding right under your nose like a burst of feathered shrapnel, and blinking out of sight before you can get your gun to your shoulder. Dave Newell's got a place down in Leesburg, Florida, where he says the quail are so thick that even the singles get up in twos and threes. That's where I'm heading as soon as the season opens."

"Why tr-r-ravel at great expense, mon," Mister MacNab objected, "when ye can hunt r-r-ringneck pheasant right at home? There's nae handsomer bir-r-rd than a pheasant with its exotic colors, long showy tail and brilliant red breast and white collar around its throat," he beamed, "and besides, luik at how much more meat ye get for the pr-r-rice of a shell."

Dexter Smeed had been standing with his wet rear end to the stove, listening to the other members in silence. He reached into the game pocket of his hunting jacket.

"Everybody's been arguing about the best kind of game," he said, "but so far I haven't seen them produce anything." He held aloft a long furry object, dangling by its ears. "At least, I got a rabbit today."

There was a concerted movement among the members, and Dexter made the front door of Uncle Perk's store just in time, as the rabbit which he had dropped in his precipitous flight came sailing past his head. Uncle Perk waited until they had taken their seats again, and order was restored.

"The best thing about upland game," he mused, knocking out

his pipe on a heel of his rubber hunting boot, "there ain't a big trophy to hunt for. You're not lookin' for a head to mount an' brag about afterwards. One pa'tridge is about's large as another, one timberdoodle is as tricky's all the rest, one quail is as fast's the next. You don't have to go to the Yukon or Tibet, 'cause the gunnin' is just's good right in your own lower forty. Everybody can shoot, an' everybody can miss. That's what makes it fun."

He reached into his desk drawer, and brought out a new jug.

"You can argue all day," he concluded, pausing to pull out the cork with his teeth, "but it ain't whether you hit a bird that matters. It's the fun you have even if you don't."

WE'LL LIVE ON ANGEL PIE

This Christmas Cousin Sid suggested that the members of the Lower Forty Shooting, Angling and Inside Straight Club should devote themselves to some worthwhile community project. Since Cousin Sid was a member of the local school board, which had just completed the construction of a fine new consolidated grade school, it was his personal suggestion that the Club might carry out the Yuletide spirit by christening the building with a real bang-up Christmas party for the kiddies.

Judge Parker fell in enthusiastically with Cousin Sid's proposal. "It is up to the older people in town to set a good example for the young, in order to help combat juvenile delinquency," he stated firmly. "I'll get Sheriff Jackson to shake down some of these big ten-wheel Diesel jobs that haul groceries through town, and nab a few crates of oranges or bananas that happen to be on the load." His eyes glowed with Christmas fervor. "Those trucks have been getting away with murder lately, breaking speed regulations and exceeding the legal load limit, and it's time we taught them a little law and order, not to mention getting some free supplies to gladden the kiddies' hearts at this festive season."

"By a for-r-rtunate circumstance," Mister MacNab offered, "I happen to hold a mortgage on the local movie theater, on which the interest is long overdue, and I am sure I can per-r-rsuade the proprietor to donate one gross boxfuls of buttered popcorn for the wee tots."

Uncle Perk scratched his head. "Last time they was an inventory took in my store," he recalled, "was when my granddaddy come back from the Civil War and wanted to see if he'd been cheated by his fambly while he was away. I don't rightly know what's down in the cellar, but last time I looked they was quite a collection of old wool boots and mouse-eaten horse collars and buggy whips, not to mention a few rusty fox traps and some illegal bean shooters and a lot of ax blades and jackknives and crosscut saws which ought to make them young uns quite happy when they find them in their stockings."

It was Doc Hall who solved the problem of delivering the gifts. It seems that Doc had a rural client who owed him five years' back bills, and Doc volunteered to put the bite on this delinquent for a pair of Shetland ponies and an open sleigh. "We can paint the sleigh red," Doc suggested, "and put a red blanket on each pony and strap a set of deer antlers on his head. Think how the youngsters' faces will light up when Santa Claus drives right into the school gymnasium, at the height of the festivities, with a whole sleighful of presents."

"Who's going to be Santa Claus?" Cousin Sid asked.

"That," said Judge Parker, with a meaningful glance at his wife's nephew, "is just the job for Dexter Smeed."

Every afternoon, as Christmas drew nearer, the members worked feverishly to help old Orion Bean, the school janitor, get the gymnasium ready. A wide plank runway was erected from the gym's main entrance, leading down over the tiers of seats to the basketball court, and at Mr. Bean's request a generous layer of sawdust was spread over the floor to protect the polished hardwood surface. Sprays of pine and hemlock were festooned along the balcony and banked at the back of the hall, to conceal the emergency pair of rear doors which could be opened in summer when the gymnasium was being used for the annual automobile show. In the best Yuletide spirit, the members even sacrificed an entire night of coon hunting to cut down a large fir tree on Deacon Godfrey's posted land and erect it in the center of the gymnasium. All the members took turns holding the stepladder while Mr. Bean climbed up and hung the ornaments on the branches.

"Got to be real careful of these here glass balls and things," Mr. Bean cautioned. "They belong to the school, and Miss Peavey, the principal, she'd have conniptions if anything ever got busted—" He teetered precariously on the top of the ladder, and placed a gleaming white tinsel angel on the spindle of the fir. "—especially this here angel."

Cousin Sid, as master of ceremonies, had planned a rather short program of appropriate carols, climaxed by an address of welcome to Santa Claus delivered by Miss Peavey. Unfortunately Miss Peavey took advantage of this long-awaited opportunity to present an exhaustive report of the school's finances during the past fiscal year, including a statement of the current budget and a pointed hint to the school committee to vote an increase in teaching salaries at once. The young audience grew increasingly restive, interrupting from time to time with stamps and shrill whistles and shouts of "Bring on Santa Claus!" To make matters worse, Dexter Smeed was waiting outside in the open sleigh, dressed in a red Santa Claus suit and a white cotton beard, and he was having considerable trouble keeping the pair of Shetland ponies steady. Dexter was not very used to horses, and despite his effort they kept tossing their heads and jolting the deer antlers down over their eyes.

Dexter had just lit a cigarette to calm his nerves when Miss Peavey wound up her speech of welcome. Doc Hall gave the prearranged signal — a short blast on his duck call — and the gym doors swung open. Dexter spat out his cigarette, which lodged unnoticed in his cotton beard, and shouted: "On, Donner and Blitzen!", flapping the reins and cracking the whip. This proved to be a rather poor idea. The nervous ponies started through the door at full gallop and raced down the ramp, the sleigh gathering momentum behind them. As their hooves struck the polished hardwood floor of the basketball court, they began to skid and slide, their panic increased by the jangling of sleigh bells and the excited shouts of the audience. The sleigh slewed and sashayed back and forth in a tortuous route across the gym, strewing its contents in all directions, while Santa Claus held on desperately with one hand and beat at his smouldering beard with the other. Sizing up the situation promptly, Mr. Bean threw open the emergency rear doors in the nick of time. Without breaking pace, the ponies exited through the back of the gymnasium at a dead run, Dexter's cotton whiskers trailing smoke and flame as the sleigh disappeared into the night.

While the children gathered up their scattered gifts, the conscience-stricken members tried to console Miss Peavey, who had burst into tears at the debacle. "Now they'll never believe in Santa Claus again," she moaned.

"Shucks, ma'am," said a third-grade pupil whose father was an Air Force pilot stationed in Germany, and who spoke for all his young fellow members of the new supersonic age, "if Santa's got to do a drop mission on every school in the country inside of twenty-four hours, it stands to reason that all he can do is lower his flaps, eject his cargo as he buzzes his d.z., and then pour on the coal for the next target." He shook his head admiringly. "Personally I'll always believe in the old boy from now on, after seeing the way he cut in his afterburner when he started to pull up."

Late that night, after the party was over, the members of the Lower Forty sat in the empty gym, enjoying a few swigs of Uncle Perk's special holiday jug of Old Splitting Wedge while Mr. Bean took down the Christmas tree ornaments one by one. Doc Hall, seated at the school piano, pounded out the tune of "It Came Upon a Midnight Clear," while his fellow members joined together in the old hunting refrain:

When I can shoo-oot my rifle clear
To Angels in the sky,
Then I'll stop living on bread and beer
And li-ive on Angel pie.

Mr. Bean balanced on top of the ladder, and reached in vain for the white tinsel angel. Judge Parker picked up his semi-automatic .22, drew a bead, and severed the spindle neatly. The janitor caught the angel as it fluttered down into his cupped hands, descended the ladder, wrapped it in cotton batting and replaced it carefully in a box on which Miss Peavey had written "Xms.Angl." The Judge acknowledged Mr. Bean's grateful thanks with a modest wave of his hand.

"When I can shoo-oot my rifle clear," the members sang in unison as Doc Hall hammered the piano keys, "to Angels in the—" Doc Hall stopped for a moment, struck by a sudden thought. "By the way, Judge," he asked, "wha'ev'r happened to

[79]

Dexter?"

"Las' I heard," shrugged the Judge, "he was seen heading for the North Pole, still shouting 'Whoa' and slapping at his beard."

Doc Hall nodded, and bent over the piano again. "Then I'll stop living on bread and beer," he resumed, leading the chorus of voices in a minor key, "and li-ive on Angel pie . . ."

THE CONFIRMED
BATCHELDER

Somehow the subject of wives came up again at the February meeting of the Lower Forty Shooting, Angling and Inside Straight Club. "Take my wife," Judge Parker confided to his fellow members, "she never leaves anything where it is. She always puts it back where it was. Like for instance every night I move the reading lamp over by my chair, and every morning she moves it over by the wall again, because she says that's where it goes, and when I ask her why it goes there, she says because that's where it belongs."

"The reason my wife moves things," said Doc Hall, "is because she wants to try them somewhere else instead. By the time I finish shifting all the furniture around every night, I'm so tired I fall right into bed, except it usually turns out she moved the bed."

"My wife doesn't so much move things," Cousin Sid sighed, "as she puts them away to save them. Like for instance she always saves string. Not only string but wrapping paper, and not only wrapping paper but boxes. I bet we've got an attic full of empty boxes. The trouble is that when there's something I want to put in a box, she says I can't have it because she's saving it."

"My wife saves ever-r-rything," Mister MacNab mourned,

"except money."

Uncle Perk leaned back in his swivel chair, clasped his hands behind his head, and grinned contentedly. "The more I hear you fellers talk about your wives," he chuckled, "the better off I feel bein' a batchelder."

"How come you managed to stay single all these years?" Judge Parker asked enviously.

"I'll admit ye're not too attr-r-ractive to look at, Pairk," Mister MacNab added in all fairness, "but the prosperous income ye d'rive from this store here should be hard for any woman to r-r-re-sist."

"Married life ain't for me," Uncle Perk said stoutly. "I got a shotgun, and the best durn rabbit dog in Hardscrabble County, and nobody complains if I come home late for supper or track my wet feet all over the house. I'm perfectly content just livin' with Old Trail."

"Haven't you ever longed sometime for the pleasure of female companionship?" asked Cousin Sid.

Uncle Perk hesitated a moment. "Wal, to be frank, there was a widow lady here in town I used to be sort of sweet on once't," he confessed, "but we busted up on account of my dog." He shook his head. "I couldn't stand the way she treated Trail."

"You mean she abused him?" asked Doc Hall, shocked.

"On the contrary," Uncle Perk corrected, "she was so nice to him I had to break off the engagement." He lapsed into reminiscent silence, while the sleet rattled against the store windows and an occasional down draft sent a puff of smoke from the Franklin stove. "It's a long story," he sighed, "but seein' it ain't a fit afternoon to go rabbit huntin' anyway, I might as well tell you."

Uncle Perk strode to the front door, turned the key in the lock, and yanked down the shade with its printed sign: "Store closed. Have went ice-fishing." He returned to his desk, pulled out the lower right hand drawer, and took a long swallow from a jug of Old Splittin' Wedge.

"I guess me and Millie was pretty serious back there for a while," he began, crossing his hunting rubbers on the desk blotter. "She'd come over and cook supper for me every night, and whenever we'd go huntin' together she'd sit in the car and never say a word even if I was gone three-four hours, and on the way home she'd let Trail sit in her lap, muddy paws and all. She said she knew how much I thought of the dog, and when we got married she was going to make him a nice home, and we could all sleep in the same bed like one happy fambly. That should of made me suspicious right off, but you know how it is when a feller gets romantical, he don't stop and think sometimes.

"Just about then my uncle died in Californey, and I had to go out there a couple of months and settle the estate. Naturally I wondered what to do with Trail, but Millie said not to give it another thought, she'd look after him while I was away. She kep' writing and telling me he was all right and not to worry. She met me at the train when I got back, and the first thing she said was: 'I got a surprise!'

"I noticed she had a funny kind of expression on her face. 'How's Trail?' I ast.

" 'Wait'll you see him,' she smiled, 'you won't even know him.'

"I tell you what's a fact, I actually didn't recognize him at first. He must of put on twenty pounds, he was so fat he couldn't wag his tail without standing up, and he had a red ribbon around his neck and she'd even curled the hair on top of his head. He was lying on a special sanitary foam-rubber mattress, and there was a French china dog dish with *Pour le chein* on it for him to drink out of, and he had a plastic dog bone and a toy mouse that squeaked. Can you imagine the best rabbit dog in Hardscrabble County playing with a rubber mouse?" Uncle Perk groaned. "All I could do was stand there and look at him without saying anything.

" 'I knew you'd be pleased,' Millie said. 'Now watch this!'

"She snapped her fingers, and Trail yawned and unpeeled one eye. 'Roll over,' Millie told him, and so help me, he rolled over. 'Sit up and beg,' said Millie, and Trail reared up on his hind end with his front paws dangling, and Millie took a piece of candy and balanced it on the end of his nose and counted 'One, two, three!' and he flipped it in the air and caught it. 'Sit down,' she said, and so did I, because I was too weak to stand up.

" 'He's so intelligent,' Millie beamed, picking him up in her arms and smearing a little lipstick on his muzzle. 'He used to bark all the time, but I broke him of that. Remember how he chased rabbits once?' she winked. 'Not any more.'

" 'What do you mean?' I groaned.

" 'Come on and I'll show you,' she said triumphantly. 'That's my surprise!'

"So she dressed him in a nice warm dog sweater with 'Trail' knitted on it, and I followed her out to the back yard, and there was a wire coop with a couple of white Angora rabbits inside it. She put Trail right into the coop with them, and he lay down and let them snuggle up beside him, and he was just about to start lapping one of them with his tongue when I grabbed him by the scruff of the neck. I don't remember what I said to Millie, but it ended our engagement then and there. She never even spoke to me again."

Uncle Perk paused to take another swallow from the jug.

"It only took a couple of baths with disinfectant soap to get the smell of perfume out of his fur, but it was six months before I got all the fat off him so's he could hunt again, and to this day it seems to me his voice is a little higher pitched than it used to be. The worst of it is that when he chases a rabbit, I'm still not entirely sure whether he wants to catch it or kiss it." He shook his head. "I tell you, it takes a woman to spoil a hunting dog—"

Uncle Perk paused as an imperious scratching sounded at the front door. He hurried over and unlocked it obediently, and admitted an elderly and well-fed beagle. Old Trail gave him a superior glance, waddled across the store, and climbed into the chair where Uncle Perk had just been sitting. Uncle Perk covered him with his hunting coat, and sat down meekly on the floor beside him.

"So that," he concluded, watching in doting approval as Trail chewed the buttons off his coat one by one, "is why I'm still a batchelder."

A MORNING
IN APRIL

Doc Hall seemed ill at ease as he faced the other members of the Lower Forty at their April meeting. "I'm afraid I won't be able to join you fellows on Opening Day tomorrow," he informed them briskly, avoiding their eyes as he spoke. "I . . . I've got to attend a medical meeting down in Boston."

Judge Parker acted equally evasive. "I'm not going to be able to make it, either," he announced to the Club with an elaborate sigh. "There's an important court case coming up. The rest of you'll have to get along without me."

"As a matter of fact, I can't be on hand myself," Cousin Sid stumbled. "It's . . . uh . . . my wife," he invented quickly. "She wants me to take her shopping."

"Pairsonally ye'll have to include me out, too," Mister Mac-Nab shrugged. "I canna affor-r-rd the license fee this year." His effort to sound offhand was not entirely convincing. "I guess Uncle Pairk will have to open the tr-r-rout season alone."

"Not me," Uncle Perk muttered, tamping tobacco into his pipe. "Gotta stay here an' take inventory of the store." He peered quizzically at his fellow members over the flare of the match. "You know," he mused, "this is the first time the Lower Forty ever failed to fish Farmer Libbey's brook together on

Openin' Day."

The mention of Aldo Libbey's name produced a little silence. The news of his recent stroke had hit the Club hard; there was no hope, Doc Hall had informed them. Judge Parker drummed his fingertips on the counter, and cleared his throat. "Tell us the truth, Doc," he asked bluntly. "How much longer has the old codger got?"

Doc Hall shrugged. "He's sinking fast. It could happen any time."

Cousin Sid inquired in a low voice: "Does he know?"

"I haven't told him," Doc said briefly. He glanced at his watch, and rose. "Well, I'd better grab some sleep. Got a long trip to Boston tomorrow."

Bright and early the following day Doc Hall hurried to his car, glanced up and down the street to make sure he was not observed, and headed for the Libbey farm in Hardscrabble. It was a liquid spring morning: The robins were trilling, the dew glistened on the fresh green grass in the fields, and the first skunk cabbage and cowslips showed along the banks of the stream. The blue April sky was reflected in the clear water below, as his car rumbled over the wooden bridge, and a trout boiled temptingly against the far bank.

Doc gave it a longing glance, and drove on resolutely toward the big white house at the top of Hardscrabble Hill. Opening Day could wait; this morning — though Doc would be the last to admit it — he was on a sentimental mission. For years old Aldo Libbey had been a generous host and friend. On Doc's left, as he drove, was the tangled alder bottom that Aldo always referred to as his lower forty — that was how the Club first got its name — where the members hunted woodcock every fall. On his right,

Libbey's brook tumbled and cascaded down through the old man's pasture, halting now and then in its headlong course to form an occasional deep pool. These were Farmer Libbey's favorite fishing holes; he had always insisted that the members of the Lower Forty share them with him. "The most fun o' fishin'," he used to tell them, "is the folks you fish with." In later years, when Aldo was too crippled to handle a rod any more, he'd hobble down to the stream and point out to the others where the big ones lay. "Seen an ole sockdollager there last evenin', Doc. Try your fly over yonder under that cut bank . . ."

Effie Libbey opened the front door in silence, and Doc tiptoed upstairs alone to the front bedroom. Aldo's white-stubbled face looked thin, and he was breathing hard. His eyelids fluttered open as Doc bent over him. "What you doin' here, Doc?" he asked weakly. "Why ain't you out fishin' on Opening Day?"

"Just happened to be driving by, Aldo," Doc said lamely, "and I wondered if there was anything I could do for you."

"Ain't nothin' nobody can do for me." His eyes met Doc's. "You know it, an' I know it, too."

Doc hesitated, and then nodded.

"Wal, then, it ain't no sense to waste your time indoors, a purty mornin' in April like this. Get out there on the stream with them other fellows—"

The bedroom door opened, and Judge Parker strode in. His face flushed as he confronted Doc. "Thought you were supposed to be in Boston," he muttered under his breath.

"Thought you had a court case," Doc retorted in embarrassment.

"Just happened to be driving past," the Judge told Aldo self-consciously, "and I wanted to drop off this latest copy of *Field and Stream.* Maybe you'd like to read what the Lower Forty's been up to lately—"

The doorknob rattled behind them, and Cousin Sid and Mister MacNab entered the room together. They halted in confusion as they saw their fellow members. "Well, say, this is certainly quite a coincidence," Cousin Sid stammered. "I just happened to be driving out this way, and who should I bump into but Mister MacNab, and we figured while we were so handy we might drop in and say hello . . ."

"Natur-r-rally we had no intention of coming here whatso-ever-r-r," Mister MacNab insisted, "but it would be a sheer waste of gas to go back again without passing the time of day."

"By the way, Aldo," Cousin Sid said with a forced heartiness, "I brought you some wet flies and leaders. You can try them this summer after you're up and around again."

"I brought ye a dip net for when ye go smelting," added Mister MacNab. " 'Twas my son's butterfly net, but the wee tot has outgr-r-rown it of late."

The bedroom door creaked open again, and Uncle Perk shuffled in. He blinked at the others without surprise. "Sort o' figgered I'd run into you fellers here," he murmured. "Reckon we all had the same idee." He produced a familiar-looking object from the game pocket of his canvas jacket. "Brung you a jug o' my special Ole Lightnin' Rod," he said to Aldo. "Might like a swaller later when you're feeling more like yourself."

The old man's lips parted in the ghost of a smile.

"I thank ye," he said faintly. "I thank ye kindly, but I don't cal'late I'll have much call for these any more." He saw the concern on their faces, and went on quickly: "I got everything I need, boys. I'm content."

He looked down at his heavy callused hands folded on the bedspread.

"I done my share of work in my life, but I done my share of huntin' and fishin' too. I got a lot of nice things to look back on now. I can lie here an' think of all the purty mornin's like this, an' the red sunsets, and the good times I had with my fish pole or my ole cornsheller. I got my memories. That's all a man needs to content him when he comes to the end of the long day."

His eyes moved to the window. The sun was bright, and a few insects stirred in the newly opened apple blossoms.

"It's a good time for fishin' right now. Them flies will be landin' on the water, and mebbe that old sockdollager will be stirring there under the bank. Go see if one o' you can take him. It will be a nice thing to look back on someday."

The sun was high overhead as Doc straightened his line across the pool, and dropped his fly beside the far bank. There was a swirl, a square tail thrashed the water once, and his reel screamed. The other members gathered to watch him as he led the big trout to shore, and knelt beside it. He wet his hand, held the trout behind the gills, and removed the fly. He released his grip; it flicked its tail once, and darted out of sight.

"What have ye done, mon?" Mister MacNab gasped. "It's gone."

Doc was looking at the house on the hill. He said to himself slowly: "It isn't gone. I've got it to look back on some day."

MINUTES
ON THE MOVE

All the members of the Lower Forty Shooting, Angling and Inside Straight Club nodded in approval as Judge Parker offered his notion. "Only one way to combat juvenile delinquency," he insisted, "and that's to inculcate in the younger generation the principles of sportsmanship and honesty for which our club stands." He helped himself to another slab of rat-trap cheese when Uncle Perk wasn't looking. "So I hereby propose we found a Lower Forty Junior Camp, and invite a group of city kids to Hardscrabble each year for a week in the great outdoors."

"A verra guid idea, Judge," Mister MacNab agreed, "but how do ye pr-r-ropose to finance this noble endeavor?"

"From the proceeds of our book." Judge Parker pointed to a large carton filled with copies of the club's brand-new anthology. "The publishers are letting us have a hundred of these at a discount," he explained, "and the profits from their sale should take care of our Junior Camp this coming summer."

"Wal, ain't that nice o' Mr. Holt an' Mr. Rinehart an' that other feller," Uncle Perk murmured. "Now all we got to do is find a hunnerd people here in Hardscrabble who can read."

"It's a matter of the right approach, that's all." Judge Parker rose and strolled toward a customer who had just entered the store. "Good afternoon, Mrs. Peavey," he smiled, "I'm sure an intelligent person like yourself would want to buy a copy of *Minutes of the Lower Forty*."

"I'm sorry, Judge," Mrs. Peavey began, "but you see—"

"Just off the press," the Judge persisted, brushing aside her objections with a wave of his hand, "all the favorite stories of your favorite club, gathered together for the first time in one handsome volume, profusely illustrated by Walt Dower, a veritable fest of fun and frolic."

"Yes, but—"

"You'll laugh from the moment you pick up until you read it," Cousin Sid urged.

"I know, but—"

"The perfect gift for Father's Day," Colonel Cobb pointed out, "let alone a birthday or wedding anniversary or maybe your son's graduation."

"The trouble is—"

"Or else you can use it for a doorstop," Doc Hall suggested. "Or prop up the rear leg of your kitchen table with it, or set hot dishes on it, or hang it on a nail in the privy, or throw it at your husband during a family argument."

"What I'm trying to say—"

"'Tis a bar-r-rgain ye canna resist—" Mister MacNab argued —"three dollars and fifty cents for 159 pages. That's only two cents a page — the paper alone is worth the price. How can you af-for-r-rd to be without one?"

"But I've already bought it," Mrs. Peavey managed to break in. "I clipped the coupon from *Field and Stream*, and sent in my money yesterday."

Uncle Perk shook his head as the door closed behind her. "I'm afraid you ain't got the right approach, Judge." He peered over his spectacles at Hentracks Hennessy shuffling into the store. "Watch how I handle it."

Hentracks opened the showcase, took out a tin of tobacco, and dropped it into his pocket. "Just charge it," he told Uncle Perk.

"Now, hol' on a minute, Hentracks," Uncle Perk scowled. "You already run up a back bill o' fifty-three dollars and fourteen cents. 'Course I know your wife's been poorly lately, an' you're out of a job, an' your children all got slush runnin' out o' their shoes, so I tell you what I'll do." He winked at the others. "I'll let your account ride a little longer if you'll buy a copy o' *Minutes o' the Lower Forty*."

"Sure, I'll be glad to." Hentracks dropped the book into his pocket. "Just charge it," he told Uncle Perk as he departed.

There was a moody silence. "We don't seem to be getting ahead very fast," Cousin Sid sighed.

The silence was broken by the sudden alarm of the string of sleigh bells hanging inside the door. The members looked up hopefully. They lowered their heads again as Deacon Godfrey entered, his thin face set in wintry lines. "Ain't no use tryin' to sell a book to that ole tightwad," Uncle Perk muttered, leaning back in his swivel chair, "pertick'ly after what we wrote about him in it."

The deacon strode across the room and halted before him. "I'd like to buy a copy of *Minutes of the Lower Forty*," he announced, tossing his money on the counter.

Uncle Perk's swivel chair came forward with a heavy thud. "Why, that's real friendly of you, Deacon," he said when he had recovered from the shock. "I hope you enjoy readin' it—"

"I ain't a-gonna read it," Deacon Godfrey snarled, glaring at the group around the stove. "This copy is for my lawyers. I'm suing the Lower Forty for libel, defamation of character, and malicious highbowdjery."

The door slammed so hard behind him that the string of sleigh bells stood straight out. The echoes died and silence settled over the room again. "There's only one way to dispose of these books," Judge Parker concluded. "Let's take a dozen copies apiece and go out and sell them by hook or by crook. If fair means don't work, try foul." He handed out five armloads of books. "We'll report back here same time tomorrow."

"An' I'll offer this here jug of Old Stump Blower," Uncle Perk added, pulling open the lower left-hand drawer of his desk, "as a prize to the member who sells the most."

The next afternoon, Uncle Perk's hunting rubbers were crossed on his desk blotter and smoke from his battered corncob wreathed his face in a contented smile as the Lower Forty reassembled in his store.

"Nothing to it," Judge Parker told the others, cutting himself another slab of cheese. "I had the state troopers knock off some of these overweight trucks going through town, and then offered to give the drivers a suspended sentence if they'd buy a book. Got rid of six copies overnight."

"I'm one up on you, Judge," Doc Hall grinned. "My score is seven. All I did was make the rounds of my patients, and ask them which they'd rather have: a copy of *Minutes* or a barium enema. They all chose the book."

"I sold nine copies," Colonel Cobb reported with a superior smile, "by dropping a hint to a few leading citizens that I was thinking of running their names in the gossip column of the *Gazette*."

"Put me down for eleven," Cousin Sid announced. "I assigned *Minutes of the Lower Forty* as required reading in our high school English class."

Mister MacNab cackled with glee. "Well, that makes me high mon," he beamed. "I sold all twelve buiks in one feel swoop."

"Howinell did you do that?" Judge Parker said enviously.

"I was conducting an inter-r-rment sairvice this morning," Mister MacNab replied, "and in the midst of the proceedings, just as the winch was lowering the box containing the late lamented, I lean over to his next-of-kin and whispered: 'Do I let it go thoomp, or will ye buy a dozen copies?'" Mister MacNab reached for the jug of Old Stump Blower. "So I guess I take the pr-r-rize."

"Not so fast, Mac," Uncle Perk said, snatching the jug away. He pointed to the empty carton on the floor beside him. "I sold all forty books that was left over, an' I never even stirred outa this chair."

The others stared incredulously.

"I just picked up the phone," Uncle Perk explained, "an' called up the Jedge's wife, an' Doc's wife, an' Cousin Sid's wife, an' Maggie MacNab, an' tole 'em about the Lower Forty Junior Camp. They thought it was sech a worthy cause that they bought ten copies apiece to help support it."

"But—" The Judge struggled for words. "We husbands are the ones who'll have to pay for them."

Uncle Perk took a long swallow from the prize jug, and put it back in the lower left-hand drawer of his desk. "That's your problem," he shrugged. "I'm a batchelder myself."

BRINGING IN
THE SHEAVES

Judge Parker slammed the front door of Uncle Perk's store so hard that the strap of sleighbells hanging inside leapt and jangled shrilly. His accusing eye moved around the circle of members, and came to rest on Uncle Perk. "What's the idea?" he demanded, "hanging that confangled sign in your window?"

Uncle Perk slid his spectacles down the bridge of his nose, and gazed mildly over the rims at the hand-painted poster in front of the store. The delicate feminine print read:

Today!
August Bazaar of the Ladies' Circle
of Silent Workers of the First Church!!
Parish house lawn, 2:30 p.m.
Come one come all!!!

"Why, Jedge, your wife ast me to put it there," Uncle Perk remonstrated. "Seems the ladies want to raise some money to refurbish the parish house for this here new minister that's coming, they got to git the floors resanded where the knots is poking through, and the wallpaper's hanging in shreds, and the roof leaks, so they figgered to hold a church fair—"

"I know all about it," the Judge interrupted irritably. "Why do you think I got on my best suit and even a necktie for? It's bad enough to be dragged off to a charity bazaar this afternoon when I was planning to go fishing instead," he complained, "without being reminded of it everywhere I look."

"Sure wisht I could enjoy that fair with you fellers," Uncle Perk sighed with mock sympathy, "but I got to stay here an' tend the store. On the other hand, o' course," he mused, "it ain't much sense to keep the store open with everybody at the fair, so I guess I'll try that lower pool on Mink Brook while you're all away." He grinned at the glum faces around him, and took a fresh jug of Old Stump Blower from his desk drawer. "Mebbe you fellers better lug this along," he chuckled, "so's to console yourselves when them new store shoes start hurting your feet along toward evening."

Judge Parker was still grumbling as he arrived at the scene of the festivities that afternoon. The parish lawn was dotted with booths, in which the ladies of the Circle of Silent Workers were displaying their homemade wares for sale. There was an apron table, with bright-colored specimens of fancy work dangling from a string; a table beside it offered candy and jellies and piccalilli; at another stand Mrs. MacNab was dispensing pink lemonade; while at the rear of the lawn Judge Parker's wife was presiding over a long table, loaded with assorted items of second-hand apparel. The Judge glanced at the array, and his eyes suddenly widened.

"Isn't that my old fishing hat?" he demanded.

"Yes, dear," his wife said pleasantly. "It was hanging in the attic, and I thought it would be just the thing for our rummage table."

Doc Hall stared aghast at the display. "Why, that's my old fishing shirt," he exclaimed, "and my old fishing pants that are practically as good as new except the seat is missing." He turned to his wife. "No wonder I couldn't find them in the hall closet this morning."

"I knew you'd be glad to contribute them to this worthy cause," his wife nodded.

"That's my old pair of waders I was planning to patch sometime," Cousin Sid groaned, giving his wife a reproachful look. "I've been wondering where they were."

Mister MacNab uttered a stifled sound, and pointed to a stuffed deer's head with one antler missing. "Think of all the money I spent to stuff that elegant tr-r-rophy," he mourned, "not to mention the cost of the ammunition it will r-r-require to shoot a new one."

Judge Parker took a deep breath, and assumed his fiercest judicial scowl. "Now, look here, Patience," he began sternly, "we're taking these things back—"

"Why, Lyford, dear," Mrs. Parker said with a reproving glance, "would you work against the Lord?"

Judge Parker started to reply, and then let out his breath in a long sigh of defeat. The members turned away, and strolled disconsolately across the lawn. The popping of an air rifle assailed their ears, and they halted before a canvas tent. A string of tin ducks moved across the rear of the tent, and assorted kewpie dolls and boxes of cigarettes were ranged along the back wall, with numbered targets beside them. "Try ya luck, gen'lmen," the concession owner urged in a gravel voice. "Ten cents a shot."

The Judge plunked down a dime on the counter, put the air rifle to his shoulder, and aimed at a passing duck. The cork pellet missed it by a foot. "All right, gen'lmen," the owner said, pocketing the dime briskly, "who's nex'?"

Colonel Cobb watched narrowly as the other members paid their dimes, and each scored a clean miss in turn. He beckoned the group to one side. "I used to work around a carnival," he whispered. "That rifle's gaffed."

"Gaffed?" echoed Judge Parker, puzzled.

"Fixed. Rigged," Colonel Cobb explained, "so the ump-chay can't in-way. In this case, Judge," he added, "you're the ump-chay."

"Ump-chay my oot-fay," Judge Parker growled. "You fellers stand around me so the sun isn't in my eyes, and let me investigate this a little." He put down another dime, fired the rifle, and followed the course of the cork pellet. "Four inches low at seven o'clock," he confided. "That's simple. We'll just hold at one o'clock high."

The concession owner's face grew pale as the Judge picked off the tin ducks one by one, and swept up an armload of kewpie dolls. He handed the rifle to Doc Hall, who proceeded to lower the numbered targets beside the cigarettes. As Doc gathered up his spoils, and handed the rifle to Cousin Sid, the concessionaire threw up his hands.

"Gimme a break, fellas," he pleaded. "You're cleaning me out. I'll be ruint."

"I'll make a little deal with you," the Judge offered, with a sidelong glance at his fellow members. "We'll settle for enough cash to buy everything over there on that rummage table."

"It's a holdup," the owner protested. "You can all go to—"

He paused as an ominous shadow fell across the tent. Woolboot Jackson, the local sheriff, had halted at his elbow, a cigarette thrust between his lips. Woolboot struck the head of a kitchen match on the hammer of the .357 Magnum at his belt, and lit his cigarette. "If I was you, buster," he suggested, snapping the burnt match casually at the owner's chest, "I'd pay and git out."

Judge Parker snatched the proffered sheaf of bills, and galloped toward the rummage table. Mister MacNab, following at his heels, paused beside the lemonade booth. His wife was dabbing at her eyes with a handkerchief.

"Nobody's buying any lemonade," she sobbed. "I made a gallon of it and used up a whole lemon, and now it's all going to waste."

"Dinna fret, sweetheart," Mister MacNab said promptly. "All it takes is the pr-r-roper salesmanship." He stepped behind the counter, turned his back, and bent over the bowl of lemonade furtively for a moment. He straightened, filled a paper cup, and handed it to a passerby. "Try a fr-r-ree sample," he urged.

The farmer took a swallow, and his Adam's apple twanged like a musical saw. "Gimme another," he said in delight, reaching for his wallet.

"Salesmanship, that's all," Mister MacNab assured his wife, handing out free samples to all the ladies of the Circle of Silent Workers. A sizable mob was converging on the booth. "My advice is to r-r-raise the price at once."

The other members of the Lower Forty blinked in surprise as the rest of the crowd hurried past them, bound for the lemonade stand. A marked air of jollity had swept the bazaar, and several vestrymen with their arms around each other's shoulders were leading the chorus of "Bringing in the Sheaves." Judge Parker's wife swayed slightly as she drained the contents of her paper cup, her face a trifle flushed. "Mos' delicious lem'nade I ever put in my whole mouth," she assured Mrs. MacNab with a giggle that ended in a slight hiccup. "Sometime you mus' let me have the reshipee."

Judge Parker crammed his old fishing hat on his head and tip-toed unnoticed out of the fair grounds, bound for Mink Brook. "By the way, what did you do to that lemonade?" he asked Mister MacNab as the members piled into Cousin Sid's car.

" 'Twas Uncle Pairk's contribution to this wor-r-rthy cause," Mister MacNab replied. "He couldna be present in pairson," he said, "but the guid mon was here in spir-r-rit."

A CHRISTMAS
TURKEY SHOOT

What with Christmas coming along again soon, the members of the Lower Forty gathered in Uncle Perk's store late in November to decide on their annual good deed for the Yuletide season. The Club's time-honored custom of dressing Dexter Smeed as Santa Claus and distributing presents to the needy had been abandoned last year, when Dexter's cigarette had ignited his cotton beard, and this Christmas Judge Parker felt they should concentrate their efforts instead on helping the Widow Libbey. "Ever since poor old Aldo passed away last spring," he said, "she's been having a hard time making both ends meet."

Mister MacNab shook his head sympathetically. "I know how it is," he sighed. "Pairsonally it's all I can do these days to make one end meet."

"That isn't the worst of it," Judge Parker continued. "Deacon Godfrey holds a mortgage on her property, and he's planning to foreclose if she doesn't make her December payment." He paused to let the full effect of his words sink in. "You know what it would mean to the Club if he ever got hold of the Libbey farm."

His fellow members nodded solemnly. Every season the alder run in Farmer Libbey's lower forty had furnished their favorite woodcock shooting, and opening day of each trout season found them lined up along the choice section of the brook that ran through the Libbey pasture. "We might as well kiss our hunting and fishing goodbye," the Judge warned. "Godfrey would post every inch of the land the moment he laid hands on it."

"We can't let that happen," Doc Hall said, shocked. "We'll have to do something for the poor widow at once."

"Aye, 'tis a plain case of Christian char-r-rity," Mister MacNab agreed. "The only question is, where will we get the money to be char-r-ritable with?"

There was a moment of thoughtful silence, which was broken by Mister MacNab. "In answer to my own question," he said triumphantly, "how about a Christmas Tairkey Shoot? With all these out-of-state sportsmen here in town for deer season, we could attr-r-ract a sizable gate if we offered sufficient prizes."

"Supposin' them city slickers walk off with all the prizes," Uncle Perk demurred. "You can't perdict a turkey shoot."

"There'd be nae risk at all," Mister MacNab assured him with a crafty wink. "Not the kind of tairkey shoot I have in mind."

"We don't want to do anything dishonest," Cousin Sid objected.

Mister MacNab gave him a hurt look. "Now, Sidney, ye wouldna think I'd suggest a thing like that," he sighed. "I dinna mean to rig the shoot so they'd lose. All I mean is to fix it so we'd win." He lowered his voice confidentially. "There's a few simple tr-r-ricks my grandfeyther taught me . . ."

The Lower Forty's Christmas Turkey Shoot proved to be an outstanding success. Posters had advertised the event all over town, Colonel Cobb had given it generous coverage in his newspaper, and a throng of out of staters converged on the meet, eager

[106]

to test their skill against the local contenders. Mister MacNab, as Club treasurer, collected the entrance fees, and gazed at the pile of cash thoughtfully. "It doesna seem right for all this guid money to lie idle," he mused. "Pairhops our visitors can be induced to wager on the contest."

The first event of the meet was a shot-sticking contest. Six squares of cardboard were placed in a row, at a distance of sixty-five yards, and the entrants were instructed to fire in unison at the signal. Doc Hall and Colonel Cobb had drawn the third and fourth squares, and they stood on the firing line side by side, flanked by the visiting challengers with their expensive tight-bore shotguns. The order to fire was given, six guns echoed as one, and the scorekeeper tallied the number of holes in each card. "Winner is Colonel Cobb," he announced. "His score is double anybody else." He glanced in surprise at Doc Hall's square. "Doc, you didn't land a single shot in yours."

"Must have flinched just as I pulled," Doc Hall apologized.

Again the contestants lined up on six new squares, and again the scorekeeper counted the results. "It's Doc Hall this time," he said. "He's got twice as many as any other card." He peered at Colonel Cobb's square, and shook his head. "That's funny, Colonel, you didn't even get a hole this time."

"Probably I put the shell in backwards," Colonel Cobb explained innocently.

The second event of the day was a balloon-busting contest with high-power rifles at a hundred yards, miss and out, slings and scopes barred. Judge Parker was the Club entry, and he took his place with a confident smile. Dexter Smeed had been assigned as pitman, to release the balloons one by one. Just before the firing started, his head emerged from the pit for a moment.

"Which one did you say was yours, Judge?" he inquired.

"It's the third one," Judge Parker shouted, holding up his fingers. "One, two, three."

"Okay, I got it," Dexter nodded, and lowered his head out of sight again. The first two balloons were released, and drifted away untouched. As Dexter sent up the third balloon, he cocked a .22 pistol, taking up half the trigger squeeze in readiness, and held careful aim as the balloon floated a few feet over his head. At the crack of the Judge's rifle, his trigger finger tightened instinctively, and the balloon exploded with a resounding pop. The Judge lowered his smoking rifle with a contented smile.

"It's just a matter of aiming right," he explained modestly, watching Mister MacNab collect the side bets and add them to the Club's mounting total.

Third and final event was for the grand prize. A live turkey had been anchored securely behind a log, a hundred yards away, and his bobbing head presented an elusive target. Mister Mac-Nab had personally volunteered to represent the Club in this event, and the members watched dubiously as his turn arrived. To their relief, his shot decapitated the bird neatly. "I got to hand it to you, Mac," Judge Parker whispered after the congratulations were over. "It takes good aim to hit a turkey right in the head."

"Oh, I didna aim at the head," Mister MacNab confided. I held about two inches low, right into the top of the log, pr-r-roducing a fine lovely spray of splinters and bullet jacket that severed the tairkey's neck like a cleaver. 'Tis a trick my grandfeyther always used," he said proudly, "when he was poaching back in the old country."

The members were beaming with justifiable satisfaction as they sauntered into Uncle Perk's store on Christmas afternoon.

The proceeds of the turkey shoot, augmented by various side bets, had been enough to meet the Widow Libbey's mortgage payment and make her a handsome Yuletide donation. "A guid deed well done," Mister MacNab summed it up, "and now we can look forward to enjoying the widow's land for many more seasons to come."

Uncle Perk leaned back morosely in his swivel chair. "Guess you ain't heard the news," he muttered.

"What happened?" Judge Parker asked, startled.

"Wal, Deacon Godfrey was so impressed when the Widow Libbey paid up in full," Uncle Perk reported, "that he figgered she must of come into a rich inheritance somewheres. So he's been courtin' her ever since, an' on Christmas Eve she up and accepted his proposal." Uncle Perk opened the desk drawer. "I hear they're planning to get married before next trout season."

He uncorked a holiday jug of Old Santa Claus's Helper, and handed it around to the stunned members.

"It's like I was sayin'," Uncle Perk sighed. "You can't perdict a turkey shoot, any more'n you can perdict a woman."

COUSIN SID'S BLESSED EVENT

Cousin Sid was wearing a pleased smile as he strolled into Uncle Perk's store. "I'll let you all in on a little secret," he informed his fellow members. "Jennie just broke the news to me. We're going to have a baby."

"Well, congratulations, Sidney," Judge Parker said, peering owlishly over his spectacles. "First thing you got to do now, of course, you got to get your wife a puppy right away."

Cousin Sid looked a trifle puzzled. "But maybe in her condition the job of housebreaking a young dog—"

"That's just the point," the Judge insisted. "She'll be thoroughly oriented by the time the baby arrives. After a wife has learned to clean up after a frisky Labrador puppy, collecting the pieces of chewed wax paper and vacuuming the rugs and mopping the floor, why, changing a few diapers won't seem any trouble at all."

"There's another advantage, too," Doc Hall agreed. "The experience of training a pup will come in very handy when you have to forcebreak the baby later." He helped himself to a slab of Uncle Perk's rat-trap cheese. "Anybody who's ever taught a dog to obey will know how to handle a youngster. Like for instance you tie a clothesline around the baby's ankle when it begins to crawl, and then say 'Whoa!' If it keeps on crawling, just give the rope a tug, and the youngster will turn a somersault, and next time it hears the command it will stop right in its tracks."

"Some baby trainers recommend a choke collar," Colonel Cobb added, "but I always say you can do just as well with a folded newspaper. If the baby tends to be hardmouthed, you might insert a few spikes in its teething ring."

Cousin Sid paled perceptibly. "I'm afraid my wife wouldn't exactly—"

"Of course, if you're planning to keep the baby in the house and make a pet of it," Judge Parker went on, "you'll have to train it not to climb on the furniture. If it starts to yank off the table runner, say 'No!' in a firm tone of command, and at the same time step on its hind feet. Works every time," he assured Cousin Sid.

"Aye, ther-r-re's nothing like a well-behaved tot," Mister MacNab averred. "We've taught our wee bairn to fetch, for exomple, and every morning when we let him out he brings back the neighbors' newspapers and a couple of milk bottles from the back porch next door and pairhops even a fr-r-resh egg now and then. I tell ye, mon, a guid retriever like that will pay for himself within the year."

Cousin Sid shifted uncomfortably in his chair. "I don't know about all that," he said, "but I do admit a watchdog might be a protection against kidnappers."

"Wal, naow, they's two ways o' looking at that," Uncle Perk mused, taking a tin of brand-new tobacco from the show case and prying it open. "Sometimes, on the other hand, a watchdog can be a real problem." He filled his pipe, and put the tin back in the show case for sale. "Like you take what happened to

Lemuel Goss."

There was a pause while he rasped a match across the showcase glass and dragged the flame into his pipe. He flipped the burnt match casually into the flour bin beside him and exhaled a cloud of rank blue smoke. "What happened to Lemuel Goss, Uncle Perk?" Judge Parker prompted after a decent interval.

"Seems Lem had a baby, and his wife was scairt of kidnappers, so Lem figgered the on'y answer was a watchdog," Uncle Perk began, settling himself on a sack of potatoes and crossing his boots on a convenient slab of bacon. "His Uncle Amos had a fine pedigreed imported German shepherd what had won a lot of medals and was very valu'ble, so when Uncle Amos had to move out West, Lem he got hold of this valu'ble dog and brung it home. Lem's wife sort of backed up a couple of steps when she seen it, account of it had bloodshot eyes an' a set of teeth like a dinnersour, but Lem tol' her they wa'n't nothin' to worry about. 'This here dog will sleep right at the foot of the baby's crib,' he said, 'an' if it so much as opens its mouth, there won't be any kidnappers.'

" 'If it opens it big enough,' his wife said, 'there won't be any baby.'

" 'You leave it to Rin-Rin-Tin,' Lem said to her. 'He'll perteckt Junior, you wait an' see.'

"Wal, as it turned out, they didn't have to wait long. About a week after the dog arrived, things begun to happen. Several nights they heard strange noises outside the house, and they was footprints in the flower bed under the nursery window, and once't they come home late from the movies and found a skeleton key broke off in the front door. Lem kep' a revolver under his pillow, an' Lem's wife slep' with all the lights burning, but finally one night she woke up an' shook Lem and said 'Listen!'

" 'All I can hear is the baby,' said Lem.

" 'That's what I mean,' his wife said. 'There's a kidnaper!'

"So Lem listened, and over the noise of Junior's yellin' he could hear the nursery window opening and then somethin' heavy being drug acrost the floor, and Lem natchally pulled the covers over his head again, but his wife kep' shaking him and saying 'Listen!' till he coulden go back to sleep. So he got up and drest and went down the hall to the nursery, and he helt the revolver in front of him and shoved the door open and shut his eyes and said 'Stckmp!' When he opened his eyes again, there was the kidnapper standing by the open window, with a burlap sack at his feet and his both hands in the air. That give Lem a little confidence, an' he spun the revolver by the trigger guard, like he'd seen in the movies, and caught it again just in time. 'Keep reachin',' he said. 'Why did you climb in that window?'

" 'Because the door was locked,' the kidnapper said.

"Junior was screamin' so loud in his crib that Lem hadda raise his voice to make himself heard. 'I know why you come here,' he said, 'you come here to steal the baby.'

" 'Look, mister, who'd want to steal a noisy little brat like that,' the kidnapper shrugged, 'when there's a valu'ble pedigreed dog right here that's worth a lot of money?' He pointed to the burlap sack at his feet. 'I'd of had him out of here okay,' he complained to Lem, 'if that noisy little brat haddena started hollerin'—'

" 'I don't like you to keep callin' my baby a noisy little brat,' Lem interrupted him.

" 'Then whyncha teach it not to holler?' the kidnapper demanded. 'This here watchdog never made no noise at all. I coulden hardly wake it up when I slid it into the sack. All it done was lick my hand an' go back to sleep again.'

"Lem he thought a minute, mostly about what he was going to tell his wife, an' then he had a bright idea. 'I tell you what I'll do,' he offered. 'You take the dog and git out of here, on'y there's just one little thing I'd like to ast you. When you get down to the bottom of the ladder, shoot your revolver in to the air a couple of times.' He apologized: 'I'd do it myself, but mine isn't loaded.'

"So the kidnaper took the dog, and Lem he took the baby and carried it back to the bedroom where his wife was waiting, and he tol' her everything was gonna be all right. Just then they was a couple of shots, and Lem shook his head, and muttered something about that loyal watchdog what give his all for little Junior, and his wife burst into tears, and from that time on they wa'n't never bothered with kidnapers again."

Uncle Perk knocked out the ashes from his pipe into an open barrel of molasses, and gazed at Cousin Sid thoughtfully.

"So mebbe on second thought, Sid," he concluded, "you better wait to get that puppy till the baby arrives. Then the pore little dog will have somebody to perteckt it."

FISHING IS ITS OWN REWARD

Mister MacNab was the unhappiest member of the Lower Forty Shooting, Angling and Inside Straight Club as the group set out early in May for the spring run of black salmon. Not that Mister MacNab had anything against salmon. "My gr-r-rand-feyther was one of the outstanding salmon poachers in all Scotland," he assured his fellow members. "He always claimed that fishing was its own r-r-reward."

It was Cousin Sid who had arranged for the Club to have access to some excellent black-salmon waters in New Brunswick. At first the members had demurred at the expense, but Cousin Sid had pointed out they could save money by camping on the stream. "We could all share the same car," he urged, "and chip in for the gas, and maybe pay the owner a little extra cash for wear and tear."

Mister MacNab's ears had shot forward. "Did ye say cash?" he murmured. "In that case, why don't we use my hair-r-rse? The undertaking business is slack right now, and I'd be vur-r-ry pleased to furnish the vehicle for the trip."

The members had accepted his suggestion with alacrity. Mister MacNab's hearse was in excellent condition, its commodious interior would hold all their gear, and on a pinch they could sleep inside. Cousin Sid supplied a tent and portable stove and camping equipment and all the food, Judge Parker brought along his sleeping bag and a snore-ball to fasten between his shoulder blades, and Uncle Perk furnished a jug of Old Power House for the occasion. He stretched out contentedly on a pile of blankets in the rear, sharing his jug with Judge Parker and Doc Hall who sat on the jump seats on either side, while Cousin Sid rode up in front with the driver.

Mister MacNab gripped the wheel in glum silence, as snatches of close harmony rose from the interior of the hearse. He was already beginning to regret his offer. The roads grew steadily worse as they progressed through the Canadian hinterland, and the springs banged and creaked loudly. Mister MacNab groaned aloud as each new jolt shook the frame, and overhanging branches scratched the shiny paint. To make matters worse, it had started raining, and mud spattered the chrome trim as they wallowed through the sticky mire. Once they skidded against a guard rail and dented a fender, and Mister MacNab burned a half inch of tread from his tires trying to pull it out of the ditch. " 'Twill cost me a for-r-rtune to repair-r-r this vehicle," he moaned, "if I ever get it home again."

The rain was coming down in sheets as they reached the fishing grounds, and obviously it was hopeless to try to pitch a tent. They halted the hearse at the side of the road, and the members huddled inside while Cousin Sid spread a poncho under a tree and cooked supper in the downpour. "At least you won't have to wash the dishes afterwards," Doc Hall consoled him through the window. "Just leave them outside till morning."

They rolled up blankets as soon as the meal was over, and stretched out on the floor of the hearse to get a good night's rest.

Soon the other members were slumbering contentedly, but Mister MacNab could not sleep. He lay staring at the darkness, trying to figure how to levy an extra assessment on his fellow members to pay for the damage to the car. The longer he thought of the possible broken springs and damaged fenders, the more wide awake he grew. The rain drummed steadily, Judge Parker had rolled off his snore-ball, and the hearse echoed to loud strangling sounds, and a horde of mosquitoes had found their way inside and added their steady humming to the midnight cacophony. Mister MacNab sighed, and pulled the sheet over his head.

A new sound assailed his ears, and he peered out. A local farmer, obviously the worse for alcohol, was staggering along the road toward the parked car, weaving from side to side and bellowing a French drinking song. He halted abruptly as he reached the hearse, and stared at it in bewilderment.

At that moment a mosquito lit on Mister MacNab's nose, and he sat upright in his shroud and struck a match to light a cigarette. As the flame illuminated his white face, the farmer stood for a moment, transfixed with terror, and then flung his bottle away and took off down the road in a cloud of mud. Mister MacNab gazed at the shattered bottle, and sighed again deeply.

The rain had let up by morning, and the other members set up their rods and hurried down the path to the stream; but Mister MacNab decided to forego fishing until he could inspect the damage to his vehicle. He was bending over, testing the springs sadly, when a battered sedan halted behind him, and a stout woman rolled down the window. "I drove over to thank ye," she said. "My husband come home last night shaking like a leaf, and he swears he'll never touch another drop as long as he lives." She reached out and shook Mister MacNab's hand gratefully. "He's turning over a new leaf from now on."

Mister MacNab licked his lips. "Where did your mon imbibe all this alcoholic refr-r-reshment?" he inquired.

"He's been lapping it up at my poor uncle's wake," the woman sighed. "He ain't drawed a sober breath for ten days."

"Doesna that seem to be a rather lengthy wake?" asked Mister MacNab, puzzled.

"We been waitin' for the undertaker to get back," she explained indignantly. "He drove off in his hearse to go fishing."

Mister MacNab clucked in disapproval. "Can ye imagine that?" he murmured. "A self-respecting undertaker using his hair-r-rse to go fishing, particularly when there was lucrative business waiting." A crafty gleam entered his eye. "Pair-r-rhops in the emairgency I might be willing to supply this vehicle of mine to transport the deceased to his final resting place. Naturally I'd accept no more than the customar-r-ry fee . . ." The gleam in his eye brightened. ". . . plus of course some slight remuner-r-ration for coming so far . . ." His eye fairly glittered. ". . . plus any spare bever-r-rages that might be left over after the sairvices."

Mister MacNab was smiling broadly as he drove back down the road that evening. His fellow members stood at the roadside in a bedraggled group, looking weary and downcast. "Any luck?" he inquired as he halted the hearse beside them.

"Not a thing," Judge Parker grumbled. "We didn't see a rise all day."

"Now, then, ye mustna complain," Mister MacNab chided, shifting his position slightly because his right cheek was resting on his heavily stuffed wallet. "There's other things to repay a mon on a trip like this. Even if I dinna see a salmon, I'll pairsonally be the richer for this happy experience." He took a long swig from a bottle of Canadian rye, and beamed sententiously. "As my gr-r-randfeyther used to say," he intoned, "fishing is its own r-r-reward."

UNCLE PERK'S SPLITTING WEDGE

Gloom hung in a pall over the Lower Forty Shooting, Angling and Inside Straight Club. Normally June would have been a month of carefree angling, with May flies hatching and trout rising eagerly to the lure; but now a mood of black despair gripped the membership, as the date of the Widow Libbey's nuptial ceremonies drew nearer. As soon as she and Deacon Godfrey sealed the matrimonial bonds, they knew, there'd be no more hunting or fishing on the Libbey farm. "The moment that old skinflint gets his hands on her property legally," Judge Parker said grimly, "he'll put up signs over every last inch of it, just for spite."

"Including our favorite woodcock cover down in the Libbey lower forty," Doc Hall mourned. "He'll probably cut out all the alders and drain the swamp for pasture."

"He couldn't do that!" Cousin Sid gasped. "Why, that's where the Club first got its name."

"I wouldn't put anything past Ira Godfrey," Colonel Cobb frowned. "I heard the other day that he's planning to subdivide the land and sell it off for building lots."

"Maybe we could talk to the Widow Libbey," Dexter Smeed urged, "and explain that the Deacon's only marrying her for her money."

Judge Parker glared at his wife's nephew. "She'd suspect we were trying to break up the marriage so the Club could keep on using her land."

"Now, what would ever make her think a thing like that?" Doc Hall protested in a hurt tone.

"Pairhops I could pr-r-resent the Deacon with an added bill for my hairse," Mister MacNab suggested hopefully, "which he hired last year to bury his first wife Hettie. I only char-r-rged him half rate," he recalled, "because he let me use it on the return trip to tr-r-ransport a load of fairtilizer."

The Judge shook his head. "We've got to think of something better, and fast. The wedding's only a couple of days away. They're giving a bridal shower for Effie Libbey tomorrow afternoon—"

Uncle Perk opened his eyes for the first time. "You say a bridal shower?"

"That's right," Doc Hall nodded. "The ladies of the community are going to surprise the widow. All our wives are in on it."

"Wal, now," Uncle Perk mused, blinking shrewdly at his fellow members over the top of his spectacles, "mebbe the gals could work on Effie. Sometimes a female touch will succeed, where a he-male can't do nothin'. Like the old sayin' goes, the best splittin' wedge is one made out o' the same wood."

Cousin Sid hesitated. "I don't know if my wife would exactly feel like helping out the Lower Forty," he said. "She claims the Club cuts into my weekends that otherwise I might be spending with my family."

"Oh, ye'll all have to make a few concessions, o' course," Uncle Perk advised. "Like promisin' your wives you'll stay home one weekend a month, f'rinstance." He raised a hand to silence the protests of the members. "It's our only chance," he warned. "We got to get the gals to help . . ."

The bridal shower the following afternoon was a success in every way. Effie Libbey opened her gifts amid laughter and squeals of delight, and later all the ladies gathered in the farmhouse kitchen for coffee and refreshments. "I only wish poor Aldo could be here to enjoy it," the widow murmured, dabbing her eyes. "He always told me that if anything ever happened to him, he'd like me to marry again. That's the only reason that I'm—" She caught herself. "Aldo wanted me to be happy."

"So do we all, dear. We hope you'll be happier than poor Hettie was," Mrs. Patience Parker murmured. "Did you ever know Deacon Godfrey's first wife? Such a dear sweet person," she sighed. "Some ways I can't help but be glad the Lord relieved her of her suffering."

The Widow Libbey's eyes widened. "Why, I hadn't heard . . ."

"Oh, she never complained, of course," Mrs. Jennie Hall said quickly. "Not even when the Deacon refused to wipe his muddy boots before he came in, or left the newspaper upstairs in the bathroom, or threw matches in her nice clean fireplace that she'd cleaned out for the summer and filled with ferns—"

"Or insisted on bringing his favorite heifer right into the kitchen and feeding it," Cousin Sid's wife added. "Nobody ever heard a word out of her, though."

"Aye, Hettie was tr-r-ruly a saint," agreed Mrs. Maggie Mac-Nab. "Nary a pr-r-rotest the time she dented the ax blade on a r-r-railroad spike, and the Deacon made her take it out of her egg money."

"I understand one Christmas he gave her a set of handles for the chopping block, so she could lug it," Patience Parker recall-ed.

"And the next Christmas he bought her a floodlight for the woodshed," Jennie Hall added, "so she could see to split the kindling for his breakfast every morning at four-thirty."

"I . . . I don't believe it," Effie Libbey said weakly. "Ira was very fond of his first wife. He said so himself."

"Then why did he give all her clothes away, less than a month after the puir soul was laid to rest?" Maggie MacNab demanded. "I pairsonally saw a woman over in East Har-r-rdscrabble going around with Hettie's bonnet on. I'd recognize it anywhere."

"I think I know the woman you mean," Patience Parker nod-ded, and all the wives exchanged significant glances.

"He had a separate post-office box, you know," Jennie Hall informed the widow, "so Hettie couldn't keep track of his mail."

"And he always locked the glove compartment of his car," Cousin Sid's wife put in. "She never knew what was inside."

"I won't have you talking about Ira like that," Effie Libbey protested, but without conviction. "I admit he may have his faults—"

"Oh, we're sure you can handle him, dear," Jennie Hall in-sisted, "even if he gets started on one of those famous sprees of his."

"Why, Ira told me he never touched a drop of liquor in his life," Effie Libbey gasped.

"He's a vanilla drinker," Patience Parker confided in a low voice. "Every time he goes to the store, he buys an extra bottle. The big economy size," she added ominously.

"Come to think of it," Effie Libbey faltered, "Ira did tell me he was very fond of vanilla cookies."

"I understand he's quite a lady-killer, too," Cousin Sid's wife commented. "Those long trips he takes to a senior elders' convention, well, I happened to see him getting off the train once and there was definitely lipstick on his shirt."

"I suppose you've noticed," pointed out Jennie Hall, "that the last three girl organists at the church all left town rather suddenly."

"There's a boy in the next town who walks with his toes out, just like the Deacon does," Patience Parker reminded her.

Effie Libbey's face was growing tight. "So that's why he refused to have a double-ring ceremony."

"I dinna like to mention it, dar-r-rling," said Maggie MacNab, delivering the final thrust, "but there's a r-r-rumor around that he's maintaining a second establishment down in Boston." She handed the widow a photograph of a wide-eyed curly-haired baby. "This fell out of a letter he was reading the other day at the post office."

Effie Libbey caught her breath in a sharp gasp. "I knew it!" she said. "I knew it all along." She ripped the photograph into shreds, and hurled it to the floor. "Aldo never liked him, either."

There was a full attendance at the special emergency meeting of the Lower Forty in Uncle Perk's store next morning. Colonel Cobb's newspaper had carried a brief social item, announcing the abrupt cancellation of the Libbey-Godfrey wedding; and the Club's former mood of despair had changed to one of appropriate jubilation. "The only thing I r-r-regret," Mister MacNab said, "is the fact that the widow tore up that baby picture. 'Twas the only one I had of myself taken when I was a wee bair-r-rn in Scotland."

Judge Parker rapped for order. "Let's get on to the business of the meeting," he said. "I hereby move that we found a Ladies' Auxiliary of the Lower Forty—"

Uncle Perk's swivel chair banged forward with a crash. "You mean to say we're lettin' women in?"

"That was the concession our wives insisted on," the Judge admitted sheepishly. "At least, when they go fishing with us," he maintained, "we'll get to go ourselves."

BE IT RESOLVED FOR 1959

The New Year's morning meeting of the Lower Forty Shoot-ing, Angling and Inside Straight Club was held in an atmosphere of sober remorse, or anyway fairly sober. The members had plan-ned to go rabbit hunting that afternoon, but after weighing the problem of stooping over to fasten their snowshoes, it was unan-imously decided to postpone the whole expedition until the next day. "Frankly I couldn't stand the noise of those rabbits stamping around," Judge Parker sighed, placing a hand to his throbbing temple and moaning contritely. "Never again," he vowed.

"I'm going on the wagon myself," said Colonel Cobb, blinking his bloodshot eyes. "I can't remember what I did last night, but I swear it's the last time I ever do it."

Doc Hall started to nod in agreement, but desisted because the effort proved too painful. "I'm taking the pledge, too," he insisted. "This morning I stood under the shower for twenty min-utes, and I couldn't even get wet."

"It wasna the dr-r-rinks that proved so hard to resist," Mister MacNab sighed, "as the fact that they were fr-r-ree." He took out a pocket flask filled with Worcestershire sauce, gulped a long swallow, and shuddered, "From now on I'm turning over a new leaf."

"I think that's a very good idea," said Cousin Sid enthusiastically. "Why doesn't the Club celebrate the New Year by passing a whole set of good resolutions? We'll all turn over a new leaf together."

Mister MacNab stole a glance at Uncle Perk's corncob pipe, which was exuding its usual aroma of scorched galoshes, and his face turned green. "Just for a starter," he choked, "let's swear off smoking."

Uncle Perk put his pipe back in his pocket, and scowled at Mister MacNab. "How about promising to carry our own shells for a change," he retorted, "instead of borrowing them from all the other members to save money?"

"For that matter," Judge Parker suggested, gazing pointedly at Doc Hall, "how about a resolution never to claim a deer that somebody else shot?"

"Listen to me, you big baboon," Doc Hall bristled, "you know doggone well I dropped that buck cold before you even got your rifle to your shoulder—"

"Wait a minute, fellows," Cousin Sid interrupted hastily, "this is no way to start the New Year off. Let's all promise not to have any more arguments in the Lower Forty in 1959."

Judge Parker relented, and held out his hand to Doc Hall. "Okay with me," he grinned. "Let's bury the hatchet."

"Bygones are bygones," Doc nodded, gripping the Judge's palm. "We'll be friends from now on."

"Hearts linked in unity."

"Bonds of brotherhood and all that."

The other members shook hands solemnly all around.

"Maybe it might be a good idea to set some of our good resolutions down," Cousin Sid said eagerly, "so we won't forget them later." He seated himself at Uncle Perk's typewriter, and the members gathered around him as he wrote. Several of them winced slightly at the loud clatter of the keys, but they gritted their teeth manfully while his fingers raced back and forth:

LOWER FORTY RESOLUTIONS FOR 1959:

1. I swear I'll never claim that the fish which got away was the biggest one I ever hooked.
2. When I come home empty-handed, I won't insist it was because (a) the water was too low, (b) the water was too high, (c) it was too muddy, (d) it was too clear, or (e) I should have been here last Wednesday.
3. If I miss a deer, I won't blame it on the fact that somebody obviously borrowed my rifle and tampered with the sights.
4. I won't try to top another member's story by claiming that the deer I missed was bigger.
5. When a fellow member shows me his (a) gun, (b) fishing rod or (c) camera, I won't try to prove to him that my (a) gun, (b) fishing rod or (c) camera is better than his.
6. I won't set my alarm clock an hour early, when I learn that a fellow member is planning to hunt his favorite grouse cover the following morning, so I can get out there and go through the cover ahead of him.
7. If a fellow member fires at the same time I do, I promise not to yell "I got it!" before he gets a chance to yell himself.
8. When a grouse which I shoot at fails to drop, I'll admit right off that I missed it clean with both barrels. I won't hold up the hunt for half an hour because I'm positive I saw it set its wings and coast into a pile of slash.
9. I'll clean my own game, instead of leaving it for Cousin Sid to do.

10. I'll get back to camp in time to help Cousin Sid cook supper. P.S. I'll also give Cousin Sid a hand with the dishes afterwards.

Cousin Sid pulled the paper from the typewriter triumphantly, and the members affixed their signatures one by one. Uncle Perk opened his desk drawer and took out a jug of Old Stump Blower. "Here's to 1959," he offered.

The entire membership recoiled from the jug in horror, as though they had been confronted with a polecat. "Put that stuff away!" they chorused virtuously. "Not for me!" "Never again!"

The light of virtue was still shining in their faces as they headed back to Cousin Sid's camp after their rabbit hunt the following afternoon. They were a little late getting back, as it happened, owing to the fact that the members had spent half an hour hunting for a rabbit which Judge Parker was positive he'd seen tumble head over heels and crawl into a pile of slash. In addition, Mister MacNab discovered he'd left all his shells home again, Colonel Cobb missed an easy shot because somebody had obviously tampered with the sights of his rifle, and Uncle Perk's beagles put a large hare past the Judge and Doc Hall, who both fired and shouted "I got it!" at the same time, as a result of which neither of them was speaking. Fortunately, Cousin Sid had started back to camp early, and all the game was cleaned and a rabbit stew was bubbling on the stove when they showed up at last.

"That's the best part of a New Year's resolution," Uncle Perk mused, as he uncorked a second jug and passed it around after supper. "No matter how you break it, it's just as good again another year."

The members nodded contentedly as they sprawled before the fire and watched Cousin Sid do the dishes.

UNCLE PERK'S JUG

Uncle Perk scowled at the white drifts piled outside the window, tossed another chunk of birch into the potbellied stove, and slammed the lid irritably. He settled back in his swivel chair and rasped a match across the top of his desk. "On'y good thing about Feb'uary," he muttered to the other members of the Lower Forty, "is that they ain't but twenty-eight days in it." He held the match over the bowl of his battered corncob. "Pers'nally I wisht they'd substitute some other month instead," he said, sucking in the flame, "an' while they're at it I wisht they'd have it in the summer so all this pesky snow would melt."

"You have to admit the flakes look pretty coming down," Cousin Sid objected.

"They'd look a lot prettier if they were going up," Doc Hall retorted. "Then we wouldn't have to shovel them later."

"Aye, when I think of the cost of plowing my dr-r-riveway," Mister MacNab sighed, "I obsairve each new flake and add it to the total: $1.64, $1.65, $1.66."

Judge Parker nodded morosely. "Worst time of year for a sportman," he grumbled. "Too late to go hunting, and too early to go fishing. Nothing to do in winter but wait for spring."

"Maybe we could take up skiing," Cousin Sid suggested. "They say it's the thrill that comes once in a lifetime."

"Usually at the very end," Doc Hall added.

"Why go out in the cold to break your leg," Colonel Cobb agreed, "when you can fall downstairs at home where it's warm?"

"Wal, there's one thing a sportsman can allus do in winter," Uncle Perk said, pulling open the lower left hand drawer of his desk. "How about a little tetch of Ole Power Saw?"

Judge Parker tilted the jug to his lips. "This tastes just like Old Stump Blower."

"Same diff'rence," Uncle Perk shrugged. "Sometimes I call it Ole Lightnin' Rod, or Ole Dynamite Cap, or Ole Splittin' Wedge. It all depends which jug I put it in."

"It's a funny thing, Uncle Perk," Cousin Sid mused, taking a long swallow. "The Lower Forty has been drinking your Old Stump Blower all these years, but you never told us the recipe."

"It's a fambly secret," Uncle Perk said, lowering his eyes evasively. "Been handed down from generation to generation. It was invented by my Great Great Grampa Eben Perkins, way back in the Rev'lutionary War. He give some to the Minutemen, and they run the British clear out o' Boston."

"How did he make it?" Colonel Cobb asked.

Uncle Perk crossed his hunting rubbers on the desk and exhaled a cloud of blue smoke. "Wal, the basic ingre'jent was ole Medford rum. Not this newfangled rum you get nowadays that's all strained and clean, but real honest-to-God third-run rum, so thick you could spread it on bread like molasses. First my Great Great Grampa would take an empty mixin' bucket, and he'd put in two cups o' maple sugar an' about an inch o' boilin' water, an' melt it all together. Then he'd add a coupla quarts o' rum, an' a lump o' butter as big as his fist, and a handful o' powdered cinnamon, an' fill up the bucket with hot cider, an' stir it with a poker till it dissolved. Lost a lot o' pokers that way," Uncle

Perk admitted, "but it made a pow'rful drink. Great Great Grampa Eben allus kep' a jug handy till he died at the age of 103."

"What happened to him?"

Uncle Perk paused to light another match. "It seems there was a story goin' around that ole Eben finished a jug once an' went out an' rassled a catamount with his bare hands. Eben claimed it wasn't true, all he done was to slap the critter around a little mite, but sooner or later he got to believin' the story himself. So to prove it he took his jug an' climbed into a cave with a hibernatin' she-bear an' three cubs." He drew on the dregs of his corncob with a low mournful sound. "All they ever found was a coupla Continental uniform buttons an' the handle o' the jug."

There was a respectful silence, while Uncle Perk knocked the ashes from his pipe against a rubber boot heel and filled the bowl again.

"He passed the recipe along to my Great Grampa Aldo," he continued, "but Aldo made it a little diff'rent. Instead o' usin' rum, he'd take a barrel o' hard cider, an' set it out in the snow an' let it freeze solid, all but the core in the middle. Then he'd siphon off the core into a jug, an' add some beet juice to give it color."

"What did he do with the rest of the cider?" asked Cousin Sid.

"Wal, he used to leave it in the cellar, but a mouse got into the barrel one night, an' chased the cat around the house three times. So Aldo fed the whole barrelful to the hogs," Uncle Perk said, "an' when he slaughtered 'em the bacon was so strong you couldn' hardly hold it in the fryin' pan. On'y bacon I ever heared of that had to be kep' corked."

He tamped down the hot coal of his pipe with a calloused

thumb, struck another match, and blew a sentimental smoke ring toward the ceiling.

"Poor Great Grampa Aldo died durin' a barn-raisin'," he recalled sadly. "Back in the ole days when a barn was finished somebody'd volunteer to run the ridgepole to bring good luck. Wal, Aldo took a long swig of Ole Stump Blower an' said he'd run the ridge, only when he come to the end he kep' runnin'. They buried him between two barn doors, an' the recipe passed on to my Grampa Wilbur."

"Did he change it any?"

"He tried addin' a lot o' cloves an' spice to give it flavor," Uncle Perk replied, "but the trouble was that his wife could smell it on his breath. One Sad'dy night she was plannin' to take him to a poetry readin' at the Browning Club, and Grampa Wilbur wanted a drink to fortyfy himself, but his wife said no. So when she wasn't lookin' he poured some Ole Stump Blower into one o' them gelatin capsules you use to give medicine to horses, an' swallered it, an' waited. All through the poetry readin' he sat waitin' for it to take effect, but nothin' happened, an' Grampa Wilbur was bored stiff. Next day was Sunday, and he an' his wife was sittin' in church, an' right in the middle of the sermon the horse-capsule suddenly melted. Gramp lep to his feet an' started up the aisle, wavin' his arms an' singin' 'When mornin' gilds the skies, My heart awakenin' cries . . .' His wife made him swear he'd never tetch a drop again, an' he handed on the recipe to my father, an' he passed it along to me."

The other members leaned forward expectantly. "Well, what's the recipe?" Cousin Sid prompted.

"That," Uncle Perk repeated stubbornly, "is a fambly secret."

"You wouldn't even tell the Lower Forty?"

"Wal, let's put it this way," Uncle Perk explained. "S'posin' you was to go grouse huntin', an' you knew exactly where the bird was an' which way it would fly, what would be the fun o' huntin'? Or s'posin' you was to cast a fly on a stream, an' you knew just when the trout would strike an' how long it would fight an' how much it would weigh when you landed it, would you enjoy fishin'?" Uncle Perk shook his head. "Sometimes not knowin' enough is better'n knowin' too much."

Judge Parker took a long swallow and nodded thoughtfully. "I guess Perk is right, at that," he agreed. "If the rest of us could make Old Stump Blower, it wouldn't be the same, would it?"

"Cair-r-rtainly not," said Mister MacNab, draining the last drop. "For one thing, it wouldna be fr-r-ree."

Uncle Perk picked up the empty jug, opened a trapdoor in the floor, and clambered down the steep stairs into the cellar. He pulled a stopper from a cobweb-covered barrel, and refilled the jug. Hooking a forefinger through the handle, he rested it on his bent arm and put it to his lips. His Adam's apple rose and fell, and he lowered the jug with a sigh of satisfaction.

"Yep, that's the whole secret of Old Stump Blower," he murmured under his breath, as he started back up the stairs. "I don't even know how I make it myself."

POTTER'S FANCY

Their trout rods rested horizontally on nails driven in the side of Cousin Sid's camp, their wet waders hung from pegs, and the members of the Lower Forty lounged on the granite doorstep, basking in the warm June sun. The pleasant aroma of luncheon wafted from the kitchen, where Cousin Sid was frying the results of their early morning's catch. Uncle Perk reached for his jug of Old Stump Blower, and then hid it hurriedly behind a clump of ferns as a canvas-clad figure stumbled along the path toward them, weaving slightly. "Mornin', Perley," Uncle Perk greeted him.

"Mornin'," Perley Potter replied, lowering the battered fishing rod he carried over his shoulder and leaning against a tree for support.

"Think that big trout of yours will be rising this soon in the day?" Doc Hall asked.

"Figgered I'd git to the pool a mite early," Perley explained in a husky voice, "in case he gits hongry ahead o' time." He rubbed the back of a hand across his stubbled chin. "Don't s'pose you fellers got a little somethin' to wet my whistle," he pleaded. "I seem to've picked up one o' these hangovers that's been runnin' around lately."

"Sorry, Perley," Uncle Perk said firmly, "we ain't got a drop."

"Wal, in that case," Perley sighed, "I guess I'll be movin'

along. Can't never tell when ole Beelzebub might show up."

He stooped to grasp his rod, and the neck of a pint flask protruded from his hip pocket. The Lower Forty exchanged silent glances as he staggered up the path, tacking from side to side and caroming off an occasional oak.

"Sure hate to see a nice feller like Perley let himself go that way," Uncle Perk grumbled. "Used to be a real hard-workin' cuss till he took to drink."

"What started him off?" Colonel Cobb inquired.

"If you ast me, it's that tarnation trout," Uncle Perk replied. "Ever since he spotted Beelzebub a coupla years ago, he's been goin' from bad to worst. All he thinks about is catchin' that fish. He broods about it so much that he takes a drink before he starts fishin', an' then if he misses a strike he has to take another drink to console himself, an' by that time he's so orry-eyed he can't see to cast a fly, which depresses him till he has to have another drink, an' when he wakes up the fishin' is all over, so then he gets real drunk to drownd his sorrows."

"Suppose it would cure him if he caught it?" Doc Hall mused.

"He'll never catch a smart ole devil like Beelzebub unless he sobers up," Uncle Perk grunted, "an' he'll never sober up unless he catches it." He recovered the jug from its hiding place among the ferns and took a swallow. "It's the curse o' the demon rum."

"Stingeth like the adder," Judge Parker agreed, reaching for the jug, "and biteth like the serpent."

Doc Hall borrowed the jug in turn. "Look not upon the wine when it is red," he nodded solemnly, and handed it to Mister MacNab.

"Pairsonally I never touch a drop myself," Mister MacNab said, "unless it's fr-r-ree." He lowered the jug after a long moment. " 'Tis a fortunate thing we dinna suffer the same cur-r-rse as poor Pairley."

The afternoon hatch of flies was just starting as the Lower Forty, rods in hand, hurried up the path along the stream. They came to Perley Potter's favorite pool, and Doc Hall paused and pointed. Perley was stretched at the base of a dead stump, his fishing rod on the grass beside him, the pint bottle tilted to his lips. His face was downcast. "What happened, Perley?" Doc asked.

"Missed him again," Perley mourned. "He was risin' over by that far bank, an' I tried to make a cast an' hooked my fly on a hemlock an' fell into the pool an' scairt him away." His trembling fingers worked in vain to tie on another fly. "Here, mebbe you can make this thing quit jigglin' up and down," he said to Doc.

Doc Hall threaded Perley's leader through the eye of the hook and knotted it. "What's this fly called?" he asked curiously, inspecting the bedraggled woolen body dressed with chicken feathers.

"It's s'posed to be Potter's Fancy," Perley sighed, "but nowadays my hand shakes so I can't tie 'em like I used to." He consoled himself with another swig from his flask, and closed his eyes. "You fellers go ahead," he murmured, "I'll wait here fer ole Beelzebub."

Perley was still reclining at the base of the stump, his fishing rod beside him, when Doc and the others made their way back down the path at dusk. His bottle was empty, his mouth hung open, and he emitted a steady gurgling snore. Doc gazed at him in sympathy, and his eye wandered toward the stream. Suddenly he froze, staring at a small bump which appeared momentarily in the flat run over by the far bank. "Perley!" he shouted, "get your rod, quick!"

Uncle Perk peered at the slumbering figure. "He wouldn' wake up if it was half-past doomsday."

Another newly-hatched fly dropped down from the overhanging grass bank and was caught in the dark run. Again the bump showed for an instant in the smooth water, leaving barely a ripple as the insect disappeared. Doc scooped up a spent fly from the eddy at his feet and studied it a moment. "Olive dun," he nodded. He opened his fly box and riffled the contents. "This one ought to do it," he decided, "about No. 16." He tied the artificial dun on his leader, glanced once more at the inert form beside the stump, and crept cautiously toward the stream.

His first cast fell short, and he let his fly drift well below the feeding trout before he retrieved it, lifting it slightly off the water with an expert flick of his rod tip. Again he shot the line forward, stripping another foot or so from his reel. The fly lit on a tuft of grass, toppled into the run, and rode downstream. Something rolled under it, the fly was sucked out of sight, and Doc waited a fraction of a second and then tightened. A huge V raced across the pool, his reel screamed, and there was a heavy swirl and the glimpse of a green slab-side turning. Perley stirred slightly, a dreamy smile crossed his face, and he settled back in deep repose.

Doc Hall leapt in to the stream, his arched rod held high, and followed the speeding trout around a bend of the stream. A half hour passed before he returned up the path, carrying the monster squaretail curled in his landing net. "It's the grandaddy of them all," he gloated. "Ought to go four or five pounds."

"We'll take it back to the store an' weigh it," Uncle Perk suggested.

Doc shook his head. "This is Perley's trout," he said quietly. He took Beelzebub from the net, reached for Perley's leader, and hooked Potter's Fancy securely in the trout's jaw. He laid the fish on the grass beside the sleeping form, paused in thought for a moment, and then scooped some water in his hat and poured it over Perley's extended waders. Perley never stirred as the Lower Forty tiptoed down the trail toward Cousin Sid's camp.

Late that night they heard someone stumbling along the path, and the pounding of a fist on the front door. Perley Potter lurched into the room, his eyes bloodshot, holding the trout by its gills. "B'gorry, I got 'im," he said thickly. "Cotched him on Potter's Fancy."

"Put up a good fight?" Doc asked, with a wink at the others.

"Hmmm? Yeah. Yeah, I guess so." Perley's face had a blank look, as though he had stopped to worship at a wayside shrine and been hit on the head by a falling plaster angel. "My waders was wet clear up to the waist. Yeah, it must of been the fight of a lifetime."

"Wal, congratulations, Perley," Uncle Perk beamed, removing the cork from the jug of Old Stump Blower. "How about a little somethin' to celebrate?"

Perley leapt back as though he had stepped on a copperhead. "Not for me. I'll never tetch another drop as long as I live."

Uncle Perk blinked. "Wotinell's come over you?"

"I learnt my lesson," Perley said in a quavering voice. "All these years I been dreamin' about the time I'd cotch that trout, and now I done it, an' I don't remember anything about it." Tears welled in his eyes. "Biggest thrill I'll ever have, an' I missed the whole fun." His voice broke. "Now I'll never know what it was like."

He held the trout aloft, and gazed dolefully into its glazed eyes.

"I'm gonna have him mounted an' hang him on the wall," he sobbed, "an' any time I'm tempted to take a drink I'll look up at Beelzebub an' remind myself: Never again."

The door closed, and they heard his uncertain steps recede down the path. Uncle Perk picked up the jug of Old Stump blower, strode resolutely into the kitchen, and poured the remaining contents down the sink. Mister MacNab emitted a strangled sound.

"What ever-r-r are ye doing, mon?" he gasped.

"In memory of Beelzebub," Uncle Perk replied. There was a moment of respectful silence. "Besides," he added, "they's another full jug right out in the car."

A BEARDED LADY

The Alabama woods were silver in the April dawn. Honeysuckle and jasmine scented the soft air, jaybirds scuffled in the dry leaves under the oaks, and the long purple fronds of grandsir graybeard bushes stirred in the first faint breeze of the coming day. Mister MacNab hooked his shotgun over his forearm and followed his Cousin Fergus down the shadowy trail, stumbling over a fallen tree in the dim half-light. "Mind your big feet," Fergus muttered over his shoulder. "You'll scare every turkey out of the country."

Mister MacNab gritted his teeth in silence. He had only himself to blame, he reflected. Against his better judgment he had accepted his cousin's invitation to drive his hearse south for a spring gobbler hunt on the estate of Fergus's father-in-law, Senator Beauregard Beadle. To be sure, he had arranged to defray the expense of the trip by transporting the remains of a late lamented citizen of Hardscrabble part of the way; but even this saving was not sufficient to cheer him. His vacation was paid for, the weather was perfect, but there was one fly in the ointment.

The fly was Fergus.

It had been many years since he had seen his second cousin, and absence had not made the MacNab heart grow any fonder. Back as wee bairns in the old country, he recalled, they had poached the same pools together, and Fergus had always gill-netted the biggest salmon. Now that he was married to the daughter of an Alabama lumber baron, he had taken on all the airs of a rich man's son-in-law, fawning over his wife's parent in a manner that offended Mister MacNab's Scotch pride. Even Fergus's native burr had yielded to a cultivated Southern drawl, he noted in disgust. From the outset, moreover, Fergus had adopted a superior attitude toward his Yankee relative, scoffing at everything from Mister MacNab's shotgun to his hunting clothes. "Where'd y'all get that checkered shirt?" he inquired.

"Checker-r-red shir-r-rt!" Mister MacNab echoed, choking on his R's. He had imported the garment from Scotland at considerable expense, and his cousin's disloyal comment cut him to the quick. " 'Tis the MacNab tartan," he pointed out with feeling.

"It's too bright," Fergus objected. "A gobbler would spot it a mile away." His lip curled in a supercilious sneer. "There's a lot of things a dub like y'all has to learn about turkeys."

"I'm sure ye're just the mon to tell me," Mister MacNab grunted.

"The most important thing," Fergus warned, as they crept down the trail, "is not to shoot a hen by mistake. Senator Beadle would blow his top if anybody killed one of his hens."

"How can ye tell the difference?"

"Well, the hen is smaller, for one thing, and her feathers are lighter colored, and of course there's no spurs or white turban cap, but the main thing to look for is the beard. Hens don't have a long beard on their chest like a gobbler—"

The dark woods exploded before them, and a great brown shape rose out of a clump of sparkleberries. Mister MacNab swung his gun to his shoulder, following the bird to the top of the cypress trees. For a moment it was silhouetted against the pale sky, and he pulled the trigger. A wing tilted and straightened again, and the turkey sailed serenely out of sight. Cousin Fergus doubled over with laughter.

"Missed it clean," he guffawed. "Y'all waited too long to shoot."

"I wanted to make sure it had a beard," Mister MacNab explained, popping out the empty shell.

"Well, I'll have to cut your shirt-tail off, I guess," Fergus grinned.

Mister MacNab recoiled in alarm. "Ye'll nae go hacking off a piece of this expensive gar-r-rment," he announced, backing a step and dropping another shell in his gun.

"It's the custom down h'yah when somebody misses a gobbler," his cousin chuckled unpleasantly. "We'll have a little ceremony as soon as we get back to the house." He gestured toward a stump beside the trail. "Y'all set still an' don't move, and maybe some more turkeys will feed in," he said. "I'll go up to that oak ridge yonder and make a stand."

Mister MacNab squatted glumly at the base of the stump, the thought of his doomed shirt weighing on his mind. His discomfort was increased by the fact that Fergus had contrived to seat him on an anthill. Minutes lengthened into hours, the sun climbed higher and so did the ants, but he did not dare to scratch. At last he heard the blast of a shotgun in the distance, and Fergus's triumphant yell, and he rose and hurried toward the oak ridge.

The turkey was hanging from a branch, trussed by its legs, but for some reason Fergus did not seem overly happy. Mister MacNab peered curiously at the trophy. The feathers were light colored, he observed, and there were no spurs or white turban cap.

"Kind of a small gobbler, isn't he?" he remarked.

"He isn't a gobbler," Fergus groaned. "She's a hen."

Mister MacNab clucked his tongue in feigned sympathy. "My, oh, my, what ever will your feyther-in-law say?"

"It wasn't my fault," his cousin insisted. He pointed to a small tuft of hair that sprouted on the bird's chest. "Anybody would make the same mistake."

"Why, 'tis a bearded lady," Mister MacNab murmured, removing his hat in respect.

"It only happens one time in a hundred," Fergus said nervously, as they started back to the car. "I'm sure the Senator will understand when I show the beard to him . . ."

Beauregard Beadle was standing in the doorway as Fergus halted the car before the white-pillared mansion. Mister MacNab remained in the front seat beside the turkey, while his cousin raced up the front steps to explain to his father-in-law. The old man's face grew apoplectic, and he strode toward the car, with Fergus cringing in his wake. Mister MacNab noted that his cousin's voice was distinctly shaky.

"But, you see, sir, there was no way of telling." Fergus reached for the turkey, and held it up in proof. "It was feeding toward me, and I saw this beard—"

His voice trailed, and he stared at the bird in disbelief. There was no tuft of hair on its feathered breast. The color drained from his face, and his voice rose to a high whine. "But it was right there, I know it was." He appealed hysterically to Mister Mac-Nab. "Y'all saw it yourself."

"Why, Fair-r-rgus," Mister MacNab said innocently, "I dinna ken what ye-all are talking about."

His cousin's eyes narrowed in sudden comprehension. "You—

you—"

"That's enough, young man," Senator Beadle interrupted coldly. "We'll discuss this matter later." He recovered his Southern courtesy with an effort. "Tell me, suh," he said to Mister MacNab, "did y'all have any luck this mo'nin'?"

"Never saw a one," Mister MacNab sighed. He cast a meaningful glance at his cousin. "Isn't that right, Fair-r-rgus?"

Cousin Ferguus swallowed hard. "Yes, sir, that's a fact, sho' nuff," he assured the Senator. "He didn't fire a shot."

"Maybe it was just as well," Mister MacNab smiled philosophically. "I might have lost my shir-r-rt tail." He fumbled in his pocket, bent over, and pretended to pick up something from the front seat. "Could this be what ye were looking for, Fair-r-rgus?" he asked, handing him a tuft of hair. "It must have jolted off somehow during the ride."

Cousin Fergus snatched the missing beard, uttered a malevolent growl, and stalked toward the house. Old Beauregard Beadle placed a friendly hand on Mister MacNab's shoulder. "Come inside and have a tetch of bourbon and branch," he offered. "We'll drink to better luck next time."

Mister MacNab followed him up the front steps. "By the way, Senator, this tartan of mine may be a wee bit bright," he suggested. "I wonder if I could borrow one of my cousin's shir-r-rts to wear tomorrow." He watched his host fill an old-fashioned glass. "Preferably one that has a tail with a zipper."

THE DEACON
BRINGS SUIT

News of Deacon Godfrey's suit against the Lower Forty for defamation of character had spread all over Hardscrabble, and the courthouse was packed with eager spectators as the May session of the Superior Court convened. On one side of the room, the six defendants squirmed uncomfortably in their chairs and stole an occasional uneasy glance at the stern features of old Judge Philbrick, the presiding justice, seated behind the bench with a hand cupped to his ear. On the other side of the courtroom, the lone plaintiff exchanged winks now and then with his lawyer, and an ill-concealed smirk wreathed his thin face. Doc Hall mopped his forehead in the oppressive heat.

"Well, I hope the Deacon's satisfied," he muttered under his breath, "dragging us into court on the opening day of trout season. Think of that big squaretail in Mink Brook that's waiting for us to catch."

"I'm not thinking of trout," Judge Parker replied in a whisper. "I'm thinking of that big damage settlement that's waiting for us to pay, if this trial goes against us."

"Dinna mention it, mon," Mister MacNab groaned. " 'Twill use up all the club tr-r-reasury."

His fellow-members nodded in mute agreement. Deacon

Godfrey's charge that he had been held up to ridicule and scorn was hard to deny. The attorney for the prosecution, Mr. Homer Wattle, had introduced a collection of Lower Forty stories to prove that the Deacon's character had been defamed from coast to coast and simultaneously in Canada. All morning long he had read aloud such incriminating phrases as "parsimonious old buzzard" or "conniving skinflint" or "psalm-singing hypocrite," and had pointed out to the shocked jury that the club had publicly accused the plaintiff of every misdeed from keeping an illicit rendezvous in his fishhouse with Eloise the schoolmarm to trying to marry the Widow Libbey for her money. The Deacon cast a look of injured innocence toward the jury box as Mr. Wattle dwelt eloquently on the mental pain and anguish which his client had suffered.

"He's got us over a barrel," Colonel Cobb admitted in a low voice. "We can't claim we didn't say it because it's right in print."

Attorney Wattle concluded reading the evidence, and presented the collection of stories to Judge Philbrick with a flourish. "And now if it please your Honor," he continued in his most obsequious manner, "I should like to call a couple of reputable witnesses who will testify to the falsity of this slander." He beckoned toward the rear of the courtroom. "Miss Eloise Simpkins."

There was a murmur of excitement as the pretty schoolmarm strolled up the aisle in a tight-fitting sweater, her yellow stretch pants switching as she walked. She dimpled at Judge Philbrick, took her oath, and seated herself in the witness stand with her legs crossed, waving a trim calf toward the jury.

"Miss Simpkins," Attorney Wattle began, "will you state the purpose of your visit to the Deacon's fishhouse on the afternoon of March fifth?"

"We were discussing educational matters," Eloise replied loftily. "The Deacon is on the school committee, and I was explaining the problems of child psychology in the third grade when all of a sudden" —she glared across the room at the Lower Forty— "this gang of ruffians and hoodlums gave the house a push."

"I object, your Honor," Judge Parker shouted, springing to his feet.

"*You* object!" Eloise retorted. "How do you think *I* felt, skidding across the ice at twenty miles an hour? I'm still black-and-blue where I landed on my whoosis." She appealed to Judge Philbrick. "Would you like me to show you, your Honor?"

Judge Philbrick adjusted his spectacles, which had just slid down onto his nose. "The court will admit the evidence without visual examination," he said hastily. "Proceed with the next witness."

Attorney Wattle faced the rear of the courtroom and paused for a dramatic moment. "Mrs. Effie Libbey," he called.

The members of the Lower Forty turned in surprise as the Widow Libbey rose and hurried past them, her head averted to avoid their eyes. "Howinell did the Deacon ever talk her into testifying against us?" Judge Parker mumbled. "Now we're in real trouble."

The Widow Libbey took her oath and seated herself nervously, twisting a handkerchief in her hands and sniffling. Attorney Wattle beamed as the jury clucked in sympathy. "Mrs. Libbey," he began, "is it true that the defendants have sought to influence you against marrying my client?"

The Widow knotted her handkerchief into a tight ball. "Well, I wouldn't say they was exactly in favor of it," she admitted.

"Did they ever state their motives for preventing such a marriage?"

"They said they was afraid that if the Deacon got aholt of my land," she murmured, "he'd post it with 'No Trespassing' signs so's they couldn't hunt or fish there any more."

Judge Philbrick sat forward with a start. "Would the witness explain that statement?"

"You see, your Honor, the Deacon don't approve of hunting or fishing, he says it's wrong to murder God's poor little defenseless critters, he never does it himself, and he says so-called sportsmen like the Lower Forty ain't nothing but cold-blooded killers." Her voice trembled. "I don't know what to think—I'm all confused—"

She burst into tears, and Attorney Wattle helped her down gently from the witness stand. Judge Philbrick was peering thoughtfully at Deacon Godfrey, and a strange faraway expression flitted across his face. He reached for his gavel.

"The Court declares a recess for half an hour," he announced. "Will the plaintiff and the defendants come to my private chambers, please? I think it might help if we had a little talk together."

He strode out of the courtroom, the collection of stories under his arm, and the members of the Lower Forty followed him moodily down the corridor. "We might as well face it," Judge Parker told his codefendants frankly. "Effie Libbey's testimony swung the jury. We're as good as licked right now."

"That means we can't afford our Lower Forty Junior Camp this summer," Cousin Sid pointed out sadly.

"I'll be lucky if I dinna have to sell my hair-r-rse," Mister Mac-Nab sighed.

Uncle Perk paused outside the chambers and scanned the corridor. "I wisht Owl Eyes Osborn would hurry," he said. "He promised me he'd git here as soon as he could."

"What's Owl Eyes got to do with all this?" asked Doc Hall.

"It's just a hunch I had," Uncle Perk shrugged. "Just a hunch, is all—"

Deacon Godfrey was already seated in Judge Philbrick's chambers as they entered. The Deacon's lip curled in a sneer, and he turned his back on them. "Ain't no use my talking with these fellows, your Honor," he assured Judge Philbrick. "I ain't gonna drop this suit, or discuss a settlement out of court. They're agonna pay for all the things they done to me." His voice was hard. "I don't forgit easy."

Judge Philbrick packed tobacco in a curved brier pipe, and studied the Deacon over the flare of the match. The same faraway expression crossed his face again. "I don't usually forget either, Deacon," he said. "Are you perfectly sure you've never hunted or fished yourself?"

"I don't believe in killin' God's critters," the Deacon insisted.

"That's funny," Judge Philbrick mused, exhaling a cloud of smoke. "I seem to recall that you were charged ten years ago with jacking a ten-point buck."

"Oh, yes, I do remember now," the Deacon said quickly, "but it was all a frameup. I happened to be in the woods with a spotlight looking for mushrooms, and I seen this poor deer that somebody'd killed, and I drug it out so the meat wouldn't go to waste. Unfortunately the case was tried by some narrow-minded idiot of a local judge who was a hunter himself."

"I know," Judge Philbrick said thinly. "I happened to be that judge. What's more, I'd been stalking that same ten-point buck fair and legal all season." He pointed the stem of his pipe at the Deacon. "It isn't the hunters and fishermen who are killers," he began, "it's the nonsportsmen who ignore the law and—" He paused as a knock sounded on the door. "Come in."

Owl Eyes Osborn shouldered into the room, clad in his official game warden uniform. He removed his broadbrimmed hat and stepped up to the Judge's desk. "Pardon me, your Honor," he said, "but may I have your permission to make a criminal arrest in your chambers?"

Judge Philbrick blinked. "Whom do you propose to arrest, warden?"

"Deacon Godfrey," Owl Eyes replied grimly.

The Judge's face was impassive. "Well, I certainly don't want to stand in the way of an efficient officer who is performing his sworn duty."

"Thank you, your Honor." Owl Eyes place a hand on the Deacon's quaking shoulder. "I hereby charge you with taking trout before the season opened, without a license, and by the use of dynamite."

"That's a lie," Deacon Godrey stammered. "I never bought a stick o' dynamite in my life."

"Naow, Deacon, ain't you gittin' a mite forgitful again?" Uncle Perk said. "I was goin' over my store records last night, and I seen where you purchased several sticks o' dynamite an' caps an' waterproof fuse just a month ago. So on a hunch I phoned Owl Eyes an' tole him about it."

"Oh, yes, I do remember now," the Deacon stammered. "I used it to blow a beaver dam that was flooding my lower meadow."

"That so?" said Owl Eyes. "Then how do you account for the fact the beaver dam is still standing, as I noticed when I looked over your property this morning while you were here in court? I also noticed a piece of waterproof fuse lying beside the best pool in your brook, not to mention a couple of dozen nice trout under the sawdust in your icehouse."

Deacon Godfrey's face was working convulsingly. "Can't we—can't we settle this thing without a lot of publicity?"

"Well, now, that might be arranged, Deacon," Judge Parker nodded. "Your case will come up before me in magistrate's court, and I might be persuaded to file it without date—" He paused a moment, and glanced at his fellow members. "Provided you drop this damage suit of yours."

"And pay all the legal fees and cour-r-rt expenses," Mister MacNab added.

"And make a small donation of a hundred dollars for the Lower Forty Junior Camp," Cousin Sid suggested.

Deacon Godfrey swallowed a couple of times, and his eye shifted from Owl Eyes to the Lower Forty to Judge Philbrick, smoking placidly behind his desk. He snatched a checkbook from his pocket, wrote a check and tossed it on the desk, and stalked out of the chambers in silence. The members of the Lower Forty rose to leave.

"By the way, gentlemen, would you mind telling my clerk-of-court that by agreement this case has been declared a nonsuit?" Judge Philbrick asked. He leaned back in his chair, put on his spectacles, and picked up the collection of Lower Forty stories. "I'm looking forward to reading the evidence, now that the trial is over."

A MATTER OF SPORTSMANSHIP

Judge Parker paused in the entrance of the cook tent and gazed over his shoulder contentedly at the Lower Forty Junior Camp grounds, bathed in warm morning sunshine. A dozen half-naked youngsters in trunks and sneakers were busy scrubbing tin breakfast dishes and airing blankets and lugging firewood. Trout dimpled in the stream that flowed at the edge of the clearing, and the camp mascot, a tame Canada jay, pecked unconcernedly at crumbs in front of the tent. The Judge smiled and pushed through the canvas flaps.

"A few more days here," he observed to Cousin Sid as he poured himself a cup of coffee, "and these city kids will be as much at home as that whiskey jack."

Cousin Sid nodded in happy agreement. Thanks to Deacon Godfrey's grudging contribution in settlement of his lawsuit, the club had been able to bring a group of underprivileged teenagers to the country for a week's camping trip. Mister MacNab's hearse had met the excited contingent at the Hardscrabble station and transported them to this remote wilderness spot near the Canadian border. Already their lean bodies had begun to harden, and their city pallor had been replaced by a healthy tan; and under the tutelage of the Lower Forty members they were fast learning the rudiments of woodcraft and firearms safety and survival in the outdoors.

"They're learning something even more important," Cousin Sid added. "They're learning to be sportsmen—"

There was a thud outside the tent, a squawk of pain, and a frantic beating of wings that died away into silence. Doc Hall entered, carrying the limp form of the Canada jay in his hand. He laid the carcass on the table. "Somebody nailed it with a slingshot," he said grimly.

Judge Parker whirled and strode out the door. A circle of youngsters had formed at the far end of the campsite, and in their midst the Judge could see two boys rolling in the dirt, legs kicking and fists flailing. He shoved his way through the onlookers, grabbed the shoulder of the boy on top, and hauled him erect. The smaller boy clambered slowly to his feet, wiping a smear of blood from his nose. He was a snub-nosed youngster of sixteen, with a shock of unruly red hair and a look of rebellion in his blue eyes. His bare upper body was covered with scratches, and a discolored lump was swelling on one cheek. He clutched a slingshot in his fist.

"What's your name?" Judge Parker asked.

"Chick Keenan."

"Let me have that slingshot."

"It's mine," Chick said sullenly, hiding it behind him.

The Judge's face clouded. "Go wait in your tent, Chick," he said. "The rest of you can take your morning dip."

The other members of the Lower Forty looked up in silence as Judge Parker seated himself beside the collapsible tin stove in the cook tent. "I'm afraid we'll have to get rid of that Keenan boy," he frowned. "He's nothing but a troublemaker."

"I can't figure him out," Cousin Sid sighed. "Always staying by himself, never mixing with the rest."

"Last night I caught him shooting cr-r-raps in his tent," Mister MacNab reported. "Not only that, but the young rascal took me for four dollars and thair-r-rty-two cents."

The Judge turned to Colonel Cobb. "You brought him here, Cobbie. Had you known him before?"

"I used to know his father," the Colonel said. "He was my tail gunner in a B-17 back in England, the best sergeant I ever had, but he sort of went to pieces after the war. His wife walked out on him, and he took to drinking, and after he died the kid started running wild. I got the parole officer to sign him over to me for a week in hopes that—"

"What was he on parole for?"

Colonel Cobb hesitated and fingered his close-cropped grey moustache. "Shooting swans in the Boston Commons," he admitted. He appealed to the others. "He's my responsibility," he pleaded. "Give me one more chance with him . . ."

Chick squatted cross-legged on his cot, his thin arms hugging his knees, as Colonel Cobb shouldered stiffly into his tent. The boy's bruised face was defiant. "Tell me, Chick," the Colonel asked, "what were you fighting about?"

"That's my business."

The Colonel seated himself thoughtfully on the edge of the cot, trying to fathom the hostility in the boy's eyes. There was something behind that belligerent front, he sensed, something that was reaching out to him. His brusque military manner softened. "Don't you like it here, son?" he asked.

"What's to do here?" Chick shrugged.

"I'll tell you what's to do. Let's go fishing together."

"All I ever done was spear goldfish in the Public Gardens."

"All right, then, come along and watch me." The Colonel rose. "I'll show you how."

Colonel Cobb led the way along the bank, and Chick followed in silence. They halted beside a likely pool, and the Colonel set up his rod and opened an aluminum fly box. Chick peered curiously over his shoulder. "Why don't you put on a worm?" he asked. "I should think the least you could do, before you knock off a fish, is to give it a square meal instead of a mouthful of feathers."

Colonel Cobb selected a small Gray Bivisible, and threaded it onto his leader. "I don't like worms," he explained.

"I bet a fish does. I bet he likes a worm better'n one of them things."

"That's just it," the Colonel said, daubing a spot of mucilin on the hackle and blotting it carefully. "It's too easy that way." He waded cautiously into the stream, whipped the slender rod a couple of times, and sent his tapered line skimming across the pool. "I'd rather get him on a fly."

"What difference does it make how you get him, as long as you get him?"

The fly landed lightly beside the far bank and rode downstream with the current toward a deep eddy. "You see, Chick," the Colonel began, turning back to face the figure on the bank, "it's a matter of sportsmanship—"

The pool exploded, and a massive silvery form rocketed into the air, the sun glinting on its great slab sides. Too late, the Colonel lifted his rod to take up the slack. The trout flung itself downstream, the leader parted, and the limp line settled on the stream as the ripples widened toward shore. The Colonel waded back to the bank and collapsed, his hand shaking. "That was the biggest rainbow I ever hooked," he whispered in awe. "I'd have given my right arm to land that trout."

"It was on account of me," Chick said slowly. "You turned around to speak to me and—"

"I shouldn't have taken my eyes off the fly," Colonel Cobb mourned. "I'll probably never have a chance like that again." A low rumble of thunder sounded in the distance. "Well," he said disconsolately, "we'd better get back to camp before the storm."

Rain drummed steadily on the canvas of the cook tent that night, and Uncle Perk rose and shoved some more sticks into the stove. "Gittin' a mite chilly," he observed, lighting his pipe with the end of a burning stick and replacing the lid. "Mean night to be out." He glanced at Colonel Cobb, slumped in his chair. "Hadn' you better turn in like ev'rybody else an' git some sleep?"

Colonel Cobb shook his head. He was still brooding over the trophy he had lost that afternoon through his own carelessness. In his mind's eye he could see the huge form arcing over the pool in a shower of iridescent drops, his Gray Bivisible embedded in its lower jaw. Well, the better man had won, that was all. Mentally he tossed a salute to the trout. One soldier to another.

A flashlight bobbed in the dark outside the tent, and the canvas flaps rustled as they parted. Chick stood in the entrance, his red hair plastered in streaks over his grinning face. His soaked T shirt clung to his skinny body, and water seeped from his soggy dungarees and made a puddle on the floor. He dragged an enormous trout behind him, and laid it proudly on the table.

"Here's that fish you wanted," he said to Colonel Cobb.

The Colonel stared aghast at the mutilated rainbow. Blood ran from a cruel gash in its silver side, its head had been battered with a boulder until it was flattened, but there was no mistaking the tiny Gray Bivisible still embedded in its jaw. Chick held up a long pole, with a hunting knife lashed to the tip.

"I speared him with this," he said, "when he come to my light."

Colonel Cobb removed the fly from the trout's jaw, an dropped it into his aluminum box. "I guess this settles it, Chick," he announced cripsly. "You're not a sportsman."

The grin disappeared from the boy's face and his blue eyes widened. He turned and bolted from the tent. Uncle Perk knocked the ashes from his pipe in the ensuing silence, and filled it again. He rasped a match across the stove, and blinked at Colonel Cobb over the flame. The Colonel shifted uneasily under his gaze.

"I'm sending the boy back to the Orphan Home tomorrow," he insisted. Uncle Perk did not answer. "What else can I do?" Colonel Cobb asked him defensively. "Spearing trout, shooting the camp mascot, starting a fight—"

Uncle Perk emitted a slow cloud of tobacco smoke. "This afternoon I happened to overhear some o' the kids talkin' about that fight," he murmured. "Seems the bigger boy stole Chick's slingshot an' killed the bird. That's why Chick lit into him."

"But why didn't he say so?"

"Mebbe it's his idea o' sportsmanship not to tell on somebody." Uncle Perk tamped the coal of his pipe with a calloused thumb. "Mebbe he's used to goin' it alone. Mebbe he never had nobody he could trust before."

Colonel Cobb rubbed his grizzled moustache in bewilderment. "You mean he trusts me? Why, I can't even get close to him."

"Why do you think he went an' snagged that trout for you?" Uncle Perk asked, striking another match. "He figgered it was somepin' you wanted."

Colonel Cobb shoved back his chair, pulled on his army trench-coat, and hurried across the rain-swept campsite toward Chick's tent. The other occupants sat up in fright as his flashlight played across their faces. It came to rest on the empty cot at one side of the tent. "Where's Chick?" he asked.

"He ran away," one of the boys answered. "Said he was gonna hike through the woods and find his way to Canada." His voice trembled. "Please, mister, we couldn't stop him. It ain't our fault."

The Colonel stood in the door of the tent, the rain beating on his face. "No, it's my fault," he said huskily. "And it's up to me to find him."

The rain had stopped by morning, but low clouds hung over the site of the Lower Forty Junior Camp and water dripped dismally from the spruces around the clearing. Word of young Chick Keenan's disappearance had spread rapidly, and the other teenage campers huddled in an excited group around the bonfire, shivering in the clammy chill as they discussed the night's events. "He said he was gonna hike all the way to Canada," one of his tentmates reported. "He said he'd poke me in the nose if I tried to stop him."

"You oughta seen the Colonel's face when he heard he'd run away," another youngster whispered. "The old boy took right off after him, rain and all."

In the cook tent across the clearing, Judge Parker was busily planning the search activities. "Cousin Sid, you stay here in camp today and look after the kids while we're away. Uncle Perk, will you get some sandwiches and canteens of coffee ready? We may be gone a long time." The Judge glanced up as Mister MacNab's hearse jolted to a halt outside the tent. "Any sign of him along the highway, Mac?"

"Nary hide nor hair-r-r," Mister MacNab sighed. "His footprints would have shown in the mud if the wee bairn had gone that way."

Judge Parker frowned at a survey map on the table. "There's no habitation between here and the border," he said. "Mac, drive back to town and alert the game wardens and state troopers. Have them set up an air search as soon as these clouds lift." He rose. "Doc, you and I better get started."

They halted outside the tent as Colonel Cobb stumbled wearily across the clearing toward them. His clothes were sodden after walking all night in the rain, and his eyes were red-rimmed from lack of sleep. "Colonel, you ought to get yourself a little shuteye," the Judge advised. "You're out on your feet."

"I'm coming with you," the Colonel insisted, "as soon as I grab a cup of coffee." He squared his tired shoulders in a military posture. "Chick ran away because of me, and I'm going to find him if it's the last thing I do."

Judge Parker hurried to his tent and took his shotgun from its case. "I'll fire this in the air now and then," he told Doc, "to let the kid know where we are."

"Better not, Judge," Doc cautioned. "He'll run all the faster. He's afraid we'll send him back to that Orphan Home."

Colonel Cobb stumbled behind them, his face tired and drawn, as they set off along an abandoned lumber road that led north from camp. "It's the logical route he'd take," Judge Parker argued, "if he's heading for Canada." They trudged single file through the woods, tripping over fallen logs and sinking ankle-deep in the spongy moss. The lumber road was petering out, and it ended at last in a desolate pile of slash. Several smaller trails branched from it, half hidden by brush.

"We'd better split up here," the Judge said, taking a compass from his pocket. "I'll work due north along the stream. Doc, you take the trail that runs northeast."

Colonel Cobb peered through the mist at an overgrown path that led up the side of a steep incline. "I'll follow this one over the hill," he told the others. "It's just a hunch."

The path grew steeper as he mounted, and the Colonel paused for breath. There was no sound in the woods save the steady dripping from the rain-soaked trees, and the water squishing inside his boots as he started climbing again. His hopes were fading fast; there was only a chance in a million of finding the boy in this wilderness, he knew, but he forced himself on, thinking of Chick's thin face and wide hurt eyes. He stooped to crawl on hands and knees under a blowdown, and stared at a familiar object lying in the path. It was a slingshot.

He shoved it in his hip pocket and started running, his breath coming in sharp gasps as he neared the crest of the hill. He halted again and strained his ears. Above the steady patter of drops from the trees he made out another sound: a low strangled sobbing somewhere ahead of him. He shoved his way through a tangle of hemlocks, and felt his heart bump. Chick was huddled at the base of a tree; his ripped T shirt hung from one shoulder, his dungarees were soaked through, his teeth chattered with cold. The boy sprang to his feet as he saw Colonel Cobb, and scurried up the path ahead of him like a frightened animal, making for the hilltop.

"Chick, wait for me," the Colonel called. "Wait, Chick."

The boy crept out onto a rocky ledge. "No," he whimpered. "I'm not going back to that home. Why cancha leave me alone?"

"Listen to me, Chick," the Colonel pleaded, pausing at the foot of the ledge. The boy hesitated, poised to run. "You can trust me." He took a step forward, and the boy retreated. "Chick, I was a friend of your father's."

The boy's face suddenly contorted. "My father was a bum," he shouted. "I'm a bum just like him." His blue eyes welled with tears. "Now leave me alone, willya?"

"Let me tell you something about your father," the Colonel said in a low voice. He took another step, holding out his hand; the boy did not move. "He was my tail-gunner in the war. Our airplane was hit and caught fire, and I was jammed behind the controls. I ordered the crew to bail out, but he wouldn't leave me. He crawled up into the cockpit and pulled me out." He started across the ledge, reaching for the boy. "He was the finest man I ever—"

A chunk of soggy moss skidded out beneath his boot, and he sprawled full length on the ledge and began to slide backward, faster and faster, down the slippery rock and over the side and into black space . . .

Colonel Cobb stirred and opened his eyes. He was lying on a bed of soft balsam twigs, and several larger branches had been laced overhead to form a makeshift roof. He tried to rise and felt a stab of pain in his right ankle. He look down at his leg, puzzled; his boot had been unlaced and pulled off, and his ankle was bound with strips of a torn T shirt. Something rustled behind him, and he turned as Chick crawled through the bushes, his lean body bare to the waist. "I hope that foot is bandaged right," the boy said. "Doc Hall was showing us first aid the other day in camp."

Colonel Cobb nodded. "I'm afraid I can't walk on it, though."

"You don't have to," Chick said. "You'll be okay here till they find you." He held up a dead squirrel by its hind legs. "I borrowed back my slingshot to kill it," he apologized. "I hope you don't mind."

The Colonel started to struggle out of his coat. "You're shivering. Put this on."

"Nah, you need it, lying on the ground. I'll be warm enough as soon as I get a fire going."

Colonel Cobb took a waterproof match case out of his pocket and shook his head. "Where can you find any wood that will burn?"

"Judge Parker was saying to always look for a hollow tree, sometimes there's dry stuff inside." Chick put his shoulder to a small dead pine, and it toppled with a crash. "I think I can get enough out of this to start it."

The Colonel reared on an elbow, and watched the boy dig out some punk with his fingers. He held a match to the heap, blew the smouldering spark to life, and added a few slivers from the interior of the tree. They watched the coal redden and build to a small steady blaze.

"I'll set these bigger branches above it so they'll be drying, like Cousin Sid was telling us at camp," Chick said. "Then we can roast this squirrel."

"Did you ever roast a squirrel before, Chick?"

"Oh, sure, plenty of times," Chick shrugged. "I used to shoot them in the park." He caught himself guiltily. "I guess you wouldn't call that very sporting."

Colonel Cobb leaned back on the bed of balsam twigs, his hands laced behind his head. "You know, Chick—" He swallowed a lump in his throat. "There's a lot I'm learning about sportsmanship."

The clouds had lifted, and the column of smoke rose straight up, brown and heavy in the clear still air. They heard the drone of a motor in the distance, and a small reconnaissance plane flew toward the signal. It circled them, dipped a wing, and headed back to town. The boy's eyes followed it as it disappeared.

"Well, Chick, they've spotted us," Colonel Cobb said slowly. "They'll be here pretty soon to carry me down the hill." He gazed at the small naked back, bent over the fire. "Hadn't you better get going?"

"I'm staying here," Chick muttered. "I'm not leaving you."

Colonel Cobb hobbled into Uncle Perk's store, rested his crutches against the counter, and settled himself into a chair, his plaster cast stretched out in front of him. "Nice job you did, Doc," he said to Doc Hall. "Only problem is that I can't drive for a while."

"That's no problem," Doc remarked, watching through the window as the Colonel's car pulled away. "Chick's a better driver than you ever were."

The Colonel turned to Judge Parker. "Something I want to ask you, Judge," he began in his crispest military manner. "Will you start drawing up papers so I can adopt the boy? He can work for me in the printshop and learn the publishing business and—" He hesitated and fingered his close-cropped moustache. "You see, he hasn't got a father—" His military pose faded, and he concluded awkwardly: "—and I haven't got a son."

"Wal, naow, that's a real fine idee," Uncle Perk grunted,

reaching for his jug of Old Stump Blower. "It's time we got some new blood in this here Lower Forty."

THE GLOR-R-RIOUS FOURTH

Not that the Lower Forty objected to taking part in Hardscrabble's annual Fourth of July parade. They were only too willing to serve as living statues on the patriotic float of the Sisters of Samantha Circle of Silent Workers, particularly when Cousin Sid pointed out the negotiable value of such cooperation. "If we do this little favor for our wives," he reminded them shrewdly, "maybe they won't kick about being left home when we take our fishing trip to Canada next month."

It was the float itself which they viewed with misgiving. The Sisters of Samantha had hit on an original conception called "The Spirit of Seventy-Six," in which Judge Parker, portraying George Washington, would read the Declaration of Independence to his Colonial troops. All week long the womenfolks had cut and stitched Continental uniforms and draped red-white-and-blue bunting over a pickup truck in the Judge's garage, confident that their novel idea would take first prize. The members of the Lower Forty, donning their homemade costumes on the morning of the parade, were less sanguine. Judge Parker shook his head dubiously as he pinned on a pair of cardboard epaulettes, fringed with curtain tassels.

"What chance have we got of winning?" he grumbled. "The Godfrey Insurance Agency is entering a float this year, and the judges are all friends of the Deacon." He fastened a gilded wooden sword to his belt and adjusted his white cotton wig. "At least, we can enjoy the fireworks display afterwards."

"Guess you fellers ain't heard," said Uncle Perk, as he wrapped a ketchup-stained bandage around his forehead. "This here's gonna be a safe an' sane Fourth. There won't be no fireworks."

Doc Hall started so violently that he almost dropped his little son's drum. "Whyinell not?"

"Godfrey talked the selectmen into refusin' to sign a permit, that's why not." Uncle Perk tootled a few experimental notes on a toy flute. "Guess he don't want to risk any accident, in case his company might have to settle an insurance claim."

"I'd like to lay hands on a few old-fashioned skyrockets," the Judge fumed, "just to spite that conniving skinflint."

Mister MacNab set a dented derby on his head, its brim cut in three places and pinned back to form a tricorn hat. "It so hoppens I know a gun trader just across the state line," he said thoughtfully, "who bootlegs fir-r-reworks on the side. Pairhops we might work out an illegal tr-r-ransaction over a jug of Uncle Pairk's Stump Blower."

Judge Parker glanced at his watch. "Parade starts in a couple of hours." He strode briskly toward Mister MacNab's hearse. "We'll have to hurry."

Mister MacNab's acquaintance proved to be a hard trader, and both time and the jug were running low as the Lower Forty

[174]

headed back to Hardscrabble, a box of bootleg fireworks tied on top of the hearse. To add to their difficulties, Mister MacNab had endeavored to keep up with his friend, drink for drink, and was now slumped on a jump seat with his tricorn hat over one eye, puffing a large cigar and humming "Yankee Doodle" in an off-key falsetto. Cousin Sid mannned the wheel instead and drove at breakneck speed; but as they neared town they heard a telltale "Oom-pah!" and the distant roar of the crowd. Main Street was blocked off, and a state trooper held up his hand to halt the hearse. Judge Parker leaned out the window.

"I've got to get over to the other side of town," he explained. "Our float is in my garage." He pointed to his epaulettes. "I'm Washington."

The trooper saluted respectfully. "Sorry, General," he apologized, "but nobody ain't allowed to cross Main Street til the parade's finished."

The Judge's protests were drowned by the blare of the approaching High School band, drums beating and fifes squealing. Behind them came a group of uniformed soldiers and sailors and airmen, followed by the members of the Grange and the 4H Club and the Patrons of Husbandry, slightly out of step. Next in line was the riding class from Idawanna Camp for Boys, mounted on white horses and led by a dapper instructor in gleaming polo boots. A cheer went up from the sidewalk throng as the local chapter of the American Legion passed in trim ranks, rifles shouldered and eyes straight ahead. Here and there a World War I uniform failed to button across a bulging paunch, but the veterans marched erect and proud, and as they drew abreast of the Post Office flag their rifle butts came down smartly together. Judge Parker peered down Main Street at a long undulating line of Boy and Girl Scouts tagging after them, stretching as far as he could see.

"We'll never get across," he groaned. "What will our wives say?"

Another cheer rent the air, and the Hardscrabble Fire Department's brand-new pumper rolled up the avenue, its crew in rubber boots and oilskins clinging to the sides. The wail of its siren was punctuated by the shrill beep-horn of a flashy red Corvette Sting Ray that followed close behind, driven by the enterprising Chevy dealer. In his wake was an elderly resident in a linen duster, seated proudly at the wheel of an equally ancient Stutz-Bearcat with wire wheels. The Judge jerked a thumb in disgust at the next exhibit.

"Here he comes, slogans and all," he grunted.

A polite patter of handclapping sounded as the Godfrey Insurance Agency float hove into view, bearing a huge streamer the length of the truck: "Eternal Vigilence is the Price of Safety." In the center of the platform body was an antique dollhouse, surrounded by an artificial grass lawn dotted with miniature figures representing a happily insured family with the children and dog. Presiding over this peaceful scene was the Deacon himself, clad in his best black suit and holding aloft a canvas sign reading: "Your Home is SAFE when Godfrey Insures It." As he passed the halted hearse, his face wrinkled in a smug smile.

Judge Parker cast another glance down the avenue, and his eyes lighted. The next float was the Order of the Eastern Star; on it a group of ladies in white dresses stood pointing at a silver star suspended from a tall pole. Unfortunately the star had become entangled in the branches of an elm, and the truck had halted for a moment while the driver shook it free. The Judge nudged Cousin Sid at the wheel.

"Get into line, quick," he whispered. "We'll ride along with the parade a couple of blocks, and then duck out again at my street. It's our only chance."

Cousin Sid stepped on the starter and slipped into the temporary gap, and the hearse moved up the avenue amid the laughter and hoots of the crowd. Mister MacNab, aroused by the applause, lurched to his feet and staggered out onto the rear platform, beaming at the onlookers. "Luik at us, boys," he shouted, brandishing his cigar, "we're a-float!" He made a sweeping gesture with his arm, and the cigar butt flipped unnoticed into the open box on top of the hearse. A small trickle of smoke rose as he climbed back inside. Judge Parker, peering intently ahead, prodded Cousin Sid and pointed.

"Here's my street," he yelled. "Turn off!"

"I can't," Cousin Sid replied over his shoulder. "They've got a sawhorse across it."

Mister MacNab settled himself on the jump seat and reached for Uncle Perk's jug. "Aye, mon," he crooned, " 'tis a gr-r-rond and glor-r-rious—"

A muffled boom shook the hearse, and an instant later there was an earsplitting crackling and a series of explosions high overhead. Several more booms followed, filling the sky with the erratic bursts of rockets and Roman candles. The crowd screamed and scampered for cover, and pandemonium swept the parade as the marchers broke ranks in panic. Behind the erupting hearse, the driver of the Eastern Star truck slammed on his brakes, and the group of ladies sat down abruptly in unison, still pointing at the star. The Camp Idawanna riding class, bouncing conscientiously in their saddles, grabbed for leather and took off across the landscape in all directions, leaving their instructor sprawled on the near side of a privet hedge. A bomb exploded directly over the head of the Chevy dealer, and he gave a startled glance aloft and carpeted the throttle. As his Corvette roared ahead at full speed, he heard the strident bellow of a Klaxon behind him, and the Stutz-Bearcat passed him in a blur, the owner's linen duster flapping as he streaked up the avenue and out of sight.

Mister MacNab lifted the jug to his lips again. "As I was saying," he began, " 'tis a gr-r-rond—"

A mighty boom interrupted him, and a three-stage rocket headed straight for the float in front of them. Deacon Godfrey ducked in time, and the missile zoomed through a window of the dollhouse. Its first stage exploded, and the lace curtains started to smoulder. With a yelp of anguish, the Deacon stooped to extinguish the sparks, leaping back with another yelp as the second stage let go. Smoke curled through the miniature chimney, and he tried in vain to beat out the growing conflagration with his "Your Home is SAFE" sign. The third stage of the rocket went off with a shattering detonation, flames crowned through the dollhouse roof, and the Deacon beckoned wildly to the crew of the Fire Department pumper. "Save my house," he screamed. "It isn't insured."

Still sputtering and launching an occasional pyrotechnic shower, the hearse sped up the deserted avenue past the reviewing stand, beneath which the judges had crawled for refuge. Mister MacNab, gazing through the rear window, nodded in approval as the pumper shot a stream of water toward the blazing dollhouse and sluiced the Deacon backward off the platform. He lifted the jug once more. "—and glor-r-rious Fourth," he concluded, and shut his eyes contentedly.

Cousin Sid drew up in front of Judge Parker's house and halted the hearse, its metal top blistered and charred, and the members of the Lower Forty slunk into the garage in glum silence. The Judge seated himself on the running board of the Sisters of Samantha truck, festooned with red-white-and-blue bunting, and unbuttoned his General's blouse disconsolately. "Well, we might as well forget that fishing trip to Canada," he sighed. "When our wives get home—"

Uncle Perk sauntered through the door of the garage. "Dunno what there is to worry about," he shrugged. "We won first prize."

Judge Parker shoved back his cotton wig, and passed a hand across his forehead in bewilderment. "How do you know?"

"One of the jedges just tole me," Uncle Perk replied. "He said there wa'n't nothin' else they could do. We was the only float left in the parade."

ROCKABY, KITTY

A bitter February wind seeped through the cracked windows of Uncle Perk's store, and the members of the Lower Forty shivered and turned up their coat collars against the icy draft. The potbellied stove was glowing red, but a large blanket had been draped around it like a tent, deflecting all the warmth to a wicker basket on the floor. Mister MacNab gazed enviously at four beagle puppies snuggled inside. "Can't ye shift that contr-r-raption a wee bit so the rest of us can get some heat?" he complained. "I'm colder than a br-r-ross monkey."

"Law's been repealed that says ye gotta stay," Uncle Perk replied tersely, pouring a saucer of cream and setting it down in the basket. "This here is ole Belle's last litter, an' I ain't takin' no chanct o' them li'l tykes catching pneumoney."

Colonel Cobb blew on his fingers to thaw them. "You're spoiling those pups, Perk," he grumbled. "They'll turn out to be nothing but house pets. You'll have to carry them through a rabbit swamp so they won't get their feet wet."

"That's the trouble with all these modern parents," Cousin Sid agreed, emitting a frosty breath. "The way they pamper their children nowadays—"

"Grandparents are even worse," Doc Hall observed, with a meaningful glance at Judge Parker.

The Judge bristled. "In case you happen to be referring to

Lyford III," he retorted, "he's going to grow up and be a real red-blooded outdoorsman just like his father and grandfather."

"Not if his mother and grandmother have anything to do with it," Doc warned him. "Why, they're coddling that grandson of yours half to death."

Judge Parker shifted uneasily in his chair. "Nothing to worry about," he maintained stoutly, trying to hide his concern. "I'm getting him a shotgun and a hunting dog and—"

"You're too late, Judge," Doc Hall shrugged. "Your wife was in here the other day and she asked Uncle Perk to find her a kitten for Lyford to play with."

The Judge's chair came forward with a crash. "A *kitten*!" he gasped. "Not in my own house!" He fixed Uncle Perk with an accusing glare. "Why didn't you tell me before?"

Uncle Perk lowered his eyes guiltily. "She asked me not to say anything, Jedge," he explained. "She wants it to be a surprise."

Judge Parker rose in silence and stalked across the store, his face stricken. The string of sleighbells jangled as the door slammed behind him. Uncle Perk shook his head in sympathy.

"Wisht I could think o' some way to help," he sighed, taking off his jacket and spreading it over the puppies to protect them from the chill. "I allus hate to see people spoil their young'uns . . ."

Judge Parker's expression was still grim as he halted the car before his house and strode up the front steps. His wife and daughter-in-law were waiting in the doorway, bundled up in furs. "You're just in time, dear," Patience Parker greeted him. "We've got to go on an errand, and we need the car."

"Where are you going?" the Judge asked suspiciously.

"It's a surprise for Lyford III," Patience said, with a wink at the baby's mother. "You can look after the little cherub till we get back. Just change his training panties and give him a drink of orange juice when he's thirsty and sing him a nursery rhyme if he misses his Grandma too much. We won't be gone long."

The sound of the car's exhaust faded down the street, and Judge Parker poured himself a highball and sank morosely onto a chair beside the crib. It was his own fault, he realized. Little Lyford's father had been called to Florida on Air Force assignment, and the Judge was busy in court all day, and the entire upbringing of the youngster had been left to the women folks. No wonder they had — what was Doc's phrase? — coddled him half to death. Buying him a kitten, though — that was too much. He gazed sadly at his grandson, playing with his toys, and his eyes widened in disbelief. The baby was holding a stuffed flannel cat, stroking and hugging it fondly. "Nice kitty," Lyford cooed. "Nice kitty."

A muscle hopped in the Judge's jaw. "*Bad* kitty," he corrected, snatching the stuffed cat and spanking it. He dropped it back in the crib. "*Bad! Bad!*"

"Nice kitty," the baby repeated, kissing it on its flannel nose.

Judge Parker glanced around desperately, and his eye came to rest on a framed Oriental print that his son had brought home from his tour of duty in Japan. An evil-looking Siamese cat was stalking a bird with infinite patience, its red jowls dripping. The Judge took down the print and set it on the floor beside the crib.

"*Bad* kitty catch *nice* bird," he explained.

"Nice bird," his grandson dimpled.

"See, here comes the *bad* kitty like this." The Judge crouched on all fours and waddled across the living room in a slinking feline lope, uttering a bloodcurdling "Maraow-wow-wow." His grandson chuckled happily. "And here's the *nice* bird just minding its own business." Judge Parker hopped up and down several times, and stole a glance at his appreciative audience. "And now here's Grandpa with his *nice* Model 70 Winchester chambered for .375 H & H." He fitted an imaginary rifle to his shoulder. "Grandpa sights through the Lyman Alaskan scope and lets his breath half out and *squeezes*." His right shoulder rolled back with the simulated recoil. "KA-POW!"

"Kapow, kapow," his grandson echoed, clapping his hands in glee.

"*Nice* bird fly away." The Judge flapped his arms. "And *bad* kitty go like this." He stretched flat on his back on the floor; his legs kicked once or twice convulsively, then gave a spasmodic jerk and were still. "Now Grandpa gets shovel," he continued, clambering to his feet again, "and digs a big hole." He excavated an imaginary hole in the living-room rug, dropped the imaginary cat into it, and piled back the imaginary dirt and tamped with his feet. "So now the *bad* kitty won't catch any more *nice* birds."

Judge Parker sank back into his chair, exhausted by his performance, and poured himself another highball. Lyford III gurgled and pointed to a blue Delft china cat on the mantlepiece. "Kapow," he begged.

"I dunno, buster," the Judge hesitated, "Your Grandma thinks a lot of that antique."

His grandson's lower lip wobbled.

"Well, okay, if you insist," Judge Parker said, striding over to his gun cabinet. He took out his twelve gauge over-and-under Browning and dropped a shell into one barrel. The baby's eyes followed him intently as he picked the china cat off the mantle,

[184]

opened the front door, and flipped the antique high into the air. There was a single blast, and bits of shattered china flashed in the setting sun.

"More, more," Lyford III chortled.

"Only have to shoot once if you aim right," the Judge informed his grandson with professional pride. He opened the breech, caught the smoking shell case as it ejected, and tossed it into the crib. "Now, buster, it's time you had a little nap."

The baby curled dutifully on the blanket with his eyes closed, clutching the empty shell in his fist. Judge Parker took a long gulp from his highball, leaned back in his chair, and began to croon in an off-key falsetto:

Rockaby, kitty, in the treetop.
When the wind blows, the branches will rock.
When the gun shoots, the branches will fall,
And down will come ki-i-itty, branches and all . . .

The front door opened, and footsteps sounded in the hall. Patience Parker hurried into the living room. "How's Grandma's precious sweetheart?" she asked.

Judge Parker held a finger to his lips, and pointed to the crib. "He's asleep."

"Oh, dear, I brought home a little surprise for him."

Her daughter-in-law followed her into the room, carrying a pasteboard box with its top punched full of holes. A faint mewing sound emerged from within. "It's a present from Uncle Perk."

Judge Parker let out a stifled groan. "Why, that lowdown doublecrosser—"

"It was so cute I couldn't resist it." Patience opened the box, and held up a beagle puppy by the scruff of its neck. "Isn't it sweet, dear?"

The Judge removed his spectacles and passed a hand slowly across his eyes. He did not trust himself to speak.

"I was planning to get Lyford a kitten," she sighed. "But now I guess he'll have to settle for a dog."

"I think he'll like it just as well," Judge Parker said weakly.

"I'll give it to him as soon as he wakes up." Patience put the puppy back in the box and bent over the crib. "Look at that innocent expression," she whispered. "I wonder what he's dreaming."

Lyford III's fist was still clenched tight on the empty shell, and his face was wreathed in a beatific smile. He stirred in his slumbers and murmured "Kapow, kapow," his right shoulder rocking back slightly. Patience reached down and tucked the blanket around him.

"When he smiles like that," she said sentimentally, "do you suppose he's looking at an angel in the sky?"

Judge Parker nodded. "Yes, dear. Right through the Lyman," he murmured, sipping his highball contentedly.

LO, THE WILY REDSKIN

Colonel Cobb cut the outboard motor and slid alongside a crude log pier, and young Chick steadied the skiff as the Colonel and Mister MacNab clambered out and mounted the trail to a cabin on the bluff overlooking the lake. They peered at a sign on the door: J. Ansel Blatt. Private, Keep Out, and Colonel Cobb knocked uncertainly. There was a muffled oath, a chair scraped, and the door was opened by a heavy-jowled individual in a T shirt, his potbelly sagging over his belt.

"Mr. Blatt?" Colonel Cobb inquired politely.

Ansel Blatt nodded without replying and took a sip from the cup in his hand. The tempting aroma of coffee wafted through the cabin, but he made no move to invite them inside. His small eyes surveyed his visitors with hostility.

"My name's Cobb," the Colonel introduced himself, "and this is Mister MacNab. Our Lower Forty Club is camped down the shore a little ways." He paused, but Ansel Blatt did not respond. "We heard this was a good fishing lake—"

"Used to be," Ansel Blatt interrupted sourly, "till all these dam' tourists from the States started comin' here."

Colonel Cobb's face flushed an ominous red, and Mister Mac-Nab gave him a warning glance. "Sorry to intr-r-rude on ye, Mr.

Blatt," he apologized, "but we heard about ye way back in Kenora. They all say ye're the best muskie fisher-r-rman in Ontario."

"That's right enough," Ansel Blatt nodded. "Got the record one last season." He took an old newspaper clipping from his wallet, and displayed a photograph of a giant muskellunge hanging from a peg beside his cabin door. "Went forty-seven pounds."

"Aye, 'tis a ver-r-ra fine specimen," Mister MacNab remarked enviously. "Ye see, we're strangers here, and we hoped an expairt like yereself would tell us where to try a little casting."

Mr. Blatt's eyes narrowed. "Sure, I'll tell you." He pointed to the far end of the lake. "See that rocky point? There's a dead pine struck by lightning, you can't miss it. Turn right and follow a little stream a coupla miles or so, and you'll come to another lake. That's where the big ones are."

"Well, we sure appreciate your advice," Colonel Cobb said gratefully.

"Always glad to help a fellow fisherman," Ansel Blatt nodded and shut the door.

Mister MacNab grinned amiably as they hurried back down the trail to the waiting skiff. "As my grandfeyther used to say," he informed Chick, "there's nothing like a little flatter-r-ry sometimes."

His grin faded slowly as the skiff forced its way mile after mile through the tangled lilies and muskie cabbage that choked the stream. Chick crouched in the bow, peering ahead for snags in the channel. Mister MacNab mopped his perspiring brow in the oppressive heat, and brushed vainly at the black flies and midges hovering around his head. "Are ye sure we're not following the wr-r-rong stream?" he murmured.

"We turned right at the rocky point with the dead pine," Colonel Cobb insisted, swinging the tiller back and forth to avoid the heavy weed patches. "That's what Mr. Blatt told us."

"We've been going for hours," Mister MacNab observed, "and still there's nae sign of a lake ahead. Let's tur-r-rn around before it gets too dark."

Colonel Cobb swung the skiff in a circle through the weeds, and the outboard motor coughed suddenly and was silent. He glanced ruefully over the stern. "Prop's tangled up again," he grumbled. "Give me a hand while I clear it."

Mister MacNab lumbered to the stern and bent over as the Colonel lifted the outboard. The boat tilted suddenly, and the motor slid off its rack and plunged into a patch of muskie cabbage with a resounding splash. They gazed stricken at the widening ripples. "How will we ever get back to camp?" Colonel Cobb sighed.

"I'm not wor-r-ried about that," groaned Mister MacNab. "I'm wondering how we'll pay for a new motor."

"I'll dive down and look for it," Chick suggested, peeling off his shirt.

Colonel Cobb shook his head. "No chance of finding it in this mess of weeds, son," he said. "We'll have to row back."

"There's only one oar," Chick reported.

"In that case," said Mister MacNab, "we'll all take turns."

The air grew more sultry as they sculled the skiff through the weeds, hour after hour. Swarms of flies settled like soot on their faces and arms, their hands were blistered, their backs ached. Darkness was settling when they reached the rocky point, and a few raindrops pelted their flushed faces. A little wind had sprung up, whipping the surface of the lake into whitecaps. "Blowing

[189]

right in our direction," Colonel Cobb sighed, "and we've got at least two miles of open water."

"Listen!" Chick held up his hand. "Isn't that an outboard motor?"

The thudding grew louder, and they shouted and waved frantically at a small skiff coming down the lake through the gusts of rain. It headed toward them and halted alongside. A swarthy Indian in a battered felt hat and greasy jacket gazed at them stolidly. "Me Joe," he said. "What happen?"

"Well, we were looking for a second lake," Colonel Cobb began, "that Mr. Blatt told us about—"

Joe broke into loud guffaws. "He tell everybody that. No lake there. Just swamp."

"Why, that double-cr-r-rossing pre-r-revarcating r-r-rascal," Mister MacNab rattled.

"Tow you back," Joe offered. "Two dollar."

Mister MacNab started to expostulate, then recalled his blistered hands. He handed the painter to the Indian and watched him make it fast to the stern of his skiff. "I'll climb in Joe's boat," he told the others, "to distribute the weight. Just shout if ye tip over."

He stepped across the gunwales into the other skiff, and caught his breath. An enormous muskellunge lay on the floorboards, its great green body washing back and forth in the oily water. "How did ye ever get that monster-r-r?" he gasped.

"Catch'm in trap," Joe informed him. "Forty-nine pound." He started his motor. "Take'm back to sell."

"Where can ye sell a muskie around here?" Mister MacNab asked curiously.

"Mr. Blatt," Joe replied. "Last year pay ten dollar for forty-seven pound."

"So that's how he got his record one!" Mister MacNab's face assumed a crafty expression. "Joe, I'll pay ye eleven dollars cash for that fish."

"Okay," Joe shrugged.

Mister MacNab's eyes glittered. "And I'll pay ye another dollar," he added, "if ye'll let me bor-r-row your hat and coat when we get to camp."

Night had closed in and the rain was falling hard as Mister MacNab mounted the trail to Ansel Blatt's cabin, dragging the muskie behind him. The other members of the Lower Forty followed silently. He halted out of sight of the cabin, put on Joe's battered hat, and pulled down the brim to hide his eyes. "Do I luik like our wily r-r-redskin friend?" he asked.

Judge Parker studied the effect critically. "The picture's not bad," he observed, "but there's a sort of burr in the sound track. Try to talk more Indian."

Mister MacNab turned up the lapels of Joe's evil-smelling jacket around his face. His nose wrinkled. "Ugh," he shuddered.

"That's better," Doc Hall nodded. "Just say ugh."

The rest of the club members hid in the bushes as Mister MacNab hammered on the cabin door. Ansel Blatt flung it open, held up a kerosene lantern, and peered through the rain at the shadowy figure outside. "That you, Joe?"

"Ugh," said Mister MacNab.

"Whaddye want?"

Mister MacNab struggled to lift the heavy muskellunge. "Ugh," he grunted.

The lantern light gleamed on the broad green side of the fish, and Ansel Blatt nodded in approval. "How much does it weigh?"

"For-r-rty nine—" Mister MacNab caught himself in the nick of time. "Almost fifty pound," he corrected.

Ansel Blatt took out his wallet. "I'll give you ten dollars."

"Ugh," Mister MacNab protested. "Sell'm twenty."

"Too much."

"Okay," he shrugged, "sell'm instead to the Lower-r-r—to other camp down lake."

Ansel Blatt handed him the money. "It's a holdup," he grumbled, as he hung the muskie on the peg beside the door.

"Oh, I wouldna say that, mon," Mister MacNab smiled, pocketing the money and removing Joe's hat and jacket. Ansel Blatt stared at him stunned. "Counting the eleven dollarrs I paid Joe for this fish, plus another dollar for the r-r-rental of his garments, plus two more it cost to be towed back from that imaginar-r-ry lake ye sent us to," he explained, "that leaves me only six dollars pr-r-rofit on the whole deal."

"Give me that money back," Ansel Blatt shouted, advancing menacingly. He paused as the other members of the Lower Forty emerged from the bushes, and his small eyes moved from one threatening face to another. His jowls sagged in defeat. "Don't let this get around, will you, fellas?" he pleaded. "If they ever hear about it in Kenora, I'll be ruined."

"Always glad to help a fellow fisher-r-rman," Mister MacNab said pleasantly. "All we ask in exchange is this outboard motor of yours which I hoppen to notice lying here."

"But—but where will I get another motor?"

"There's one just like it," Mister MacNab told him, "lying at the bottom of that little stream ye r-r-recommended. Luik for a rocky point with a dead pine str-r-ruck by lightning. Ye canna miss it."

Ansel Blatt opened his mouth in protest, then shut it again. "Ugh," he said, and slammed the door.

"Wal, naow, Mac," Uncle Perk chuckled to Mister MacNab as they started back down the trail, lugging the motor between them, "I calc'late this here catch o' yours calls fer a special jug of Ole Stump Blower." He paused for breath. "Bet it goes a hundred pounds."

THE WORTHY TARGET

The other members of the Lower Forty watched in critical silence as Cousin Sid dropped a shell into the breach of his over-and-under Browning, closed the breech, and called "Pull-l-ll" in a lazy voice. Mister MacNab flicked the hand trap, and a clay pigeon scaled across the meadow and rose in a slow arc. Sid's gun tracked it, the sight moving up and past and then on top of the climbing bird, and his eye and brain said "Now!" The primer popped, and the target was a puff of black dust hanging in the air.

"You let it get too far out," Doc Hall objected. "If that'd been a grouse, you'd have only dusted it."

He took Sid's place on the firing line, loaded his side-by-side Parker, and gave a professional grunt. Mister MacNab sent the target in a high right-hand climb, the muzzle of the gun rose and halted, and the bird shattered into three sections. As the largest one fell, the muzzle dropped with it, and the piece disintegrated. Judge Parker snorted.

"Two shots to nail one bird," he taunted Doc. "That's because you didn't swing with it and follow through. Here, let me show you."

The Judge strode to the line, grasped his Winchester slide-action, and then lowered it irritably as a battered jeep bounced across the meadow toward him, right in the line of fire. Deacon Godfrey's saturnine face loomed behind the wheel, regarding the group with ill-concealed dislike. "I s'pose you fellers know that gunnin' season ain't open till next week," he reminded them.

"We're just practicing," Cousin Sid explained. "Trying to get our shooting eye in for opening day."

"Ain't a bad idea," the Deacon commented sourly, glancing at a couple of unbroken clay birds in the grass. "Looks like you need a lot of practice."

Judge Parker bristled. "Maybe you could do better."

"Mebbe I could," the Deacon said, "if I had anything to shoot with." He reached in the back of his jeep. "All I got is this beatup wreck I took in today on a mortgage payment."

The Judge glanced at the dust-covered shotgun, and his eyes widened in disbelief. It was a beautiful Greener, in mint condition. He grabbed it from the Deacon, and his hand moved covetously over the smooth walnut stock and delicate tooling on the lockplate and trigger guard. "Whereinell did you get this?"

"Offen old Clem Swasey. He didn't have enough cash to meet his payment, so I took his gun that was hanging over the mantle, to make up the difference. Just wanted to help the poor feller out," Deacon Godfrey added sanctimoniously. "Figger this old clunk's worth anything, Judge?"

A veiled look came over Judge Parker's face. "Oh, you might get a couple of bucks from a junk dealer, if you're lucky." He handed the Greener back to the Deacon with elaborate unconcern and shot a meaningful glance at his fellow-members. "Why don't you borrow my Winchester, if you'd like to break a few birds with us?" he suggested. "We'll each put up a buck, and the winner takes the pot."

The Deacon's eyes narrowed with suspicion. "I'll watch the rest of you shoot first," he said, "an' then I'll decide if I want to get in."

"That's fair enough," Judge Parker nodded, producing a dollar from his wallet and stepping forward with his Winchester. Mister MacNab scaled a bird past him, the Judge fired without bothering to aim, and the pigeon sailed unharmed across the meadow. "Guess I was behind it," he murmured, and winked at the others.

Cousin Sid added his money to the pile, stepped to the line and fired his Browning at a second bird, which coasted away unscathed. "Must have been ahead of it," Sid apologized. A third bird sped past Doc Hall, and he blasted his Parker at the sky. "I was a little over it," he admitted. Colonel Cobb missed a fourth bird and looked properly crestfallen. "I was a little under it."

Deacon Godfrey's face cracked into a grin. "Shucks, you fellers couldn' hit a bull in the tail with a fryin' pan," he jeered. "Here's my dollar. Judge, lemme borrow that cornsheller of yours."

Mister MacNab gave him a nice slow straightaway, and the Deacon smashed the bird as it hesitated at the top of its rise. He swept up the pile of bills, and stuffed them into his pocket. "That gun o' yours shoots real nice, Judge," he chuckled. "Like to put up some money for another round?"

Judge Parker peered into his wallet and sighed ruefully. "I'm all out of cash," he said, "but I'll make you a sporting proposition. My new Winchester against that old clunk of yours."

Chuckling to himself, the Deacon fitted the Judge's gun to his shoulder and yelled "Pull!" At a signal from the Judge, Mister MacNab sent a left-hand grass-cutter skimming low across the

[197]

meadow. The Deacon's first shot gouged a clump of turf, his second removed the top branches of an alder, and the bird scaled intact in the bushes. The Deacon stared after it, his jaw sagging.

"Wal, naow," Uncle Perk observed, "that's the first time I ever see anybody shoot under an' over an' behind an' in front of a bird at the same time."

Judge Parker stepped forward, gave a curt "Hi!," and another pigeon sped past him. It took a quick upward flip as a gust struck it, and the Winchester smashed it and churned the pieces. The Judge lowered his gun with a satisfied smile and took the Greener from Deacon Godfrey's jeep. The Deacon's lip curled.

"You're welcome to that piece of junk," he sneered, climbing behind the wheel. "I'm still four bucks ahead. Easiest money I ever made," he chortled as he drove away.

Uncle Perk waited until the jeep was out of sight, then shook Judge Parker's hand. "Wal, Jedge, I gotta congratulate ye," he said admiringly. "That was the nicest bit o' highbowdjery since they shot Jesse James." He produced a jug of Old Stump Blower and examined it critically. "Jug's most empty," he noted, "but I got another full one right here. Let's celebrate."

Cousin Sid tilted the jug. "Why, that Greener's worth at least five bills," he exulted. "A good auctioneer might bid it up to a grand."

"One dollar for five hundred," Mister MacNab cackled, reaching for the jug. "That's what I call a vair-r-ry sound proposition."

"Wait a minute, Mac," Doc Hall said. "We've each of us invested a dollar in the gun." He took a sip and passed the jug to the Judge. "Let's flip a coin and decide which one of us it belongs to."

Judge Parker drained the last swallow and set the empty jug

on the ground beside the full one. He faced his fellow members thoughtfully. "Let me tell you something about this Greener," he began. "I'll admit I've had my eye on it a long time. I knew Clem Swasey was getting old, and his hands were so crippled with rheumatism he couldn't shoot it any more, and the other day I asked him if he'd sell it to me. Well, he thought awhile, and then he looked up at the gun, hanging in the center of his mantle like a family portrait, and he shook his head. 'I couldn't do it, Judge,' Clem said to me. 'I guess it's like when you've been married to a woman all your life, you have a lot of memories you share together. This Greener is like that. It belonged to my dad, and he handed it on to me. I remember the day he taught me to shoot it, and the first pa'tridge I got with it that October, and all the other Octobers I've gunned with it. Now I can't shoot it any more, but I got it to remember with.' " The Judge paused. "This gun belongs to Clem," he said gently, "and we're taking it back to him."

The others nodded in silent agreement. Judge Parker picked up the Greener, fitted it to his shoulder, and swung it toward an imaginary grouse in the sky. He hesitated.

"I don't think old Clem would mind if I fired one round, just to get the feel of it," the Judge murmured. He dropped in a shell and closed the gun, hearing the smooth sure click, and turned to Mister MacNab. "Mac, toss up that jug as high as you can."

The jug sailed over the trees, and Judge Parker laid his cheek against the smooth stock, sighted along the barrel, and squeezed the trigger. The jug exploded with a clap of thunder, followed by a sudden cloudburst of dark-brown rain. The liquid spattered down onto the leaves and dripped to the ground, and a pungent aroma of Old Stump Blower filled the air. Uncle Perk fixed Mister MacNab with an accusing eye.

"Ye knucklehead," he choked, "that was the full jug ye tossed."

Mister MacNab collapsed on the running board of his hearse, his face hidden in his hands. The Judge patted his quaking shoulder. "It's all right, Mac," he consoled him. "A gun like this deserves a worthy target."

THE FIRST RULE

The tantalizing aroma of rabbit stew wafted through Cousin Sid's camp, and a steady rattle of pots and pans emerged from the kitchen where the Lower Forty's chief cook and bottle washer labored alone over the stove. His fellow members, licking their chops impatiently around the living-room fire, looked up in relief as the headlights of an approaching car flashed in the window. "Well, the Judge is here at last," Colonel Cobb muttered. "Now maybe we can have our game supper."

Boots stamped off snow on the front doorstep, and Judge Parker backed into the room, carrying a large pasteboard box with its top punched full of holes. He set it down carefully, lifted the lid, and removed a woolen blanket, a tufted quilt, a rubber ball, a mechanical mouse, a porcelain dish labeled "Pour le Chien," a bag of dog biscuits, a red leather leash, and finally a three-months-old beagle puppy, squirming and panting. Uncle Perk blinked in surprise.

"Whyinell are ye luggin' yer grandson's pup around?" he demanded.

"My wife won't let me keep him in the house," the Judge explained. "She says Piper will have to stay somewhere else till he's housebroken."

"But he's s'posed to be a present for Lyford III to play with."

"That's what I tried to tell my wife," Judge Parker replied

sadly, "but she says she's sick and tired of mopping up after him all day. She told me this morning she's decided to put her foot down, if she can find any place in our house where it's safe to put her foot down."

"Why, it's easy to housebreak a dog," Doc Hall scoffed. "It's the same as training little Lyford."

The Judge sighed. "He isn't housebroken, either."

"I'm surpr-r-rised at ye, mon," Mister MacNab chided him. "How can a wee pup like that cause any tr-r-rouble?"

"Trouble!" Judge Parker echoed, depositing the pup on the sofa and reaching for Uncle Perk's jug. "He chews up everything he can get hold of." He poured himself a stiff drink. "I took him to court today, and he chewed up two law books, the prosecuting attorney's spectacle case, and the handle of my gavel." He glared at Piper, who was busily chewing the upholstery buttons off the sofa arm. "Hey, leave those alone!" he yelled.

"You shouldn't try to suppress him, Judge," Doc Hall advised. "Medical experts warn that you're apt to build up inhibitions that way. Why not use a little modern child psychology?" He handed the pup an embroidered silk cushion. "Give him something else to distract his attention."

Piper sank his teeth in the cushion, gave it a pleased shake, and a blizzard of white feathers filled the air. Judge Parker snatched the pillow away, and slapped him on the rump. Doc Hall shook his head.

"You're going about it all wrong," he informed the Judge. "Force-breaking isn't the approved method of training today. Simply remove the source of temptation, that's all." He lifted the puppy off the sofa, and set him gently on the floor. "That's what I mean by psychology."

Piper yawned and stretched himself, ambled across the room, and squatted contentedly in the center of Cousin Sid's Oriental rug. Judge Parker stared aghast at the widening puddle, and grabbed the pup by the scruff of his neck. "Why, you little rascal—"

"Now, hold on, Judge," Doc Hall remonstrated. "If you punish him, the psychology books say, you'll only destroy his confidence. The answer is to give him a regular place to do his business." He took a ledger book from Cousin Sid's desk, ripped out several pages of neatly inked figures, and placed them in a corner of the room. "That's the first rule in housebreaking a dog."

Piper sniffed curiously at the papers, strolled over to the bear rug before the fireplace, and squatted again. Mister MacNab pointed to the second puddle, and winked at Doc owlishly. "Evidently the pup hasna read those psychology buiks," he murmured.

"We'll take care of that," Doc Hall insisted. He tore the rest of the pages from the ledger, and spread them all over the floor. "He's bound to hit one sooner or later."

Cousin Sid appeared in the kitchen doorway, wiping greasespots from his spectacles. "Well, fellows," he began, "supper's almost—" The sentence trailed as his startled gaze moved around the littered living room. He put on his spectacles in disbelief, and his eyes focused on the scattered pages at his feet. "That's my annual school report," he groaned, gathering them up. "I've been working on it for a month."

"Youre interfering with Piper's lesson," Doc Hall said severely. "How can he learn to use those papers if you take them away?"

Cousin Sid shoved the torn pages back into the ledger. "The least you could do is tie him up while he's learning," he complained, snapping the leash onto Piper's collar and looping the other end around one leg of a mahogany side table. "There, that ought to keep him out of mischief."

He started back toward the kitchen, and Piper trotted playfully after him. The leash snubbed taut, the side table tilted, and an antique china reading lamp teetered majestically, executed a slow arc, and shattered into fragments on the floor. Piper yelped and scurried across the room toward the kitchen, his tail between his legs. Doc Hall fixed Cousin Sid with an icy glance.

"Now you've gone and frightened him," he accused. "Probably you've given him a psychological block. It would serve you right if he grew up disliking you."

Cousin Sid opened his mouth, shut it again helplessly, and strode into the kitchen. There was a muffled thud, a moan of anguish, and Piper raced back into the living room, carrying a dripping rabbit leg in his jaws. Cousin Sid reappeared after a moment and leaned against the door jamb, struggling to control himself.

"I put the stew on the table to cool," he reported in a shaky voice, "and he grabbed a corner of the cloth and tipped the whole thing over onto the floor."

"At least, it shows he likes rabbit," Colonel Cobb pointed out cheerfully. "He's got the right instinct for a beagle."

"But—but what are we going to have for supper?"

"Wal, naow, they say these here puppy biscuits ain't half bad," Uncle Perk shrugged, taking one from the bag and nibbling it thoughtfully. "Partic'ly now that Piper don't need 'em."

Doc Hall watched the puppy devour the last of the rabbit leg.

"By the way, Judge," he suggested, "it might be a good idea to walk him outside for a few minutes after he's eaten. The first rule in housebreaking a dog—"

"The fair-r-rst rule in hoosebreaking a dog," Mister MacNab corrected, "is to break him in somebody else's hoose."

The wall phone jangled, and Cousin Sid lifted the receiver off the hook. "Who? Yes, he's right here." He beckoned to Judge Parker. "It's your wife. She sounds a little upset."

"Hello, dear . . . What?" A curious expression came over the Judge's face. "Why, of course, darling. No trouble at all, sweet. Yes, honey, I'll be back right away."

He grabbed his coat, picked up the pup in his arms, and started toward the door. "She says little Lyford is crying and having a tantrum," he informed the others. "He won't go to sleep until he has his puppy. She swears she'll never let Piper out of the house again."

"If I was you, Jedge, I'd leave the trainin' o' that pup to your grandson," Uncle Perk called after him, "seein' how well he's trained your wife."

The door closed, and the headlights of the car receded in the darkness. Uncle Perk reached for his jug of Old Stump Blower. His face fell.

"That confounded pup went an' chewed up the cork," he grunted. "Now we'll have to kill this whole jug."

Mister MacNab beamed in approval. "I dinna ken why anybody needs to tr-r-rain Piper," he observed. "He's smar-r-rt enough already."

THERE'S
ALWAYS DAMES

The August sun was hot, but the tempers of the Lower Forty were even hotter. For months they had been planning this salmon-fishing trip to Canada. They had traveled five hundred bone-jolting miles in Mister MacNab's hearse to cast a fly over their favorite stretch of Old Man River, only to find the waters leased by one Jeb Colton and closed to all public angling. "Why, we've fished these same pools every summer for years," Judge Parker said, glowering at the posting notice. "Whoinell's this guy Colton anyway?"

"Just a guy with enough money to rent the best section of the Old Man," Doc Hall grumbled. "There's nothing we can do but try downstream where it's still open."

Colonel Cobb followed the other members in gloomy silence, young Chick Keenan trudging at his side. The Colonel stole a sidelong glance at his foster son and sighed to himself. Ever since he had rescued Chick from a Boston orphanage last year and brought him to Hardscrabble, he had counted on the day when they would fish for salmon together. He had coached the boy each afternoon on the lawn behind the house, teaching him to handle the heavy salmon rod, to cast a long even line, to strip it in with short erratic jerks in order to give the fly the proper action.

The youngster had been a willing pupil, his freckled snub-nosed face always alert, his grin widening whenever he made a good cast. More than anything else in the world, Colonel Cobb wanted Chick to strike his first salmon, to feel its surge and solid weight, to see that unforgettable leap which would make him a fanatic the rest of his life. They passed the final posting notice, and the Colonel halted at an open stretch directly below.

"Try this pool, Chick," he said without conviction. "Maybe one of Jeb Colton's salmon will drift down to you." He clapped the boy's shoulder. "Good luck."

Chick waved as the rest of the party disappeared around a bend in the river, and set up his rod eagerly. The morning was growing hotter, and he peeled down to shorts and sneakers and waded out cautiously into the pool. For the next hour he cast and re-trieved his line and cast again regularly, letting the fly swing downstream in an arc and bringing it back with the little jerking motion which the Colonel had taught him. The sun blistered his bare back, his right arm throbbed, his rod moved more and more slowly. The Old Man was such a big river; how could a salmon ever spot his little fly in all that expanse of shimmering water? Probably no fish here at all. His eagerness was fading fast. He had pictured salmon-fishing as exciting, but this was backbreak-ing work; the perspiration dripped off his chin and trickled down his chest, and his arm was numb with fatigue. Try as he might to concentrate, his mind kept turning to other thoughts, or, to be more accurate, to one particular thought. It was an enticing thought, with honey-colored hair and blue eyes. He had spotted her in town yesterday, driving away in an open convertible just as their hearse halted at the local filling station. He had asked the attendant her name. "Her? That's Jill Colton. Daughter of some millionaire that's rented a lodge upriver."

Chick frowned and resumed his casting. What chance would he ever have to meet Jeb Colton's daughter? Forget her, he told himself, lifting his weary arm and sending the line out again across the pool. He glanced at the watch on his sunburned wrist. Two hours so far. How much longer would he have to keep this up? He could think of a lot of things he'd rather be doing right now — sitting in a convertible, for instance, beside a girl with honey hair and blue eyes . . .

He felt a tug on his line and yanked it toward him. The leader snapped, leaving his fly embedded in a sunken snag in the center of the pool. Muttering to himself, he reeled in his line and waded back to shore. He took another of Colonel Cobb's hand-tied patterns from his fly box, and stooped to tie it onto the leader.

The pool exploded before him, and he looked up in time to see a great silver shape twist out of water and stand for a moment on its tail. The light glinted on a gut leader that ran from its jaw to a slanting enameled line that cut the water as the salmon dove again and raced downstream. A hundred yards above him, he saw a rowboat following the salmon's mad rush, a halfbreed guide splashing the oars and an elderly angler standing in the bow with rod bent almost double. Chick looked back at the pool and caught his breath. The salmon had passed over the sunken snag, and the line was tangled in a protruding brach. Chick cupped his hands to his lips. "Hold it!" he yelled to the approaching boat. "You're hung up."

He ran down the bank and dove into the pool, swimming with long sure strokes toward the snag. His exploring hand found the line and followed it to the branch, and he lifted it free. The frightened salmon raced across the river to the far shore, swung around in a circle, and settled at his feet, wallowing in the reeds. The boat was still fighting in the current midstream, and the fisherman in the bow shouted to him: "Hook's almost worked free. Grab him, quick!"

Chick's landing net was lying at the head of the pool, and there was no time to run for it. Well, there was one trick he had learned as a kid, poaching carp on the Boston Commons. He slid his arm underwater, closed his fist around the stub of the spreading tail, and heaved it onto the bank. He knocked it inert with a rock, and rose to his feet, lifting the salmon by its gill. He held it aloft, speechless at the enormous weight. He had never seen such a fish before. His eyes moved in awe over the silvery slab side, streaked with blood, and he was only half conscious of a keel grating on the pebbles behind him. Reluctantly Chick surrendered the salmon to the guide. The elderly angler clasped his slimy hand, beside himself with excitement. "Never be able to thank you enough, young man. Biggest I've ever taken. All because of you." He continued to pump Chick's hand. "I'm Jeb Colton. Come and fish my private waters any time."

Chick hesitated. "I'm with a party of friends—"

"Tell 'em they're welcome." He gave Chick's hand a final grip and released it. "What's your name?"

"Chick Keenan, sir," he replied, watching the guide carry the salmon toward the rowboat.

"Why don't you drop around to my lodge this evening and get acquainted?" Jeb Colton turned to follow the guide. "Got a daughter about your age, name of Jill," he added over his shoulder. "Like to have you meet her."

The evening shadows were lengthening as the members of the Lower Forty hurried to their favorite pools on Jeb Colton's leased waters. Judge Parker nudged Colonel Cobb and winked: "That Chick boy of yours deserves to be elected president of the club, getting us invited to fish this stretch. Too bad he isn't with us to enjoy it."

"He's got something else to enjoy," Doc Hall chuckled. "I caught a glimpse of that Colton gal yesterday, and she's a living doll."

Colonel Cobb nodded with a rather weak smile. He couldn't blame Chick, of course. Romance comes first, when you're that age. He left the others and made his way alone through the bushes toward the stream. Perhaps some other year he and Chick could fish for salmon together.

He heard a step behind him, and Chick shouldered through the bushes, clad in his fishing waders. Colonel Cobb blinked as the boy set up his rod and ran the line through the guides. "I—I thought you had other plans this evening, son."

Chick caught his eye, and his freckled face broadened in a grin. "There's always dames." He stepped to the edge of the pool.

"Watch and see whether I'm casting right," he said. "Maybe you can tell if I'm ever going to be a salmon fisherman."

"You're a salmon fisherman," Colonel Cobb murmured.

A TASTE OF
PARTRIDGE PIE

The afternoon shadows had lengthened and there was an October chill in the air as the members of the Lower Forty piled their bird dogs into Mister MacNab's hearse and headed for the final cover of the day. They bounced and jolted in contented silence over the rutted backroad, bound for their favorite alder swale on the other side of Moose Mountain. Mister MacNab pointed to an abandoned farmhouse set in a weed-grown clearing, and heaved a sigh as he passed. "Forgive this sentimental tear-r-r," he apoligized, dabbing his eye. " 'Tis the original Mac-Nab homestead."

Uncle Perk peered through a side window at the dilapidated building, its roof sagging, and a barn already collapsed in a dismal pile of rotting timbers. "Didn' know your folks was fr'm aroun' these pa'ts."

"Aye, we're old pioneer stock," Mister MacNab assured him. "It accounts for my pr-r-ronounced Yonkee accent." He added with pride: "My great-great-grandfeyther Remember MacNab came across with the Mayflower."

"That's the only time a MacNab ever came across with anything," Doc Hall commented.

Mister MacNab ignored him. "He settled here in Hardscrabble and founded the family fortune making horsehair scalplocks and selling them to the Indians. His son Dutiful MacNab went into the wooden nutmeg business, and his son, my grandfeyther Mordecai, studied chemistry at Harvard and operated a successful still. All their savings were invested in the ancestral monsion ye've just passed." His voice choked with emotion. "It breaks my hair-r-rt to luik at it now."

Cousin Sid nodded sympathetically. "You mean the thought of all the hard labor that went into it?"

"No," Mister MacNab corrected, a note of bitterness in his voice, "I mean the thought of all the taxes I've paid on that guid-for-nothing wairthless hunk of real estate."

"Why don't you get rid of the old place?" Colonel Cobb asked.

"There's naebody foolish enough to buy it," Mister MacNab muttered, bending over the wheel. "The land's so puir that you have to put green goggles on the cows and feed them excelsior." The hearse followed the winding road around the base of Moose Mountain. "The only thing that's ever been raised on that farm is the town assessment—"

Judge Parker, in the front seat beside him, uttered a grunt of surprise and pointed ahead. A State Highway Department truck was parked beside their bird cover, and a surveying crew was hammering down stakes with red flags along the roadside. Jim Dunne, the chief surveyor, crouched behind a tripod and dangling plumb line, sighting through his transit at a black-and-white pole in the distance. Judge Parker leapt out of the hearse and hurried toward him. "Wotinell's going on, Jim?"

"State highway's coming through here," Jim Dunne replied. "I'm not supposed to mention it, but the secret's already out. Deacon Godfrey got wind of it somehow."

A muscle hopped in the Judge's jaw. "What's he been up to?"

"Haven't you heard? He's put in a bid for this whole tract of land where you're going to hunt. Says it's a perfect site for a motel, with the new road running right by."

The members of the Lower Forty exchanged stricken glances. "Well, that means goodbye to the best grouse and woodcock cover in Hardscrabble," Doc Hall muttered. "He'll cut down all the alders, and post the rest of it just for spite." He beckoned to the others. "Come one, let's have one last farewell hunt."

Jim Dunne watched them enviously as they took their dogs and guns from the hearse. "Wish I could knock off work and come with you," he sighed. "Haven't gunned for years. I'd do anything to taste a partridge again."

Mister MacNab paused, and a curiously thoughtful expression came over his face. "Would ye, noo, Shamus?" he cooed. "Weel, that gives me an idea." His eye had a crafty glint. "Have ye ever tasted one of Cousin Sid's par-r-rtridge pies? Ye dinna ken what eating is like till ye try it. Tell him how ye make it, Sidney."

"Well, first you parboil the birds," Cousin Sid explained, "and use the gravy to make a cream sauce, and add onions and sliced hard-boiled eggs and butter and ground pepper and just a pinch of oregano and a little sherry to taste—"

"Pairhops half a bottle," Mister MacNab interrupted. "I tell ye, mon, 'tis even better that haggis." He stole a quick glance at the surveyor's drooling lips. "Why don't ye drop over to Cousin Sid's camp tomorrow night and share it with us?"

Jim Dunne beamed. "Sure appreciate the invitation," he said gratefully. "If there's any little favor you fellows ever want—"

"As a matter of fact, Shamus," Mister MacNab said innocently, "it just so hoppens there's one wee thing ye could do for us."

"Name it."

"Tomorrow's Saturday, and yere crew willna be wor-r-rking. Take them over to my old farm on the back road, and have them drive some stakes with red flags in the front yard. Ye might set up yere tr-r-ripod and be taking some measurements," he added, "just in case Deacon Godfrey drops by."

The succulent aroma of partridge pie wafted from the kitchen of Cousin Sid's camp, and his fellow members relaxed in comfortable chairs before the fireplace, sipping Uncle Perk's jug while their host prepared the evening repast. They looked up with interest as Mister MacNab strode through the door, cackling with glee. "My little ruse wair-r-rked like a charm," he reported, reaching for the jug. "Old Godfrey fell for it huik, line, and sinker."

He collapsed in a paroxysm of mirth at the recollection, and the other members waited impatiently. "What happened?" Judge Parker prompted.

"I managed to drop a hint to the Deacon that they were planning to relocate the new highway on the other side of Moose Mountain, right past my farm," Mister MacNab continued when he was able to control himself. "He jumped into his jalopy and drove out to see for himself. The surveying crew was working there, sure enough, and he raced back to town and canceled his bid for our alder cover, and then he rushed over to my mor-r-rtuary parlor and told me he was willing to buy the old homestead and take it off my honds."

Mister MacNab choked with laughter, and had to take another swig of Old Stump Blower to regain his voice.

"Fair-r-rst he offered me five hundred, and then six, and finally eight, and I was fearful he might quit at that, so I told him I was entertaining several other bids, and he settled for a gr-r-rond. Paid me cash, and I signed the deed this afternoon." The State Highway Department truck pulled up in front of the camp, and he greeted Jim Dunne with a broad smile. "Shamus, I'll ne'er be able to thank ye enough."

"You fellows've got more to thank me for than that," Jim Dunne said mysteriously. He watched Cousin Sid bring the partridge pie from the kitchen, its crust a flaky golden brown, and waited till everyone was seated around the oilcloth-covered table. "I've got some good news for you," he announced, helping himself to a steaming portion. "You don't have to worry any more about the state highway going past your pet bird cover."

Mister MacNab borrowed the spoon and transferred a generous helping of pie to his own plate. "Shamus, ye're a mon after my own hair-r-rt," he chuckled, poising a forkful at his lips. "How did ye ever monoge it?"

"Well, I got to looking over that back road while I was out there today," Jim Dunne replied, "and it's a much better route. Cuts out some bad grades and saves a couple of miles. We're putting the highway right through that old property of yours."

The fork landed on Mister MacNab's plate with a dull clank.

"Of course, the Deacon will probably hold up the state for a healthy sum," Jim Dunne admitted. "He's got us over a barrel. I hear he's planning to ask ten grand."

He took a mouthful of pie, swallowed it reverently, and smacked his lips. "Best partridge I ever tasted," he said, nudging Mister MacNab. "Wait till you try it."

Mister MacNab shoved back his plate untouched. His face was a sickly gray. "I seem to have lost my appetite," he murmured.

[217]

MANY HAPPY RETURNS

The front door of Uncle Perk's store was bolted and pad-locked, a hand-lettered sign in the window read "Closd 4 Inventary," and the shades were drawn, emitting a mere crack of yellow light. Silence reigned inside the store, broken only by the scratching of pencils and an occasional stifled moan from the members of the Lower Forty, perched on counters and crates and flour sacks in attitudes of rapt concentration. Even Uncle Perk had removed his hunting rubbers from his desk, and was poring over a Federal tax form in front of him. "Wisht we could put off these here returns till later," he groaned. "Ev'ry time I add up what I gotta pay, it costs me more."

"Not a chance," Judge Parker said. "They're due the fifteenth of April, and that's tomorrow."

"Which also happens to be opening day of trout season," Doc Hall reminded him, "so we've got to get them filed and out of the way." He studied his form intently. "Let's see, we're allowed to deduct up to ten percent of our income for health. That should include hunting and fishing trips, of course."

Judge Parker was tabulating a sheaf of receipted bills. "If we take off the excise tax we've paid on shotgun shells and ammo, it ought to be a little more saving."

"That's an idee," Uncle Perk nodded. "Mebbe I could deduck the exercise tax on my Old Stump Blower, too."

"What tax?" Doc Hall jeered. "You never sell it."

"All the more reason to claim a business loss," Uncle Perk growled, "also the wear an' tear on my counter where you fellers are allus sittin' on it—" He glared at Doc Hall, who was helping himself to a a slab of aged cheddar. "—not to mention the depreciation of my cheese an' crackers."

"How about deducting our phone bills," asked Cousin Sid, "when there's a late hatch and we have to call up our wives and tell them we won't be home for dinner?"

Colonel Cobb was thumbing through a printed manual. "It says here you get $600 allowance for a dependent," he murmured. "Do you suppose I could claim my old beagle Nancy? She's so dependent that I have to chase her rabbits for her."

Judge Parker glanced at Mister MacNab, who was measuring a road map with a slide rule. "Wotinell are you trying to do?"

"Ye're allowed ten cents a mile for business travel," Mister MacNab explained, "and I'm figuring out how far I've gone in my hair-r-rse."

"You can't get away with that," the Judge frowned. "All you use that hearse for is to take people hunting and fishing."

"It comes under the head of public relations," Mister MacNab argued. "I've got to presair-r-rve their guid will, so they'll give me their trade after they're dead."

Uncle Perk tossed his pencil stub on the desk, and slumped back in his swivel chair disconsolately. "The way this here adds up," he sighed, "they won't none of us be able to afford any more huntin' an' fishin' trips this year. We'll have to work seven days a week to pay them infernal revenue boys what we owe 'em."

Mister MacNab lifted his head suddenly, as an idea struck him. "Ye know, I wonder-r-r if—" His voice trailed, lost in pleasant speculation.

"Wonder if what?" Doc Hall prompted after a moment.

"Of course," Mister MacNab apologized, "it's just a wee thought, mind ye."

"Spill it," Doc said impatiently.

"Weeeell, now, why couldna we call hunting and fishing our business?" he suggested cannily. "Naebody in this Club ever does any other wair-r-rk that I've seen. If we list it as our pr-r-rofession," he pointed out, "we could deduct travel expenses wherever we go, as well as all our meals if we can prove that over fifty-one percent of our conversation was devoted to hunting and fishing discussion."

"That ought to be easy," Cousin Sid said. "My wife would testify it's about ninety-nine percent."

Judge Parker's face brightened. "If a workman can get an allowance for special tools and uniform of his trade not supplied by his firm," he said, "we could deduct our fishing boots and hunting jackets and bamboo rods and shotguns and outboard motors—"

"As well as our outlay for trade journals," suggested Colonel Cobb, "such as our subscriptions to *Field and Stream*—"

"And of course we could claim taxes and upkeep on any part of the house used for business purposes," the Judge added, "such as our gun room, or fly-tying workshop, or our bedroom if the hunting dog sleeps there—"

"Aye, and dinna forget losses due to business accidents," Mister MacNab reminded the others. "Say for instance I hoppen to have a flask inside my waders, and I slip in a shallow stream, I could claim the loss of the flask, plus the waders that were slashed so they couldna be patched, likewise medical expenses for r-r-removing the bits of glass where I sat doon."

Judge Parker cast a covert glance at Doc Hall. "Why don't you put in for all those trout flies you leave in the tops of hemlocks?"

"For that matter," Doc retorted, "you should be able to deduct the cost of all those shotgun shells you fire without hitting anything."

Colonel Cobb chuckled. "Cousin Sid could list that pair of pants he ripped on barbed wire last summer trying to crawl into some posted land after a woodchuck."

"Of course, Colonel," Cousin Sid replied evenly, "you don't want to overlook that fine you had to pay last fall for having one more duck than your bag limit."

Uncle Perk completed his figuring and beamed at Mister Mac-Nab. "Y'know, by gorry, if we deduck all we spend for huntin' an' fishin' in a year, the gov'nment'll end up owin' us."

"You're a financial wizard, Mac," Judge Parker agreed. "How can we ever express our gratitude?"

"Dinna mention it, mon," Mister MacNab smiled modestly. "All I want is your thanks, plus the usual tax consultant fee."

"Look at all the money we've just made," Doc Hall gloated. "I move we spend it on a real wingding opening day party."

"A ver-r-ra guid idea," Mister MacNab said, reaching for Uncle Perk's jug. "We can always deduct it as a business expense on next year's retair-r-rn."

THE DEACON'S
UP A TREE

Word of the public hearing had spread to every backcountry farm, and the Hardscrabble Town Hall was packed on Sunday evening, reeking with the blended aroma of perspiration and damp woolens and manure-caked boots. Deacon Aldo Godfrey, presiding over the hearing, stood on the platform and leveled a bony forefinger at the audience. "And so, my fellow citizens," he declaimed in a high-pitched voice, "I've drawn up this here petition to be presented at town meetin' on Tuesday." He unfolded a sheet of note paper, and adjusted his spectacles. "Resolved, that there shall be an ordinance forbidding the use of firearms henceforth in Hardscrabble Township."

He paused a moment as some elderly ladies in the crowd applauded, and his eyes moved across the hall to the members of the Lower Forty, standing in sullen silence at the rear. A sardonic smile flitted over his face, and he put the paper back in his pocket and shoved his spectacles down on his nose.

"It's our duty to safeguard the youth o' Hardscrabble," the Deacon urged, "by votin' to outlaw all shotguns and rifles" — he cast a covert glance at Uncle Perk — "and prohibit the local sale o' these killer weapons."

Uncle Perk leapt as though he had been stung. "Naow, hol'

on a minute," he interrupted, waving his fist for attention, "it ain't the weapon that's a killer, it's the feller that uses it."

The Deacon banged his gavel on the table beside him. "The chair has not recognized the speaker," he admonished.

"Oh, ye hain't, eh?" Uncle Perk snapped. "Wal, I dam' well reconnize you, you're the ole skinflint that still owes me $62.49 in back bills, an' by God if you're aimin' to run me out o' business—"

Deacon Godfrey noted the shocked expression of several pious members of the audience, and took prompt advantage of his opportunity. "The chair rules you out of order," he said severely, "for using profanity on the Sabbath."

" 'Tain't no worse to swear an' mean no harm," Uncle Perk retorted, "than 'tis to pray an' mean no good."

The Deacon flushed, and rapped his gavel again. "If there's no further discussion—"

"You haven't even heard the other side yet," Judge Parker objected, starting down the aisle. "Maybe you can tell me what possible good a firearms ban would do. All the hoods and stick-up men would get bootleg guns anyway, and the rest of us wouldn't be able to protect our own homes."

"If you want to get rid of dangerous weapons," Doc Hall shouted, "why don't you start a petition to outlaw the automobile? That kills more people than all the shotguns put together."

"How about a ban on all hammers and hatchets and single- and double-bitted axes," Cousin Sid suggested, "not to mention such lethal implements as icepicks and fire tongs and pinchbars—"

"—And also butcher knives," added Colonel Cobb, "and jack handles and baseball bats and sash weights and coils of rope."

Mister MacNab glowered. "Next thing ye know," he fumed, "ye'll be pr-r-roposing an ordinance against br-r-roken bottles."

Deacon Godfrey hammered the table to quell the rising clamor of voices. "I hereby declare this public hearing adjourned," he said. "You'll all have a chance to vote on the ordinance next Tuesday."

The members of the Lower Forty halted in a disconsolate group on the front steps of the Town Hall, shivering in the chill March night. Owl Eyes Osborn, the local warden, tried in vain to cheer them. "Nothin' to worry about," he insisted without conviction. "He'll never git away with it."

Judge Parker peered at the determined faces of the ladies filing down the steps past him, and shook his head. "I wouldn't be too sure," he said. "He's got all the church groups and ladies' clubs and do-gooders behind him." He scowled as Deacon Godfrey emerged from the hall. "Frankly, now, Aldo," he began, grabbing his arm, "you know the only reason you're doing this is for spite."

The Deacon withdrew his arm. "I haven't got time to argue," he retorted. "It's late, and I've got a long walk home."

"You walkin', Deacon?" Owl Eyes asked incredulously. "Guess you ain't heard about that big rogue bear that's been sighted on Back Road near your place. Last night it got into Peavey's barn and made off with a young shoat, and when Peavey tried to chase it the bear put him right up a tree. Better carry a gun to defend yourself."

Deacon Godfrey's lip curled in a superior sneer. "I don't approve of firearms," he replied, "and what's more there won't be none in this town after Tuesday."

The Lower Forty watched him stride down the muddy street.

"Wisht that b'ar would tackle him tonight," Uncle Perk sighed. "Mebbe he might change his mind about guns."

A faraway look came over Judge Parker's face. "Why not?" he murmured thoughtfully. He snapped his fingers. "Listen. You know that bear rug in my front parlor? Well, if somebody would wrap it around him and jump out at the Deacon and say 'Grr'—"

"I nominate Mac," said Doc Hall. "He can get more R's in a 'Grr' than anybody else."

The Judge nodded to Mister MacNab. "Okay, Mac, pick up the rug and drive out to Back Road," he said briskly. "You can park your hearse behind Peavey's barn so the Deacon won't see it. Just hide in the bushes till he walks by. I'll be following right behind him . . ."

Judge Parker moved cautiously down Back Road, keeping safely out of sight. The night was inky black, and Deacon Godfrey's lanky form was barely visible ahead of him. He disappeared around a bend in the road, and the Judge heard a blood-curdling growl, a sound of crashing branches, and then the Deacon's piercing shriek: "Help! Help!"

Judge Parker tried to control his laughter. "What's the matter?"

"I'm into a bear," the Deacon yelled. "Come quick!"

The Judge hurried around the bend, straining his eyes to see. Deacon Godfrey was dangling from the limb of a spruce tree, his suspenders caught in a branch above him and his feet kicking emptily at the air. At the foot of the tree crouched a dark furry shape, emitting very plausible "Gr-r-rrrs." The Deacon caught his breath as one strand of his suspenders snapped, and he sagged a little lower. "Shoot him," he groaned. "I can't hold on much longer."

"I haven't got a gun," Judge Parker said sadly. "It's a killer weapon. Don't you remember that petition of yours?"

"I'll withdraw it tomorrow," the Deacon pleaded, his teeth chattering. "I'll tear it up, I promise. I'll do anything if you'll only save me."

Smiling to himself, the Judge walked toward the black shape and called "Scat!" There was an answering growl, and he lowered his voice. "All right, Mac," he whispered, "beat it before he recognizes you." The dark shadow wagged its head back and forth in perfect imitation of an angry bruin. "Get moving, I said," the Judge repeated irritably, delivering a swift kick at the shaggy rump. The shape lumbered away into the shadows, just as the Deacon's second suspender strap parted and he landed in a heap at the bottom of the tree. He clambered to his feet and galloped panic stricken down the road, holding up his pants with one hand.

The Judge was still chuckling as he made his way back to the hearse, parked behind Peavey's barn. He opened the front door and blinked in surprise. Mister MacNab was slumbering behind the wheel, a jug of Old Stump Blower on his lap. "Howinell did you get back here so fast?" he inquired.

Mister MacNab struggled to collect himself. "I took a wee drap to for-r-rtify myself," he apologized, "and I must have dozed off. What happened?"

"Worked like a charm," Judge Parker reported. "The Deacon never caught on. Promised to withdraw the petition tomorrow." He grinned. "You sure were convincing."

"But—but I never left the hair-r-rse."

Judge Parker's knees buckled, and he collapsed on the running board. "And I walked right up to it," he recalled hollowly, "and kicked it in the—" He reached for the jug with trembling fingers, and took a long pull. Gradually the color returned to his ashen cheeks. "That's the last time," he muttered, "that I'll ever go out without a gun."

MY COUSIN FAIR-R-RGUS

The members of the Lower Forty gathered in a curious group at the rear of Uncle Perk's store, watching Mister MacNab at work. Lips pursed in concentration, he opened an ancient can of Bulk Smokeless powder and poured a small amount onto a postal scales whose balance had been honed down to a knife-edge. He weighed it carefully, added one or two more grains, and funneled the powder into an empty shell case. Judge Parker frowned. "Don't you know that gunning season's over?"

"These shells are for next year," Mister MacNab explained, "in case I go quail hunting again with my Cousin Fair-r-rgus."

The Judge's frown deepened as Mister MacNab untied a canvas sack and took out a handful of double-O shot, so old that the lead was gray from oxidation. "If you're hunting quail," the Judge demanded, "then whyinell are you loading buckshot?"

" 'Tis a ver-r-ra sad story," Mister MacNab sighed, "which I'd be willing to relate, provided I could have a wee drap of Auld Stump Blower to ease the pangs of memory."

Uncle Perk handed him a jug, and he took a deep swig and gazed dolefully at the circle of fellow members.

"It all started a couple of weeks ago, he began, "when I received an invitation from Fair-r-rgus to shoot on his feyther-in-law's plantation down in Alabama . . ."

He had his doubts from the outset, Mister MacNab admitted to his listeners. Fergus MacNab was his cousin once removed, which Mister MacNab privately felt was not far enough, and there had never been any love lost between them. Moreover, he recalled only too well his unpleasant experience last spring when Fergus had invited him for a gobbler hunt on Senator Beauregard Beadle's estate. But the prospect of a week's free meals and board outweighed his misgivings, and he had piled his hunting gear into his hearse and headed south, hoping for the best.

His doubts proved to be well founded. Cousin Fergus's condescending manner and superior sneer were more obnoxious than ever. Since he had married the daughter of Alabama's leading lumber baron, his native Hibernian burr had been supplanted by a cultivated Southern drawl that grated on Mister MacNab's ears, and his Scotch pride was further offended by the way Fergus groveled and fawned over his wealthy father-in-law. Whenever Senator Beadle voiced an opinion, Fergus would agree with an obsequious "Yes suh, raht suh, sho'nuff suh," which was an insult to the whole MacNab clan. To make matters even more unpleasant, the Senator had insisted on accompanying them the first morning. "Reckon somebody better come along and kill a few birds," he jeered as they climbed into the hunting jeep. "Never met a Yankee yet that could shoot."

The morning was balmy, the pointers ranged back and forth expertly in front of the jeep, but Mister MacNab sat in dour silence, glowering at his host. Beauregard Beadle was short and bandy-legged, weighed down by a large canvas shooting vest studded with shells, but he could move with surprising speed when the dogs came to a point. Invariably he managed to flush the covey before Mister MacNab was near enough to get a shot. Not only that, but if he missed a bird he invariably insisted that it was down. "Saw it fall over yonder, isn't that raht, Fergus?" And Fergus would invariably agree: "Raht, Senator, yes suh," and they would spend the next half hour looking for the nonexistent quail.

Only once did Mister MacNab have a chance to shoot first. A single jumped wild in front of him, and he nailed it with the near barrel. As it started to drop, Senator Beadle fired a split second later and then hurried to pick it up. "Reckon it's mah bird," he said to Mister MacNab. "Y'all never teched it. Raht, Fergus?"

"Tha's raht, suh, he missed it clean," Fergus agreed, stuffing the quail into the Senator's game bag, which he was carrying.

Mister MacNab was smouldering with rage by the time the hunt ended. Senator Beadle had accounted for a dozen plump quail, whereas he had nothing but a pocketful of empty shell cases that, in his frugal Scotch manner, he had picked up after the Senator ejected them. Beauregard Beadle kept crowing over his score all the way home. "Always said a Yankee couldn't shoot," he taunted. "Reckon Ah'll have to come along again tomorrow and show y'all how."

That night, in his guest-room cot, Mister MacNab lay wide awake staring at the ceiling. If only there were some way he could take that pompous blowhard down a peg. If he could just make him miss a few birds . . . He sat bolt upright as a sudden thought struck him, and a crafty smile came over his face. Shouldering into his dressing gown, he bolted the door, opened his suitcase, and got out his reloading equipment. The antiquated kit had been the bottom number in a line put out by a long-defunct

Bridgeport firm, and he had taken it in part payment for handling the interment of an elderly duck hunter who had been caught off balance in his punt when his mail-order 12 gauge doubled on him. He took one of the Senator's shell cases from his coat pocket, knocked the primer out with a 20-penny spike carefully sharpened to size, and measured some powder from his can of Bulk Smokeless. "The regular load is 3^1/$_8$ grams," he murmured to himself, "but he should be content with three."

Humming a snatch of "Bringing in the Sheaves," a trifle off key, he selected the proper wad from the collection in his kit, and pressed it down with an old-fashioned wad rammer. From the canvas shot bag he took some double-O buck, counted out nine pellets, and dropped them into the shell. He put another wad on top, and closed the shell with a venerable crimper, operated by a wheel that turned by hand. His smile grew broader as he dipped the end of the shell in some hot candle wax. "If the Senator hits a quail with this pattern," he chuckled, "it's the bair-r-rd's own fault."

It was midnight when he finished a dozen shells, and the house was very still. Furtively he tiptoed downstairs to the front hall where the Senator's shell vest was hanging, removed the top row of Number 9's, and substituted the buckshot loads. As he started back upstairs, he saw Fergus standing in the upper hall, peering over the banister suspiciously. "I was just in sair-r-rch of a glass of water," Mister MacNab assured him as he passed.

"Didn't know you ever touched the stuff," Fergus commented darkly, and closed his bedroom door.

The following morning the hunting party left the jeep and walked along a piney ridge, the dogs quartering in front of them. One of the pointers bumped a large covey, well out of gunshot,

[232]

and Mister MacNab saw the singles fan out and settle on the ridge. Senator Beadle gave Fergus a meaningful glance. "Ah marked 'em all down in that brier thicket below us, didn't you, Fergus?"

"Yes, suh," Fergus said dutifully, and turned to his cousin. "Y'all work the center of the thicket, Angus, and the Senator can walk the ridge in case any birds fly this way."

Muttering to himself, Mister MacNab forced his way through the dense tangle of catbriers. Something snorted just ahead of him, and a large buck leapt to its feet and crashed away through the undergrowth. Instinctively he brought his gun to his shoulder, then lowered it again as he remembered his light loads. He watched helplessly as the deer bounded toward the ridge. A moment later there was a loud explosion, and the animal did a cartwheel off the ridge and landed back in the thicket almost at his feet. Senator Beadle's whoop of joy blended with Mister Mac-Nab's heartfelt groan.

"Quick, Fergus," the Senator shouted, "go down there and make sure he's daid."

Fergus bent over the carcass, staring at the gaping hole that could only have been made by a clumped pattern of buckshot. He fixed Mister MacNab with an accusing glare. "So that's what you were up to last night—"

Mister MacNab held up a warning hand. "Now, Fair-r-rgus, I wouldna mention it to anybody if I were you," he whispered. "If yere feyther-in-law ever found out ye had a wair-r-rthless guid-for-nothing cousin who'd pull a trick like that, he'd disown ye without a penny."

Fergus nodded thoughtfully, and began to dress out the deer. Mister MacNab made his way up the ridge toward Senator Beadle, who was strutting and puffing his wattles like a spring gobbler.

"First time anybody ever dropped a buck at forty yards with Number 9's," he gloated. "Even a Yankee'll have to admit that's real shooting." He grabbed Mister MacNab's arm, and led him back to the jeep. "Reckon it calls for a couple of mint juleps, raht?"

"R-r-raht, suh, sho'nuff," Mister MacNab said glumly.

Mister MacNab concluded his story and heaved another sigh. "That's why I'm pr-r-reparing these buckshot loads," he said, "so I'll have the right shells next time."

His eye moved to the jug of Old Stump Blower on Uncle Perk's desk.

"Could ye spare me another wee drap, Pair-r-rk?" he asked. "Just to take that mint taste out of my mouth."

ANOTHER MEMBER OF THE CLUB

Judge Parker rose and faced the other members of the Lower Forty, who were seated on flour sacks and kegs of pickled tripe around Uncle Perk's store, and rapped the counter with a bungstarter. "Seems to me about time we held a formal meeting of our worthy organization," he announced, "so I hereby call this group to order, or a reasonable facsimile of same." He glared at Doc Hall, who was munching one of Uncle Perk's soda crackers. "As President of the Lower Forty—"

"Who ever said you were President?" Doc interrupted.

"Can you tell me anybody else who is?" the Judge demanded. His eye swept the circle of silent faces. "Our first order of business today," he continued, "is the election of new members. Since I'm Chairman of the Admissions Committee—"

"What do you mean, Chairman?" protested Cousin Sid.

"Is anybody else Chairman?" There was no response. "All right, then, I have here a nomination by Colonel Cobb, who proposes the name of Chick Keenan for membership. Colonel, would you care to say anything in favor of your candidate?"

"I admit I'm prejudiced," Colonel Cobb apologized to the others, "seeing as how Chick's my own adopted son, but he's going to be seventeen tomorrow, and I've been coaching him to handle a fly rod—"

"Can he qualify as a fisherman?" the Judge asked, scowling over his spectacles in his best judicial manner.

"Well, of course, he hasn't had much previous experience, being reared in a Boston Orphan Home. All he ever did was spear goldfish in the Public Gardens."

"A verra guid training," Mister MacNab nodded in approval. "When I was a wee bairn back in the old country, I used to gill-net salmon out of the Queen's pr-r-rivate waters. 'Tis one reason I left for America in such a hurry."

Judge Parker fitted his fingertips together. "I think it's only fair to put our young candidate to the test," he said. "We're all going out on the stream tomorrow to get some trout for our annual club supper. Let's see what Chick brings back to Cousin Sid's camp in the evening." He turned to Colonel Cobb. "No coaching, mind, or showing him what fly to use," he warned, "He's strictly on his own."

The afternoon shadows were lengthening, and Chick trudged disconsolately along the backroad, his trout rod over a shoulder and a pair of Colonel Cobb's wading boots flapping around his thin shanks. It had been a discouraging day. All the best pools on Mink Brook had been worked over before he arrived, and Beaver Meadow, steaming in the hot May sun, had yielded only a couple of chubs. He wished that Colonel Cobb were here to help him; but that was against the rules, the Colonel had explained. Chick paused before Gramp Perkins' farm, and then trudged up the path to the ramshackle old house.

Gramp was sitting in a rocker on the front porch, a blanket around his legs. He was Uncle Perk's cousin, a lone widower, and Chick had often carried groceries to him from the store and helped him lug firewood since the old man became too crippled with arthritis to do his own chores. Gramp twisted around painfully in his chair at the sound of Chick's footsteps, and smiled as he recognized him. "Afternoon, son." He noticed Chick's rod and creel. "Any luck?"

"No, sir," Chick sighed, "that's the trouble." He hesitated. "I was wondering if you'd let me try that little creek of yours down at the bottom of the meadow. I wouldn't ask, Gramp, only it's very important."

The old man's crippled fingers fumbled to light a pipe. "Why's it so important?"

"Well, you see, they'll let me join their club if I can show 'em I'm able to bring back a good trout tonight. It would mean a lot to the Colonel," he said unhappily, "but so far I haven't had a nibble."

"Wal, naow, son—" Gramp hesitated, and dragged on his pipe with a long sucking sound. His eyes were looking back across the years to the time he was Chick's age. "Why don't you try for Old Wilder?"

"Wilder?"

"That's what I call him. He's a big brownie that's been livin' in my creek so long he must be as old as I am, pretty near. Once ev'ry spring I go down to his pet hole, an' fool him into grabbin' a fly, an' net him, an' then put him back again. It's sort of an annual date we have with each other, like old friends gettin' together, but now I'm too lamed up to fish any more, so—" He hitched the blanket higher around his legs. "You'll see a dead hemlock on the far bank with a dark run just below it, and that's where Old Wilder's waiting right now." Gramp bit down hard on the stem of his pipe and steadied his voice. "Just tell him I'm sorry I couldn't keep our date this year."

Chick hurried down the meadow and crept on all fours to the edge of the little brook, then reared his head cautiously over the grass tops. Below the dead hemlock the brook flowed swift and deep against the far bank, and, as he watched, a small bump showed for a moment in the center of the run, barely leaving a ripple in the water. Upstream Chick saw another olive-colored fly riding on the current. The big trout nudged the surface again, and the fly disappeared.

Chick crawled backward quickly, opened the fly box that Colonel Cobb had given him, and selected an Olive Dun of the right size. His fingers trembled as he threaded the leader through the eye and tied it with the knot that the Colonel had taught him. He rose cautiously, lifted his bamboo rod to make a long cast, and lowered it again without letting out his line. His freckled face wrinkled in a frown. Somehow it didn't seem right. Wilder wasn't his fish. Wilder belonged to Gramp.

The old man, dozing on the porch, opened his eyes as Chick raced toward him. He blinked in surprise. "Where's your rod?"

"Down by the creek. Look, Gramp," Chick panted. "I don't know much about fishing, and I'm afraid I'll scare him, and I—I thought maybe you wouldn't mind coming and showing me."

"Don't know if I could make it all the way down that meadow."

"I'll help you. You can lean on me. Please, Gramp," he begged, "you know how to fool Wilder."

They moved slowly down the meadow, the old man feeling

his way uncertainly through the tall grass, and paused near the stream. Chick picked up his rod and handed it to Gramp. "Let's see the way you do it."

"Why, son, I can't hardly see no more, I couldn't even make out where I was putting it."

I'll cast for you." Chick lifted the rod and sent a long line a little upstream, dropping the Olive Dun deftly at the head of the run. He handed the rod to Gramp. "Now show me how to handle the fly."

"Ain't nothin' to handling a fly, really," Gramp explained, holding the rod high. "just so's you let it drift natural-like over the—,,

The tip of the rod yanked down, and Gramp instinctively lifted at the same time and set the barb. The great trout rolled once and thrashed, and left a V-shaped wake as it bore downstream. Gramp yelled to Chick: "Here, son, take this rod."

"He's your fish," Chick shouted back, racing to the bottom of the run and splashing into the creek to head off the trout. "Show me how to land him—"

It was almost dark when Gramp led the exhausted trout toward shore, and Chick slid a landing net beneath it and scooped it up. The old man sank on the bank beside it, and wet his hand and grasped the fish gently and lifted it out of the net. With his other hand he extracted the fly, and held the trout upright in the water, facing the current. Its gills began to move regularly, its tail switched back and forth. "Guess mebbe I won't be seein' you again, Wilder," Gramp murmured, "but you got a date with this here young feller next spring."

He spread his hand, and the trout moved a little upstream, balancing in the current. There was a sudden rush and the swirl of a brown shape underwater, and Wilder was gone.

Judge Parker and Doc Hall and Mister MacNab had gathered at Cousin Sid's camp that night and added their respective catches to the mess of trout in the kitchen sink. Cousin Sid, both sleeves rolled to the elbow, started to clean the fish, and his fellow members strolled into the living room and settled themselves before the fire. They glanced up as Colonel Cobb trudged through the door. "Where's Chick?" they asked.

"I left him back home," the Colonel said briefly. "He told me he didn't take a trout today, so—" He handed his creel to Cousin Sid and sank heavily onto a sofa. His face was lined with disappointment. "I guess he doesn't qualify for the club yet."

The front door banged open. "What d'ye mean, he don't qualify?" Uncle Perk demanded.

He strode into the room, dropped a loaded creel onto the floor and sat down to pull off a patched rubber boot. He grunted as it came free, and stretched his damp sock toward the fire.

"I happened to stop by Gramp's place on my way back tonight," Uncle Perk said, leaning over to remove his other boot. "He tol' me that Chick had a chance for a real sockdollager this afternoon, but he passed it up so's the old man could catch a trout once more afore he was through." Uncle Perk yanked off the other boot. "If that kid ain't elected anonimously, by God, I'm resigning from the Lower Forty right now."

Colonel Cobb rose and hurried to the door. His face was averted from the others, and his voice sounded choked. "I'll be right back," he said huskily. "I want to get Chick and bring him to his first meeting."

"Ain't no hurry," Uncle Perk called after him. "Cousin Sid won't have them fish cleaned an' cooked for a coupla hours.

Meantime," he said, opening his creel and taking out a jug of Old Stump Blower, "let's us toast our new member."

SMARTER THAN A BEAVER

Owl Eyes Osborn, the local game warden, paused to take a healthy swig of Old Stump Blower. He wiped his lips with the sleeve of his uniform coat, settled himself again on the counter of Uncle Perk's store, and resumed his wildlife lecture. "Yessir, it's like I was saying before," he told the members of the Lower Forty, "they ain't a smarter critter in the woods than a beaver."

Judge Parker nodded and reached for the jug. "When it comes to engineering and figuring out building costs and estimates plus time-and-a-half for overtime," he agreed, "they've got it all over these government contractors."

"Aye, and another advantage," Mister MacNab nodded, borrowing the jug from the Judge, "they dinna char-r-rge for their wairk."

Owl Eyes helped himself to a slab of rat-trap cheese. "Take f'r instance an old King Beaver that's been in the construction business a long time," he said. "He'll walk back and forth on top of a dam in his corduroy pants and high-laced boots, carrying a roll of blueprints and sighting with his surveyor's transit, and now and then he'll wave his paw and holler a little more to the right, boys, now just a mite to the left, and finally he'll shout 'Let 'er go!' and all the young beavers grunt and shove together and there goes another log into place. It's quite a sight to see."

Uncle Perk retrieved his jug from Mister MacNab and took a swallow. "I knowed one ole boss beaver," he recalled, "who was so smart he didn't lay the logs one on top o' t'other so they'd roll off again. No, sir, not that wise ole he-hooper. He arranged to have 'em gnawed in spirals, so the young beavers could stand 'em on end an' twist 'em around and around with their paws, an' screw 'em right into the ground."

"That's what I mean by smart," Owl Eyes nodded.

Doc Hall picked up the jug, shook it experimentally, and drained the last of the contents. "Never forget a King Beaver I saw once," he said. "His work crew kept dropping the trees downstream so they'd catch in some boulders, and the old King watched them and shook his head and then he wandered off up the hill, and pretty soon he came back with a King Beaver from another colony. Well, those two old codgers put their heads together and studied out the whole problem and talked it over back and forth, and then they strolled back up the hill together and shook hands and the old King came down again and, so help me, the crew gnawed the next tree on the other side so it would fall upstream instead."

"Wish the State would hire a few beaver to build their dams for them," Colonel Cobb grunted, "instead of letting the Army Engineer Corps ruin all the good trout streams."

"Some states do it all the time," Owl Eyes said. "Take Maine and Nebraska, they plant beaver whenever they want another fish pond. They even parachute 'em by air. It's quite a sight, I tell you." He removed the cork from another jug of Old Stump Blower, and paused a moment for refreshment. "All the young beavers hook up and stand by the door, and when the pilot chops the throttle and the red light comes on, the King Beaver yells 'Geronimo!' and kicks 'em out one at a time. Then he buckles on his own 'chute, and waves to the pilot 'See ya, Mac,' and drops out after 'em."

"What happens if one of them lands in a tree?" Cousin Sid asked.

"No trouble at all," Owl Eyes replied. "He just reaches his head around and chews the tree down, and brushes off the sawdust, and goes to work." He glanced at his watch and stood up. "Speaking of work, I better get started myself. Uncle Perk, can you let me have a dozen sticks of dynamite?"

"Going to blow another dam?" Judge Parker inquired.

Owl eyes nodded. "Hate to do it," he sighed, "but Deacon Godfrey wrote the state and complained that the beaver were flooding his lower meadow."

Judge Parker's chair came forward with a jolt. "You mean he wants to ruin that pond on Back Road that's full of little trout? Why, that's where all the kids in town go to fish. It isn't even on Godfrey's land."

"Water's backing up on it, though. He's requested the State to blow all the dams that threaten his property. Nothing I can do about it," Owl Eyes shrugged. "I got my orders from the department."

"Why, that no-good psalm-singin' hypocrite," Uncle Perk scowled. "After all them beaver done for him, too. You know dang well he steals the logs from their dam every winter an' burns 'em in his stove. Saves havin' to cut his own firewood. Ain't he got no gratitude?"

"How about that other big pond in the upper meadow above his house?" Doc Hall asked. "That's got some three-four pound squaretails in it, I bet. I sneaked in and started to fish it the other day, but the Deacon ran me off. Are you going to ruin that, too?"

"He never mentioned nothin' about that dam," Owl Eyes said.

Judge Parker leaned back in his chair, his fingertips fitted together, and a crafty expression came over his face. "Tell you what, Owl Eyes," he offered, "we'll just come along with you today. You can explain to the Deacon that we're deputy wardens you hired to help you . . ."

Deacon Godfrey stood on the front steps of his house, glowering as Mister MacNab's hearse halted in the dooryard. Owl Eyes Osborn greeted him pleasantly. "Mornin', Deacon. I've come to blow them beaver dams you complained about."

The Deacon's lean face clouded as the members of the Lower Forty climbed out of the hearse, laden with crowbars and sledges and coils of fuse and a case of dynamite. "What are you fellers doin' here?"

"We came along to give the warden a hand," Judge Parker explained. "It's going to be quite a job blowing that big dam up the hill."

"Up the hill?" Deacon Godfrey glanced in alarm at the pond above his house, covering an acre of his upper pasture. A small stream of water trickled from the dam and flowed down a gulley past his barn. "I don't want that one touched."

"Sorry, Deacon," Owl Eyes said. "You asked the State to get rid of all the beaver dams on your property. It's in your own handwriting."

"I'd suggest you start getting your tractor out of the barn and moving your cattle out of danger," the Judge advised. "Can't tell what will happen when that wall of water comes roaring downhill."

"Might be a good idea to take everything out of your house, too," Doc Hall recommended. "It's right in the line of the flood."

"I'd better move my hair-r-rse," Mister MacNab said. "This whole far-r-rm is likely to be washed away."

Deacon Godfrey licked his lips. "Now, wait a minute, boys," he pleaded. "I didn't really mean that letter I wrote the State. Let's forget the whole thing."

"Too late, Deacon," Owl Eyes said sadly. "Orders is orders."

Judge Parker rubbed his chin in thought. "There's one way out, Deacon," he murmured. "I've got a little influence down in the State Capital, and maybe I might persuade them to destroy your letter. Of course, there's a small favor you could do in return."

"Anything you want, Judge," the Deacon moaned.

"I understand there's some nice trout in that upper pond of yours," the Judge said, "and I know you wouldn't mind if the Lower Forty puts a fly over it now and then."

"Only too happy to have you fellers," Deacon Godfrey assured them with a forced smile. "Come fish it any time—"

Owl Eyes Osborn perched on a jump seat of Mister MacNab's hearse as they headed back to Uncle Perk's store, and balanced a jug of Old Stump Blower on his bent elbow. "It's like I allus say," he reflected, "there ain't no smarter critter than a beaver." He paused for a long swig. "Exceptin' maybe the Judge," he added.

A FISHERMAN
NEVER LIES

Uncle Perk leaned back in his swivel chair, a pair of rubber-bottom boots crossed comfortably on his desk, and glowered at Judge Parker over a copy of the Hardscrabble *Gazette*. "Whyad-dye mean, ye want to set here in my chair?"

"Just for a few minutes," the Judge assured him. "Cousin Sid asked me to give one of his pupils a lecture on honesty, and I don't think it will seem very judicial if I deliver it sitting on the cheese counter."

Uncle Perk rose, grumbling, and settled himself on an up-ended crate beside the other members of the Lower Forty. "What's the kid done?" Doc Hall inquired.

"Faked his mother's name to an excuse, Sid says," Judge Parker replied, sinking into the swivel chair with a creak of springs, "so he could play hooky from school this afternoon. Sid happened to recognize the signature and caught him just in time." The sleigh bells inside the front door jangled, and he gave his fellow members a warning glance. "Everybody look stern."

Cousin Sid advanced across the store, followed by a freckled youngster with tousled red hair. "Your Honor," he said formally, "this is Coley Nason."

Judge Parker scowled at the culprit over his spectacles in his best courtroom manner. Coley cringed, gazed helplessly at the grim circle of Lower Forty members, and dug his fists into the pockets of his tight jeans. "Well, young man," the Judge began, "what's this I hear about your writing a false excuse to cut school today? That's the same as telling a fib, isn't it? That isn't right, is it?"

"Yes, sir," Coley stammered. "I mean, no, sir."

"You want to grow up and be a sportsman, don't you?" the Judge intoned solemnly. "Well, then, the first thing to learn is to be upright and honest and a man of your word. A sportsman always tells the truth."

"I'm sorry, Judge," the boy pleaded, "but I wanted to go fishin'."

"Tomorrow's Saturday," Judge Parker pointed out. "If you'd waited one more day, then you wouldn't have had to lie."

"Oh, but I couldn't wait, sir," Coley said. "I spotted this big ole lunker in Mink Brook, an' I was afraid somebody else might get there first."

The Judge's eyes narrowed. "How big would you say it might go?"

"Two, three pounds, anyway."

The swivel chair came forward with a crash, jolting Judge Parker's spectacles down onto his nose. He readjusted them, taking advantage of the opportunity to gain control of himself, and his voice was carefully casual. "That sounds like quite a fish, son." He beamed at Coley innocently. "Where did you spot him?"

"In my favorite pool," Coley replied.

"Remember, son, a fisherman never lies," the Judge purred. "Now, then, which pool is your favorite?"

Coley hesitated. "It's the—you know the ole covered bridge, sir? Well, about a quarter-mile above it there's a long flat run, with a big rock at the head of it. Sucker Pool, it's called. Know where I mean?"

"Yes, I believe I do," the Judge murmured, fitting his fingertips together before his face to conceal the trace of a smile. "And now you run along home tonight to think it over. I can see you've got the makings of a fisherman."

"Thank you, Judge," Coley said.

"Just remember what I've told you, son," Judge Parker said, "and you'll grow up to be an honest sportsman."

The boy hurried across the store, and the sleigh bells clanged as the door closed behind him. Doc Hall burst into hearty guffaws.

"'An honest sportsman,'" he jeered at the Judge. "That's a hot one, coming from you. All the times I've heard you lie your head off when some other hunter asks about your pet grouse cover. You always tell him there hasn't been a bird there in years. I suppose that's being truthful and upright and a man of your word."

Judge Parker reddened. "Anyway, it isn't as bad as claiming you took that big rainbow last year on a Quill Gordon, and neglecting to mention that you put a grasshopper on the barb of the fly."

"I just happened to snag that 'hopper on my back cast," Doc Hall protested.

Colonel Cob cast a sly glance at Cousin Sid. "Some sportsmen I know keep insisting that their bird dog never chased a rabbit."

Cousin Sid whirled indignantly. "Yes, and other sportsmen I know will swear they knocked a woodcock down, when every-

[251]

body else saw it fly away," he reminded the Colonel.

"If a spor-r-rtsman always tells the truth," Mister NacNab added meaningfully, "how come a trout weighs half a pound more on Uncle Pair-r-rk's meat scales?"

"I got to set 'em a mite ahead," Uncle Perk explained, "if I'm agonna make any money."

"Aye, and then keep yere hond on the scales to make cair-r-rtain," Mister MacNab chuckled. "That's honesty for ye."

" 'Tain't no wuss'n buyin' a shotgun offen that poor Widow Durgen, an' payin' her fifty dollars," Uncle Perk accused, "when you knowed it was wuth five hundred dollars."

Mister MacNab's smile faded. "That's a lie," he shouted indignantly. "It's wair-r-rth six hundred dollars at least."

Judge Parker shoved back the swivel chair. "No sense sitting here all night arguing," he said, clambering to his feet. "Let's all head home and get our gear ready. We want to be out on that covered bridge pool bright and early tomorrow, before anyone else gets there first."

The sun was high overhead, and perspiration rolled down the faces of the Lower Forty members, casting in vain over the long flat run. Judge Parker lowered his rod a moment to rest his throbbing arm, and turned his head at the sound of an approaching whistle. Coley Nason sauntered along the trail, carrying a handsome three-pound squaretail. "Any luck?" the boy inquired cheerfully.

The Judge's jaw sagged. "where did you get that trout?"

"In my favorite pool," Coley replied.

"But—but you said that here—"

"Ain't seen a rise in that place you're fishin' for years," Coley shrugged. "That's why they call it Sucker Pool."

The members gazed in silence as the boy strolled down the path past them, swinging the trout in his hand and whistling to himself. Judge Parker took out his red bandanna and wiped his forehead. "As I was saying," he grinned at the others sheepishly, "that kid's got the makings of a fisherman."

KEEP IT CLEAN

It was a perfect May morning. Fleecy clouds dappled the sky, nesting birds twittered in the maples around the Swasey homestead, and a benign sun warmed the green meadow that sloped toward Mink Brook. Mister MacNab halted his hearse in Zack Swasey's dooryard, and the members of the Lower Forty assembled their fishing gear and started down the path through the meadow, bound for their favorite pool. Judge Parker cast a sidelong glance at the house as they passed. "Seems funny not to see Zack there in the doorway," he mused. "The old codger always used to wave at us and wish us luck."

"He'll be back home again soon," Doc Hall assured him. "I checked in at the Veterans Hospital yesterday, and he's raring to leave. Says he can't stand that clean room he's in."

His fellow members grinned in appreciation. Zack Swasey had many virtues, but cleanliness was not one of them. An old bachelor, he lived in a perpetual clutter of empty tins and broken crockery that littered every inch of floor. It had been a handsome colonial homestead once, but the paint was peeling and the rooms were piled so high with trash that its fine traditional lines were obscured. "I don't believe Zack has swept out the place in twenty years," the Judge said, leading the way to the stream. "Claims he likes it the way it is—"

His voice trailed, and he stared ahead incredulously. The high bank of Mink Brook was heaped with an unsightly collection of sagging bedsprings, seatless chairs, boxes, and cartons. Some of the junk had spilled down the bank into the stream, and their choice pool was choked with rusty kitchen utensils and cracked china and old rubber boots. Judge Parker's teeth were clenched. "I'd like to find the no-good so-and-so who's been using this stream for a village dump."

Colonel Cobb retrieved an oval blue platter from the pool. "This looks like Zack's plate," he said. "I remember seeing it on his kitchen table. First time it's ever been clean," he added, starting to toss it back into the water.

"Careful, mon," Mister MacNab cried, catching the platter as it fell. He inspected it more closely. "My wife collects antiques," he said, "and I'd guess this is wair-r-rth a guid sum of money."

Cousin Sid scanned a series of telltale wheelbarrow tracks in the meadow, leading down from the homestead to the stream. "But who could get into Zack's house and cart out all his rubbish? He gave us his key when we took him to the hospital. Nobody else has one" — he thought a moment — "except Deacon Godfrey, of course. He holds the mortgage on the place."

"Speaking of the Deacon," Colonel Cobb recalled, "he came into my newspaper office yesterday to put in a social item about some wealthy real estate clients of his from New York, a Mr. and Mrs. Triplett. They're driving up this weekend to look over some property in Hardscrabble."

Judge Parker had a faraway look. "You know, I've been wondering." There was a little pause.

"Wondering what?" Doc Hall prompted.

"Well, Zack's been sick, and maybe he hasn't been able to meet his mortgage payment. Maybe the Deacon's planning to foreclose," he mused. "Maybe he sees a chance to sell the house, and clean up."

"That's why he wanted to get rid of the old man's junk," Doc Hall nodded. "So it would look nice and neat for his clients to see."

Judge Parker sprang into action. "Mac, see if you can back your hearse down the meadow to the stream." He gestured to the others. "Start gathering up all this mess in the pool. If anybody's going to clean up," he added grimly, "it won't be Deacon Godfrey."

The following morning a sleek black limousine with New York license plates and a uniformed chauffeur halted before the Swasey house, and Mr. and Mrs. Triplett emerged, accompanied by the Deacon. He escorted them up the path to the front steps, exuding oily charm. "Frankly, I consider this place a real bargain," he confided. "It's a charming home, been in the family for generations, but the owner's ill, poor old chap, and has to get rid of it at a sacrifice price. Needs a coat of paint, of course, but everything inside is in perfect condition, all spick-and-span." He turned the key in the front door and pushed it open. "Neat as a pin—"

His Adam's apple bobbed as he swallowed convulsively. The interior of the house was a shambles. Sagging bedsprings and dilapidated items of furniture were scattered at odd angles around the rooms, and the floors were strewn ankle-deep with water-soaked rags and rusty tableware and tin cans. Mr. Triplett let out his breath in an indignant snort. "What's the big idea," he stormed, "dragging us all the way up from the city to look at a pigpen like this?"

"But it wasn't like this," Deacon Godfrey stammered. "I

cleaned it up myself."

"Trying to make a quick sale and put one over on us, eh?" Mr. Triplett glared at the Deacon. "I'm finding myself another real estate agent."

He turned on his heel and almost collided with Zack Swasey, leaning on a cane in the doorway. Mister MacNab's hearse was parked in front, and the members of the Lower Forty sauntered up the path behind him. "Wotinell are these folks doin' in my house?" Zack asked the Deacon.

"Well, I thought — that is, they were thinking—"

"Not any more," Mr. Triplett interrupted. He beckoned to his wife. "Come, Gloria."

Mrs. Triplett was bending over the kitchen table, inspecting the oval blue platter. "Just a minute, dear," she told her husband. "This is the very pattern I've been collecting." She beamed at Zack Swasey. "I'll give you five dollars for it."

Mister MacNab sidled into the room. "Par-r-rdon me, madam," he said politely, "but I've been luiking at that plate myself. Tell me, Zack, would ye par-r-rt with it for ten dollars?"

Mrs. Triplett gave Mister MacNab a devastating glance. "I'll pay you twenty," she said to Zack.

"Thair-r-rty," Mister MacNab countered.

"Forty," called Mrs. Triplett.

"I'll make it for-r-rty-five," Mister MacNab offered. "Going, going—"

"Fifty," Mrs. Triplett shouted, and pulled the bills from her purse. Mister MacNab shrugged his shoulders in an elaborate show of defeat, and Mrs. Triplett snatched up the platter with a triumphant smile and followed her husband to the car. The chauffeur slammed the door, and the limousine rolled down the road. In the ensuing silence Zack Swasey counted the bills into Deacon Godfrey's hand. "There, that covers the installment on the mortgage that's due ye," he said. "Now git offen my property."

The Deacon pocketed the bills. "If you're late on your payment again," he snarled, "I'll make trouble."

"And if you make trouble," Judge Parker warned, "I'll let it be known how you polluted Mink Brook with rubbish, which is not only against the town ordinance but would be pretty hard to explain to the Keep Hardscrabble Clean Committee of which I understand you're honorary chairman."

Deacon Godfrey opened his mouth, shut it again, and strode down the path. Zack Swasey chuckled. "Ain't no need to worry about meetin' them payments, Jedge," he confided. "Any time I need cash I'll sell another plate. Got a whole set of 'em up in the attic."

The Lower Forty began to gather up the tin cans and refuse scattered around the floor. "Sorry we had to mess up your house like this, Zack," Cousin Sid apologized, "but we'll get it straightened up in no time."

Zack scowled. "What's wrong with the way it is?" he demanded. "Ever'thing's right where it belongs." He gazed affectionately at the litter around him and sank into a broken rocker with a sigh of content. "Yessir, like I allus say, they ain't no place like home."

THE WORM THAT TURNED

Saturday was opening day on Mink Brook, and the Lower Forty, gathered in Uncle Perk's store late Friday afternoon, were beside themselves with impatience. Last fall at their request the state had set aside a section of the stream for fly fishing only. Owl Eyes Osborn, the warden, had posted the stretch and stocked it with good-sized rainbows and browns, and tomorrow the restricted water would be opened for public angling.

Judge Parker rubbed his hands together in glee. "No more worm fishermen splashing around and putting down all the trout," he chortled. "We'll start first thing in the morning. How early can you pick up us, Mac?"

"I'll nae be fishing tomorrow," Mister MacNab replied dolefully.

His fellow members turned and stared at him in surprise. He was seated in a far corner beside Uncle Perk's cheeseboard, nibbling in melancholy silence. His spirit was crushed. All spring he had been casing Mink Brook in preparation for this long-awaited moment. He had located the pool where he would cast his fly, and had even spotted his trout, a big granddaddy that rose regularly near the head of the pool each afternoon at dusk. The thought of some other angler taking his prize fish tomorrow was more than he could bear, and he cut himself another slab of cheese and emitted a heartfelt moan. "We'll all be thinking of you," Cousin Sid tried to console him.

"Thank ye kindly, Sidney," Mister MacNab sighed, tilting back in his chair. " 'Tis my own fault for being marr-r-ried."

He had no one to blame but himself, he explained to the others. Last month he had forgotten his wife's birthday as usual, and to make amends he had given Maggie a nursery catalog and told her to order some rose bushes for the front yard. The whole affair had slipped his mind until she received a postcard from the nursery yesterday, notifying her that the shipment was on its way and warning that the bushes should be set out as soon as they arrived. She had staked out a rectangular rose bed in the center of the lawn and insisted that Mister MacNab stay home and spade it up.

"Maggie says the gar-r-rden has to be turned over tomorrow," he concluded sadly, "and there's naebody else to turn it over to."

He paused as the string of sleigh bells inside the front door jangled. A stranger in a canvas fishing jacket entered the store and greeted them affably. "Pardon me," he inquired, "do you know where I can get some angleworms?"

The Lower Forty caught its collective breath in a gasp of indignation. "Worms?"

"Nightcrawlers," the stranger replied. "Nice big juicy ones, the kind a fish can't resist."

"Ain't no worms for sale here, mister," Uncle Perk announced coldly. "You'll have to dig your own."

"Oh, I don't mind that," the stranger said, "if I can find some place to dig—"

Mister MacNab's chair came forward with a jolt that dislodged his bridgework. An inspiration had just dawned on him. He shoved his upper set back in place and flashed the stranger a gleaming smile. "As a matter of fact," he said, "I've got the very place for ye. My front lawn is full of wair-r-rms." He appealed to his fellow members. "Isn't that so, boys?"

"Best spot in Hardscrabble," Doc Hall nodded. "It's a regular worm mine."

"They're so juicy they make a fish's mouth water," added Colonel Cobb.

"We get all of ours there," Judge Parker agreed.

"That's mighty nice of you," the stranger said to Mister MacNab, "but I don't like to go ruining your lawn."

"Dinna give it a thought, mon," Mister MacNab insisted. "One fisherman to another, ye know." He sprang to his feet. "Come along and I'll show ye the best spot to dig. I've got it all staked out." He winked at the other members over his shoulder as he led the way to the door. "Ye can start the fair-r-rst thing in the morning."

Mister MacNab was still chuckling to himself as he waded slowly up Mink Brook, casting his fly ahead into the riffles. His little ruse had worked to perfection. He had explained to Maggie that he was hiring a gardener to make sure the work was done right, left the stranger spading up the rose bed, and headed for the stream. He had spent the morning fishing well below the secret pool; there was no use trying for his granddaddy trout until late afternoon.

The shadows were lengthening as he worked his way cautiously around a bend in the stream and halted aghast. The worm-digger was standing waist-deep in the center of the pool, his rod bent in an arc. Mister MacNab watched the taut line cut the water toward him, and the granddaddy trout swirled almost at his feet and darted back upstream. Mister MacNab found his voice. "Hey!" he bellowed. "Hey, you!"

The stranger's back was turned, and his reel sang as the trout sped toward the upper end of the pool. He held his rod high to keep a tight line and managed to check the run. Mister MacNab clambered onto the bank and galloped up the trail to the pool, shaking with rage. The stranger had maneuvered the trout downstream again, and he reached behind him and unhooked a landing net from his belt. Mister MacNab's voice rose to a scream.

"Put that tr-r-rout back," he threatened, "or I'll have the law on ye." He pointed to a posting sign tacked to a tree. "This is for fly fishing only."

The stranger slid his net deftly under the spent trout, scooped it up, and held it aloft, flopping feebly inside the green mesh. He waded toward Mister MacNab with a pleasant smile. "I couldn't hear you above the roar of water," he apologized. "What were you saying?"

Mister MacNab opened his mouth and shut it again. His eyes fixed themselves on a small black fly embedded in the trout's lower lip. The stranger removed the bedraggled feather lure, snipped it off his leader, and blew on it to dry it.

"Number Sixteen Black Gnat," he said, dropping it into his aluminum fly box. "It's my favorite fly."

Mister MacNab asked in a strangled voice, "Then what were ye digging those wair-r-rms for?"

"Oh, those weren't for me," the stranger said casually, taking a small scale from the pocket of his canvas jacket. "I ran into some bullhead fishermen down at the motel the other night, and they said they'd pay anything for a mess of nightcrawlers." He hooked the scale under the trout's jaw and lifted it. "I finally bid them up to five cents apiece."

Mister MacNab watched the needle jiggle and halt at three pounds. The stranger beamed and slid the trout into his creel. "Certainly appreciate your letting me dig the worms on your lawn. It's loaded with them. I earned enough in a couple of hours to cover my whole trip."

"Mister MacNab licked his dry lips. "I didna catch yere name."

"Gor-r-rdon MacTavish," the stranger replied, and sauntered down the trail.

The following morning the members of the Lower Forty crowded into Judge Parker's car and drove back to Mink Brook for another day's fishing. The Judge halted at the MacNab gate and tooted his horn. Mister MacNab was in his shirt sleeves spading up the remainder of his front lawn. Ignoring the car, he stooped and picked a wriggling object out of the dirt and dropped it into a tin can at his belt. "Wotinell's got into him?" Judge Parker pondered.

Uncle Perk shrugged and pointed to a hand-lettered sign in front of the house: WAIRMS FOR SALE. "If they's one thing a Scotchman can't stand," he observed as they drove on, "it's havin' another Scotchman git the best of him."

HOW TO FISH
WITHOUT EVER
TRYING

The string of sleigh bells inside the front door jangled, and Uncle Perk swung his hunting rubbers off the desk and shoved back his swivel chair with a sigh. He rose reluctantly to greet a portly customer who waddled toward the counter, clad in a brand-new canvas jacket with the price tag still attached to the collar. "I'm starting on a fishing trip," the stranger announced brusquely. "Here's a list of groceries I need." He handed Uncle Perk a scribbled sheet of paper and turned to face the silent group at the rear of the store. "Anybody know a good place around here to dunk a worm?"

The members of the Lower Forty exchange dark glances. "The only stream in these parts," Cousin Sid began, "is Mink Brook—"

"Mink Brook!" the stranger snorted. "That's no good. Why you can't even drive your car to it. Have to walk almost an eighth of a mile, and there's blackberry bushes and fallen branches to trip over. Somebody ought to do a little stream improvement."

"Like for instance blacktopping the trail," Judge Parker

suggested thinly, "and building steps down the steep part?"

"That's right," the stranger nodded. "Make it easier for the fishermen. Cut a path along the brook, and clear out the sunken snags, and chop down all the trees on the bank where you might hang up your back cast."

"Maybe we could set up a public campsite," Doc Hall offered with heavy irony, "with picnic tables and an outdoor fireplace and a couple of restrooms, his and hers."

Uncle Perk scowled at the stranger's list and began to take the items from the shelves. "Might improve it some more to have a concession stand an' sell hot dogs an' cold tonic."

"We could put a turnstile gate beside the best pool," Mister MacNab added, "and char-r-rge an admission fee."

"You got the general idea," the stranger nodded amiably. "Fishing's no fun if you have to work for it."

"I don't know about that, mister," Colonel Cobb objected. "I had a lot of fun fishing a couple of weeks ago, but I wouldn't say it was easy."

The stranger settled himself in Uncle Perk's swivel chair. "Whereabouts?"

"In California," Colonel Cobb replied, "when I took my young boy Chick out to visit Frank Dufresne. Seems Frank had a couple of fishing partners, Jack Andrews and Tom Goodhue of Oroville, and they offered to show us the Middle Fork of the Feather River. Tom had a special jeep equipped with six-ply tires and a winch and a two-way radio in case of emergency, because he said it was sort of rough going down the canyon." He paused to light his pipe. "Maybe you'd like to hear about it . . ."

It was wild country, Colonel Cobb recalled. Frank Dufresne claimed it was one of the wildest spots in North America, and

Frank has been all over Canada and Alaska. Stands of ponderosa and giant Douglas fir, mule deer leaping the trail, and occasionally a clump of rare snowflowers, blood-red against the pine spills. Hillsides covered with manzanita bush that no man would fight his way through. A canyon filled with rattlesnakes and cougars and poison oak, and an old prospector with a .38 who took potshots at any intruder. Nary a road or habitation, nothing but the unspoiled and challenging wilderness.

They had stopped for the night on the canyon rim. The Colonel and Chick had watched in admiration as Jack and Tom made camp with the swift wordless efficiency of skilled outdoorsmen. In a jiffy lanterns were glowing, air mattresses had been pumped up, drinks were poured, and steaks were grilling over a bed of embers. They fell asleep counting the stars and hearing the far-off howl of coyotes, and breakfast bacon was sizzling when they awoke at daybreak. The sun had not yet risen over the tops of the firs as they piled into the jeep and started down the vertical canyon wall toward the river.

The zigzag trail had been hacked out during gold-rush days, when the prospectors lowered their heavy mining machinery by teams of mules. It was little more than the width of the jeep itself, heaped with loose stones and slanting toward the outer edge. The jeep tilted precariously, and Colonel Cobb, cowering in the rear, could look straight down at the silver ribbon of Feather River, a mile below them. Tom wrestled the wheel with the easy confidence of a World War II fighter jockey, and Jack sat on the front fender, ready to leap off and remove a blowdown or a jagged rock that might slash the tires. The switchbacks were so sharp that the jeep could not turn, and Tom had to back down every other one, putting the car in reverse and hoping that the right wheel would not wander too near the edge. "What if the jeep rolls over?" Colonel Cobb whispered.

"We'll get down there a helluva lot quicker," Frank said laconically.

Here and there a hand-lettered sign warned: KEEP OUT! PEOPLE ARE NO DAM GOOD! THIS MEANS YOU! SLIM. Halfway down the trail, as they halted at a switchback to reverse gears, a bearded character stepped out from behind a clump of sweet birch, brandishing a revolver. He recognized the jeep and put the gun back in its holster. Tom gave him a box of food he had brought. Slim acknowledged it with a grunt, and Tom waved and drove on. "I bring him some grub every time I come down here," he explained, "and he pays me by giving me another share in his gold mine." He maneuvered the jeep around a deep washout, one wheel hanging in space. "His claim was all worked out years ago, but these old codgers have got a lot of pride. Maybe he'll strike it rich someday. You never know."

The mining trail quit completely, still a thousand feet above the river, and they clambered out and started down a narrow goat path that wound around the sheer side of the cliff. Pebbles and dry leaves skidded underfoot, and Colonel Cobb leaned away from the edge of the precipice and tried to keep his balance. Jack had cautioned him not to grab an overhead ledge to steady himself; that was where rattlesnakes liked to slumber. The Colonel stepped up onto a boulder, and Chick, walking behind him, yelled and pointed to a coiled rattler only a few inches from where he had planted his foot. Chick dispatched the snake with a rock, and Colonel Cobb collapsed on the boulder and mopped his beaded forehead.

It was stifling in the canyon, and the Colonel's bad knee was giving out. Jack had to take one end of his aluminum rod case and help him along the path. Chick and the others had gone ahead, and Colonel Cobb stumbled and slid after them, sitting on his hunkers to toboggan down the last steep slope. He came to a halt on a sandy bar at the edge of the river, and gazed at the pool before him. Chick was standing midstream, his rod already bent to a fighting rainbow, his freckled face wearing a beatific grin . . .

Colonel Cobb shut his eyes for a moment to relish the memory. The stranger urged impatiently: "How was the fishing?"

"Out of this world," Colonel Cobb recalled. "Schools of rainbows working in the fast water, and big browns lying on the bottom waiting for the evening hatch of flies. Nothing had ever disturbed them. There wasn't a human track on that sandbar; Frank said the stream hadn't been visited all year—"

"That's what I mean," the stranger interrupted. "All that fishing going to waste because nobody can get to it. The government ought to improve the river, build a highway along the bank or rig up a chair lift down into the canyon."

"Personally I'm glad there's still a few unimproved places left in this country," Colonel Cobb retorted, "that are tough enough to make a man out of my boy."

The stranger shrugged. "What's the use of fishing if you have to go to all that trouble?" he asked, rising and strolling over to the counter. He inspected the pile of merchandise that Uncle Perk had assembled and pointed to an item wrapped in waxed paper. "What's that?"

Uncle Perk lowered his spectacles and fixed the customer with a steely eye. "That's a slab o' frozen halibut, mister," he muttered, "so you won't have to go to all the trouble o' fishin'." The front door slammed indignantly behind the departing stranger, and Uncle Perk sank back in his swivel chair and opened the lower left-hand drawer of his desk. "Tain't the streams that need improvin'," he observed, taking out a jug of Old Stump Blower, "so much as some o' the fishermen."

PERKYNS'
OLDE COUNTRYE
SHOPPE

Mister MacNab's hearse halted before Uncle Perk's store, and the members of the Lower Forty piled out, tanned and happy after a week's quail hunting in Carolina. They stopped abruptly in their tracks, their jaws sagging. Gone was the ancient handprinted sign over the front door, JNO. PERKINS, PROP., GUNS & FSHNG TCKLE BOT SOLD & SWOPT. In its place hung a name-plate in Old English lettering, PERKYNS' OLDE COUN-TRYE SHOPPE.

Judge Parker removed his spectacles and wiped them clean to make sure he had read it correctly. "Wotinell's been going on while we were away?" he muttered. "Even the windows are clean."

The Judge opened the door and winced. Instead of the cus-tomary jangle of sleigh bells, a set of gift-shop chimes tinkled decorously. The formerly dingy walls were painted a glaring white, and the familiar odor of ground coffee, harness leather, and kerosene had been supplanted by the smell of antiseptic soap. A chromium showcase had replaced the old wooden cheese counter, Uncle Perk's battered rolltop desk and swivel chair were nowhere in sight, and the potbellied stove, now polished and shining, had been relegated to a far corner. The center of the store was taken up by a battery of cameras, black cables trailed across the floor, and the overhead floodlights gave the interior an unnatural brilliance. The room was filled with strangers, and the tallest, clad in a maroon velvet shirt, with pointed shoes and a pointed goatee to match, eyed them coldly.

"Kindly step to the rear," he said in an authoritative manner. "you're in the way of the crew." He raised his voice. "Let's run through this scene once more. Uncle Perk baby, take your place."

The Lower Forty stared incredulously at a character in false gray sideburns, his face covered with pink makeup. He wore a large butcher's apron and a red shirt with sleevegarters, and he was smoking a clay pipe. Patting a sideburn into place, he stepped behind the counter, and the tall figure with the goatee peered at him through the camera lens.

"Better take off those spectacles, Perk baby," he said. "They reflect too much light." He looked around impatiently. "Where's Doc Hall?"

Doc started in surprise. "Right here."

"Not you," the tall stranger said curtly, "and please don't interrupt during rehearsal." He cupped his hands to his mouth. "Hurry up, Doc baby."

"I'll be with you in half a jiff," an effeminate voice answered, "ath thoon ath I get into theeth horrid old rubber bootth."

Doc reddened. "I'm going to sue," he said grimly, following the other members to the rear of the store.

Uncle Perk was hunched uncomfortably on an upended

cracker barrel, smoking his corncob. He put a finger to his lips in warning as they greeted him. "Sit down an' be quiet, fellers," he whispered. "Mr. Whipple don't want no noise."

"Who's Mr. Whipple?" Doc Hall demanded.

"He's a big TV director," Uncle Perk explained in a low voice. "He was readin' 'The Lower Forty,' an' he decided to rent the store fer background an' shoot a two-minute commercial." He looked down sheepishly to avoid their accusing eyes. "It's a bus'ness proposition," he insisted. "They've painted my whole store for nawthin,' and what's more, they're givin' me a genuwine color TV set, twenty-five inch rectangular screen with remote control an' glareproof glass."

"But why did they hire somebody else to play your part?"

Uncle Perk sighed. "Mr. Whipple said I wa'n't the storekeeper type. People wouldn't believe me."

"Quiet!" the director ordered, and they lapsed into dutiful silence. "All right, Doc baby, walk up to the counter. And try to correct that lisp."

A slender figure in rubber wading boots and a brand-new canvas fishing jacket minced into the circle of light. He was carrying a steel rod, and an enormous wicker creel was slung from his shoulder. As he approached the counter, the actor playing Uncle Perk greeted him with a smile. "Hello, there, Doc Hall. Did you have any luck in Mink Brook this morning?"

"Did I?" the other actor gushed. "Juth wait till I show you, Uncle Perk." He opened the creel, and proudly exhibited a couple of large frozen fish. "Thee?"

Doc gasped. "Mackerel!" he groaned. "In Mink Brook!"

"I tried to git 'em to use trout," Uncle Perk apologized. "Tol' 'em I had some nice rainbows in the ice chest, but Mr. Whipple said they wa'n't big enough. People wouldn't believe 'em.'"

"Stop that talking," the director yelled. "Okay, Perk baby."

"By gorry, that's a mighty fine passel o' fish, sure 'nough," the Uncle Perk character said in what was evidently intended for a Yankee accent. "Cal'ate this calls for a celebration." He took a couple of beer cans from the shelf behind him. "There's nothing like a refreshing can of Fo-mo, spelled F-O-M-O, to give that smooth, yummy, friendly flavor. Yes, folks, Fo-mo Beer is made from specially grown hops, double-fermented to counteract acidity, and its rich creamy goodness has made Fo-mo America's Number One favorite malt beverage. You'll love Fo-mo's easy-to-open snap top." He and the other actor opened the cans and held them aloft. "Be sure to ask for Fo-mo, the beer without burp."

They clinked the cans together and Mr. Whipple shouted, "Cut!" He scowled as the Uncle Perk character lifted the can to his lips. "Don't drink that lousy stuff," the director warned. "It's sheer rotgut." He glanced at his stopwatch. "Two minutes thirteen seconds. Have to speed up that first part a little. Let's have Doc Hall carry the fish instead of taking them out of the basket. Ready, babies?" He paused and glared at the Lower Forty. "I'll have to ask everybody else to leave," he said. "This is going to be a take."

Uncle Perk cast an appealing look at his indignant fellow members. "I'm sorry, fellers," he pleaded, "but it's the on'y way I could git the store all prettied up."

The gift-shop chimes tinkled as the front door closed behind them.

Judge Parker hurried down the street toward Uncle Perk's store, feeling a trifle guilty. It had been almost a month since he'd dropped in to see the old codger, he reflected; but pressure of court business had tied him up, and lately he'd been waging a vain fight to prevent Deacon Godfrey's real estate firm from buying up the old Bryant property, including a favorite stretch of Mink Brook. The store was deserted, he noticed, as he opened the door, and Uncle Perk was seated alone beside the polished stove in a far corner, trying to read the Hardscrabble *Gazette* in the dim light.

"See in the paper where that connivin' ole Deacon's fin'ly got aholt of the Bryant land," Uncle Perk said.

Judge Parker nodded. "Now he'll put no-fishing signs up and down the whole stretch of Mink Brook."

"Wal, we all got our troubles," Uncle Perk said morosely.

"What are you complaining about?" the Judge asked, pointing to the imitation-walnut console. "Look at that nice new television set you got for free."

"What good is it?" Uncle Perk grunted. "Can't git nawthin' on it. Moose Mountain cuts off all the color channels. Dam' thing ain't wuth a hoot here in Hardscrabble."

"At least, they fixed up your store for you," Judge Parker reminded him. "You're that much ahead."

"Ahead?" Uncle Perk slammed his newspaper onto the floor. "I'm goin' broke. Had to raise my prices to keep up with them floweressent lights an' other fancy fixin's, an' all my old customers has quit me. Claim the store's too high-falutin' for 'em. Now I hear the town's plannin' to increase my tax assessment." He rasped a match vengefully across the stove, leaving a dark streak on the bright metal, and lit his corncob. "I wisht I'd never heered o' TV."

Judge Parker's eyes narrowed. "You still got that contract they signed?"

"Right here." Uncle Perk took a crumpled legal document from his pocket. "It ain't no good except to start a fire."

"Wait a minute, now." The Judge ran a professional eye down the contract, humming to himself. "Here we are, in the fine print at the bottom." He adjusted his spectacles and started to read. " '. . . hereby agrees to reimburse the owner for any damage and restore the property exactly as it was prior to . . . ' " He folded the paper briskly, and grinned at Uncle Perk. "Just leave it to me."

The string of sleigh bells jangled reassuringly as the Lower Forty opened the front door, and they gazed in relief at the drab interior of Uncle Perk's store, the walls covered once more with grime, the windows opaque with cobwebs and soot. The dingy potbellied stove was back in the center of the floor, and a familiar odor of ground coffee, harness leather, and stale pipe smoke assailed their nostrils. Uncle Perk leaned back contentedly in his swivel chair, his boots propped on the battered rolltop desk.

"What happened to your television set?" asked Doc Hall, perching on the ancient counter and cutting a slab of rat trap cheese.

Uncle Perk winked at his fellow members. "Traded it off to Deacon Godfrey," he said, "in exchange for lettin' the Lower Forty fish that part o' Mink Brook he just bought." He clambered to his feet, hooked a forefinger through the handle of a jug of Old Stump Blower, and hung a CLOSED FOR INVENTORY sign on the front door. "Come on," he told the others, "let's git fishin'."

SMILE, EVERYBODY!

Uncle Perk leaned back in his swivel chair and closed his eyes resignedly while the Lower Forty babbled on about their Carolina quail hunt. "You should have been along, Perk," Cousin Sid insisted for the tenth time. "Beautiful country, lots of birds, everything perfect—"

"Once we escaped from Malcolm and his camera," Doc Hall added.

Judge Parker's face broke into a reminiscent grin. "You've got to hand it to Mister MacNab," he chuckled. "Not only got rid of our snap-happy host, but also that loud-mouthed Cousin Fergus. It takes a Scotchman to outsmart another Scotchman." He helped himself to a slab of store cheese and winked at Uncle Perk. "Like to hear how he worked it?"

"Not pertickly," Uncle Perk said frankly.

"All right, then," the Judge beamed, "I'll tell you . . ."

Not that their Carolina host had been lacking in southern hospitality, Judge Parker assured Uncle Perk. The members of the Lower Forty, together with Mister MacNab's ubiquitous Cousin Fergus, had descended on his plantation without warning; but Malcolm had made them comfortable in his farmhouse and invited them to hunt his native coveys. "I never shoot birds myself," Malcolm had explained, "so I'll just tag along and snap a few pictures. I'm an amateur photographer," he admitted.

"You'll probably shoot more birds with your camera," Cousin Fergus jeered, "than these Yankee dubs will ever hit with a gun."

Judge Parker ignored the thrust. "I'm sort of a camera bug myself," he told Malcolm, "I have a box Brownie."

"Hm? Oh, yes. Very nice," Malcolm remarked politely. "Personally I prefer a helical type with rigid barrel." The Judge's jaw sagged. "Very simple to operate," he continued, "all you have to remember is to adjust the stop opening to the emulsion speed, which is synchronized with the filter factor in inverse ratio to the depth of focus. I'll show it to you tomorrow."

The Lower Forty set out bright and early the following morning, trailed by their host. Malcolm's slight frame was bowed down with photographic appurtenances. An exposure meter dangled from his neck, a telephoto lens hung beside it, his pockets were stuffed with assorted filters and sunshades and light bulbs and spare film, and a black case was slung from his shoulder, crammed with wide-angle lens and closeup attachment and a flash gun. "I won't be in the way," he promised, his camera equipment swaying and clanking as he walked behind them. "You-all go ahead and hunt as if I weren't here."

The dogs banged into a solid point at the edge of a weed patch, and the Lower Forty gripped their guns in readiness and moved in behind them. Malcolm brandished a hand in warning.

"Hold it, everybody," he shouted. "Let me get my exposure right." The hunters stood rigid while he consulted his meter, adjusted the opening, and then glanced at the sky. "Think I'll put on a yellow filter to make it more contrasty." The guns of the hunters were beginning to waver as he completed his preparations and peered critically through the viewfinder. "Move a couple of feet to the right, Judge; you're blocking Doctor Hall. Tilt your hat back so I can see your face." He studied the effect again and frowned. "Somebody break off that twig; it's hiding one of the dogs."

"Hurry up," Judge Parker muttered through clenched teeth. "The birds are running."

"There goes the sun behind a cloud," Malcolm sighed. "Guess I'd better use a flash. Hold it, now, don't move." He took the flashgun from his case, fastened it to the camera, and hooked up some dangling wires. The hunters' arms were sagging, and the barrels of their shotguns were doing figure eights in the air. "Try to hold those guns still so they won't be blurred," Malcolm complained, inspecting the scene once more through his finder. "All right, smile, everybody!"

A pair of quail flushed from the far side of the weed patch, and the arm-weary hunters tried in vain to steady their guns and take aim. The birds sped away unscathed, and Fergus emitted an unpleasant guffaw.

"Told you a dam' Yankee couldn't hit a quail," he chortled.

Malcolm was gazing ruefully at his camera. "I forgot to remove the lens cap," he apologized. "Well, we'll try again on the next point."

The Lower Forty's collective smile hardened into a grimace as the morning wore on. Hour after hour they stood and held it while Malcolm checked his exposure meter and changed his speed and adjusted his stops and fiddled with his focus. Whenever the dogs made a find, Malcolm insisted on arranging them so the light would be on their faces. Blinded by the sun, they fired emptily at the sky. They wound up the morning hunt without a bird, and Fergus's laughter rang in their ears as they drove back to the farmhouse.

"Maybe you'll shoot better after a little lunch," he taunted. "At least, you couldn't shoot any worse."

The afternoon hunt proved even more frustrating. Mister MacNab parked his hearse at the edge of a beanfield, and the dogs cast in a wide circle. Abruptly they froze in a double point, their flanks quivering, their heads extended toward a feeding covey. Malcolm took prompt command of the situation. "I want the guns over there on the other side of the dogs," he ordered, "so the birds will be flying into the camera. That's right. Now everybody stand still until I get focused." He adjusted the range and shook his head. "Maybe I better pace off the distance just to be sure. Hold this a minute, Fergus."

He handed Fergus the camera and started toward the dogs. There was a violent explosion of wings, and the entire covey rose and made straight for Fergus. The Lower Forty held their guns high, unable to shoot, and the birds sailed into a tangle of cat brier. Fergus handed the camera back to Malcolm a little sheepishly.

"I'm sorry," he apologized. "I clicked it without meaning to."

"That's all right," Malcolm said. "It was the last exposure on the roll, anyway. I'll put in another one and try again." He felt in his coat pocket, and his face grew puzzled. "That's funny, I thought I had several extra rolls with me." A hasty search of his camera case proved futile. "I must have left them back at the house."

"Here's the keys to the hair-r-rse, Fairgus," Mister MacNab offered. "Ye can drive Molcolm back while the rest of us stand here and hold it."

He watched the hearse roll away in a cloud of dust, and beckoned to the others. "All right, men. Now let's star-r-rt hunting."

"What's the use?" Doc Hall asked. "Malcolm will be back as soon as he finds his film."

"He'll nae find it," Mister MacNab said owlishly, and patted the bulging pocket of his hunting jacket. "I gathered it up during lunch, and stowed it all here in my poke. Not only that, but the nearest camera store is sixty miles away. We'll have the whole afternoon to ourselves . . ."

"Worked like a charm," Judge Parker concluded to Uncle Perk. "We each got our limit, and were back at the house that evening before Malcolm and Fergus showed up." He chuckled with delight. "As I was saying, it takes a Scotchman to outsmart another—"

The string of sleigh bells inside the front door jangled, and Mister MacNab strolled dejectedly into the store. His tam-o'-shanter was pulled down over his ears, and his face wore an expression of glum defeat. "I've just had a letter from Cousin Fairgus," he reported. "D'ye ken that picture of the covey rise he took by accident? It turned out so well he sold it to *Field and Stream* for a handsome fee. Says it paid all the expenses of his tr-r-rip."

He opened the lower left-hand drawer of Uncle Perk's desk and took out a jug of Old Stump Blower.

"Aye, and that's not the wair-r-rst of it," he added. "Listen to the caption that Fair-r-rgus wrote for the picture." He unfolded the letter and adjusted his spectacles. "'Quail fever,'" he read aloud. "'Members of the famed Lower Forty were so shaken by this covey rise that they forgot to shoot.'"

Mister MacNab hooked a forefinger through the handle of the

jug and hoisted it on a bent forearm to his lips.

"And to think," he sighed, "that I had that nae-guid cousin of mine right in the sights of my gun." His sigh ended in a deep and mourning gulp.

THE POCOMOONSHINE COVER

A chill wind rattled the windows of Uncle Sid's camp, and the downdraft fanned the flames in the splitstone hearth, lighting the faces of the Lower Forty members gathered around the blaze. From the kitchen came the tantalizing aroma of roasting grouse and woodcock, which Mister MacNab had furnished for the Club's game supper. "Nice mess of birds you brought back from Maine, Mac," Judge Parker remarked as the donor arrived to join the party. "Looks like you had a pretty successful trip."

"Aye, it was successful in more ways than one," Mister Mac-Nab nodded, and pointed through the front window at the drive-way. "Pairhops ye've not had a good luik at my hair-r-rse."

The group stared at the ancient vehicle in amazement. Its scarred and battered body had been freshly painted a glossy black, tasseled velvet curtains hung in the windows, and it sported a brand-new set of whitewall tires. Mister MacNab took a fistful of expensive cigars from his pocket and handed them out to his fellow members. "A wee token of the occasion," he beamed.

Doc Hall sniffed a cigar appreciatively. "What did you do,

swipe the gold fillings from a client's teeth?"

Mister MacNab ignored him. "I'm hoppy to announce," he told the others, "that I've just signed a lucrative contr-r-ract with Mr. Pottle."

"Whoinell's Mr. Pottle?" the Judge inquired.

"Dinna tell me ye've nae heard of A.B. Pottle," Mister Mac-Nab gasped, "founder and president of the Pottle Bury Yourself Inter-r-rment Plan? Biggest self-sairvice cemetery chain east of the Mississippi. Surely ye recall the slogan, 'It's Cheaper to Die with Pottle.' " He bit off the end of a choice Havana and lit it with a flourish. "A.B.'s opening a branch cemetery here in Hardscrabble," he explained, exhaling a luxurious cloud of smoke, "and as a friend and hunting partner he's given me the exclusive hair-r-rse concession."

"How did you two happen to get so well acquainted?" Colonel Cobb asked curiously.

"That," Mister MacNab replied, "is why I went to Maine." He glanced through the kitchen door. "While Cousin Sidney is basting the bair-r-rds for tonight's feast I'll be glad to tell you the story . . ."

Mister MacNab had had his eye on the Pottle concession for some time, he confessed to his listeners, but A.B. was a hard man to locate, and he had begun to despair of making a personal contact. By good luck, however, he learned that the cemetery tycoon was an ardent woodcock hunter and had a lodge in northern Maine where he spent a couple of weeks every October. To Mister MacNab's further delight, it turned out that the Pottle lodge was only fifty miles from Saleratus, Maine, the home of a distant cousin named Sandy MacNab, who worked as a hunting guide. If he were to visit Cousin Sandy, he figured, he could not only arrange to meet the elusive Pottle but also save the expense of lodging and guide during his trip.

The plan had worked out to perfection. Any slight reluctance that Sandy expressed at entertaining a nonpaying guest was overcome by Mister MacNab's generous offer to bury his cousin's whole family free of charge, and that evening he set out with high hopes in search of Mr. Pottle. He had no trouble finding the lodge, and introduced himself to A.B. as a fellow woodcock hunter in search of advice. "How are the bair-r-rds around here?" he inquired.

"No good," Mr. Pottle sighed. "They all pulled out that last cold snap."

"Doubtless they flew south to Saleratus," Mister MacNab suggested artfully. "Woodcock are so thick down there ye can barely see to shoot. Pairhops ye'd let me show ye a few guid covers tomorrow."

"I'll take you up on that," A.B. said. "Meet you first thing in the morning."

Mister MacNab and his cousin were waiting in Sandy's jeep at the appointed rendezvous when the Pottle station wagon arrived. A.B. stepped out, followed by a short, stocky character in hunting clothes who gave Sandy a baleful glance. "This is Elmer, my guide," Mr. Pottle explained casually. "I brought him along to help carry the birds."

Sandy's eyes glinted, and Elmer bristled perceptibly. Slowly the two rival guides circled each other stiff-legged, growling under their breath. Mister MacNab acted quickly to avoid an outbreak of open hostilities. "Come on, let's get started," he called to Mr. Pottle. "We'll lead the way."

Sandy stepped on the accelerator, and the jeep shot forward, jolting Mister MacNab back in his seat. They roared through the village and down the highway at top speed, the tires squalling as they took the curves on two wheels. In the rear-vision mirror Mister MacNab could see the station wagon falling farther and farther behind. "What's ailing ye, m-mon?" he chattered, bouncing up and down as they hurtled over a rutted dirt road. "We'll lose the other c-car at this rate."

"That's what I'm countin' on," Sandy muttered, bending over the wheel.

"But, Sandy, we're all supposed to be hunting together—"

"I'm not a-gonna show another guide where my woodcock are," Sandy retorted. "Let him find his own covers."

The station wagon had dropped out of sight, and Mister Mac-Nab tried a desperate ruse. "Stop! Quick!" he shouted. "There's a gr-r-rouse beside the road."

Sandy braked the Jeep, and Mister MacNab climbed out and made a great show of stalking the imaginary grouse. He delayed until the station wagon caught up with them, and Mr. Pottle inquired irritably, "What's all the hurry?"

"We canna wait to show ye that guid cover I pr-r-romised." Mister MacNab cast a look of mute appeal at his cousin. "What's the name of it, Sondy?"

Sandy's lips were compressed in a tight line. "We call it the Pocomoonshine cover," he said. "Turn off at that lumber road just ahead, and follow it in about a mile and take the right fork, and then a left, and another right. You can't miss it." His lips curled at the corners in a cryptic smile. "Me an' Angus will hunt down the road a mite so's we won't get in your way."

The smile lingered on Sandy's face as the morning wore on, and Mister MacNab had the uncomfortable feeling that something was amiss. The dog was working well, and he lowered a couple of woodcock over solid points, but his cousin's cheerful manner disturbed him, and he did not like the occasional dry chuckle that he emitted. At last he rested his gun. "Luik here, Sondy, ye're sure there's bair-r-rds in that Pocomoonshine cover?"

"Who said anything about birds?" Sandy shrugged. "I told 'em where the cover was, that's all."

Mister MacNab let out his breath in a low moan. "What's it like?"

"Nothin' but blowdowns an' slash an' cranberry bog," Sandy crackled. "Nobody ain't got a woodcock out o' there in twenny years. They'll be lucky to get theirselves out."

Mister MacNab gazed at his cousin and fingered the trigger of his gun longingly. With an effort he controlled his urge, turned on his heel, and stalked back toward the jeep, muttering over his shoulder the single word, "Tr-r-aitor." The r's rattled like shot falling on the dry leaves behind him.

That night he drove over to the Pottle lodge in hopes of making amends. A.B. was standing on the front steps as he halted the car, and Mister MacNab lowered his head contritely. "I'm sorry about Pocomoonshine, A.B., but the fact is—"

"Sorry?" Mr. Pottle ran to shake his hand. "Never had such shooting in my life. The ground was white with spatter, I got my limit of woodcock in an hour, and knocked down a double in grouse. Best day's hunt I've had all fall." He grasped Mister Mac-Nab by the arm and led him into the lodge. "Let's have a drink together, and then I want to talk to you about signing a contract for the Hardscrabble hearse concession . . ."

Mister MacNab's narrative ended abruptly as Cousin Sid

brought in the platter of birds, basted with wine and broiled a golden brown. MacNab picked one up in his fingers, bit off a chunk, and nodded appreciatively. "Ye done yerself pr-r-roud, Sidney," he beamed. "I'll have to shoot some more woodcock for ye to cook next year."

"Going back to Maine again, Mac?" Judge Parker inquired.

"Aye," Mister MacNab nodded, "I've got a date to hunt with Mr. Pottle. Maybe I can get him to show me where that Pocomoonshine cover is."

"I bet your cousin would be glad to know," Colonel Cobb smiled.

Mister MacNab bit on a No. 9 lead pellet, removed it from his mouth, and dropped it on the plate with a definite clink.

"I'll nae be telling Sondy," he said grimly. "Let him find his own covers."

EVERYBODY GETS
BUCK FEVER

Judge Parker sauntered into Uncle Perk's store, thumbed through the latest copy of *Field & Stream* on the magazine rack, and glanced at a pile of bright-jacketed books for sale on the counter. His eyes lit on the title with interest. "*Upland Game Hunter's Bible,*" he read aloud to his fellow members. "Why, here's Dan Holland's new book."

"Does Dan belong to the Lower Forty?" inquired B.D. Banks, the club's most recent initiate.

"He's president of our Vermont chapter," the Judge explained, carrying a copy over to a pile of grain bags in a corner and settling himself contentedly. "Not to mention being one of the finest bird hunters and outdoor writers in this country." He turned the pages appreciatively. "He's taken all his own pictures, too."

"If ye think so much o' that there book," Uncle Perk grumbled, "why don't you buy it instead o' readin' it for nawthin'?" He rasped a match across the desk and held it to his corncob pipe. "I ain't runnin' a liberry for a bunch o' freeloadin' moochers."

Judge Parker ignored him. "Yes, sir, when Dan'l brings up that Greener of his and centers on a bird—" The Judge stared at the page, then leaned forward with an exclamation of surprise.

"Well, I'll be damned." He reread the paragraph and scowled. "It says here he missed one."

"Gun must have jammed or something," ventured Cousin Sid.

"No, he doesn't give any excuse. Just a plain case of buck fever, he admits frankly. Listen to this." Judge Parker adjusted his spectacles. " '. . . Out of a laurel patch almost at my feet a huge turkey thundered into the air, like a ruffed grouse magnified twenty times. I emptied my double almost before it hit my shoulder, then stood there and watched the tremendous bird — a target no one could miss — sail off through the oak woods.' " The Judge shook his head. "Imagine anyone with Dan Holland's experience getting buck fever."

"Never happened to you, did it, Judge?" Doc Hall goaded.

"Of course not," Judge Parker protested. "I wouldn't lose my head or get rattled or—"

"Then how do you explain that big old gobbler down in Alabama last year?" Doc reminded him, with a sly wink at the other members. "The Judge knocked the bird over," he informed them, "and he got so excited he laid down his gun beside a tree and ran across the clearing to pick the turkey up. And just then the bird came to life again and started galloping off, and there was the Judge with his gun fifty yards away, running after his gobbler and trying to catch it with his hat." He grinned at the Judge's reddening face. "I don't suppose you'd call that buck fever, would you, now?"

"Reminds me of shootin' geese with you in a blind in Ontario, Doc," Judge Parker retorted. "You stood up and picked out a big honker, took careful aim, and dropped it into the bay with one shot. Never saw anybody so cool and collected. 'Look at Doc,' I told myself, 'he's got nerves of steel.' And then you smiled and

[292]

said to me, 'Guess I'll go pick him up,' and you stepped very calmly over the side of the blind, into ten feet of water."

Doc waited until the laughter subsided. "That's no worse than the first time we hunted quail in Carolina together," he recalled to the Judge, "and a covey exploded in front of you, and you fired both barrels right into the ground." He chuckled to himself as the Judge fidgeted on the pile of grain bags. "Later you tried to insist that the reason you missed was because you didn't close your left eye when you sighted, and our old colored guide shrugged and said, 'Gen'lman fired so fast he didn't have time to shut his eyes.' "

"It's funny how the best hunters get lock-finger sometimes," Cousin Sid agreed. "I remember last fall when a woodcock got up in front of the Colonel here" — he nudged Colonel Cobb, who shifted in his chair uncomfortably — "and it climbed to the top of its spin and hung there, like a kite on a string, while the Colonel kept yanking and yanking at his trigger until he realized his safety was still on. Easiest shot you ever missed, Colonel," he chuckled.

"Wasn't any easier than that grouse your Duke puppy froze on," Colonel Cobb insisted. "You took a couple of steps past the dog, and an enormous cock roared up and took off on a straight-way course, and you just stood still with your gun in your hand, pointing your finger at the bird and shouting, 'There it goes!' I asked you why you didn't shoot, and all you could say was, 'I never thought of it.' "

Mister MacNab slapped his knees and rocked back and forth with merriment. "Aye, the things a mon will do when he get excited," he crackled. "Like the time Dexter fir-r-red through his bedroom window at a big buck in the yard, except that he for-r-rgot to open the window fairst."

Dexter Smeed bristled. "At least I didn't fire five rounds at a deer standing in the middle of an open field, and never touch it once." He added to the others: "Mac was so dumbfounded at missing it that he stood there, holding his empty rifle, and just then the deer gave a snort and turned and ran right at him, and Mac had to jump to keep from being trampled."

"That wasna buck fever," Mister MacNab said with dignity. "I was merely estimating the pr-r-rice of the ammunition I'd wasted."

Judge Parker handed the copy of *Upland Game Hunter's Bible* to B.D. Banks, and reached for Uncle Perk's jug. "I suppose there's bound to be a time, no matter how long you've hunted," he mused, "when your stomach suddenly goes tight, and your eyes water, and the end of your gun starts doing figure-eights in the air, and you discover you're shaking just as hard as though you were sighting on your first game. It takes a sportsman to confess it, that's all."

B.D. Banks turned the pages of the book thoughtfully. "Well, if it can happen to an expert like Dan, then I guess it isn't so bad when it hits a dub like me." He handed a couple of dollars to Uncle Perk. "It makes me feel better to read that everybody gets buck fever now and then."

Uncle Perk rang up the sale on his battered cash register, sank back in his swivel chair, and emitted a cloud of rank tobacco smoke. "Way I look at it," he murmured, retrieving his jug from the Judge, "if a feller didn't get a little mite excited oncet in a while, where would be the fun o' huntin'?"

AULD LANG SYNE

"Still coming down," Judge Parker reported, peering through the window of Cousin Sid's camp at the flakes falling steadily through the beam of light. Deep drifts covered the driveway as far as he could see, and a white shroud draped the MacNab hearse, parked before the cabin. "Not a chance of shoveling out before morning," he scowled. "We're here for the night."

"Snowbound on New Year's Eve!" Doc Hall extended his stockinged feet irritably toward the blazing hearth and glowered at Cousin Sid. "Thanks to good old Sidney's bright idea."

Cousin Sid winced as the other members of the Lower Forty fixed him with dire looks. Their present predicament was his own fault, he realized. He had insisted that the club drive down here to camp this afternoon for a rabbit hunt, and the sudden blizzard had caught them without warning. They had barely managed to struggle back to the cabin before the roads were completely blocked. The hearse was marooned only a few hundred yards from the highway, but it might as well have been at the North Pole. Avoiding their accusing eyes, Cousin Sid shouldered silently into his parka, and took down a pair of snowshoes from the wall.

"Where'n'ell are *you* goin'?" Uncle Perk asked in surprise.

"Thought I'd try to break through to the road," Cousin Sid replied, "and flag down the town tractor when it goes by. Zeb

Towle's very accommodating — maybe he'll tow us out."

"It's against the law for town equipment to plow a private driveway," Colonel Cobb pointed out.

"Zeb might make an exception," Cousin Sid said hopefully, "when I explain to him that we've all got dates back in Hardscrabble tonight." He opened the front door, knocking aside a couple of icicles that dangled from the eaves. "It's our only chance."

His fellow members watched his huddled figure disappear in the stormy darkness. Judge Parker filled a tin cup with Old Stump Blower and stirred it with the tip of an icicle. "I hate to think what our wives will say," he brooded, "if we don't take them to that New Year's Eve Ball at the club."

"I not only r-r-rented a tuxedo for the occasion," Mister Mac-Nab mourned, reaching for Uncle Perk's jug, "but what's wor-r-rse, I paid for it in advance."

"A fine way to see the old year out," Doc Hall grumbled as he filled his own cup, "stuck way down here in this dreary camp."

Uncle Perk retrieved his jug. "Wal, now," he mused, "there's another way o' lookin' at it."

"How do you mean?" Judge Parker inquired.

"Some folks might figger it was more comf'table sittin' around like this in ole huntin' clothes," he suggested, "instead o' gittin' all dolled up in a boiled shirt an' tight shoes an' goin' to a dance."

The Judge's eyes widened. "I never thought of that," he murmured. "Why, I've been trying for months to think of some excuse to get out of that ball tonight."

"Nothing I hate worse than dancing," Doc Hall admitted. "I can walk ten miles through a rabbit swamp, but sliding around a hardwood floor gives me blisters."

Mister MacNab brightened. "Aye, and luik at the money we save on champagne," he chortled. "Here the dr-r-rinks are free."

The jug of Old Stump Blower made the rounds again. "After all, what's better than celebrating the new year before a fire," Colonel Cobb said sentimentally, "with a group of old friends you've hunted and fished with for the past twelve months."

"Sharing the same memories," Judge Parker nodded.

"Looking back on all the good times we've had together," Doc Hall agreed.

"Should auld acquaintance be for-r-rgot—" Mister MacNab sang, a trifle off key.

"And never brought to mind," the others joined in, their voices blending in close harmony. "Should auld acquaintance be forgot, and days of auld lang—"

They halted abruptly as a heavy rumbling and clanking sounded in the driveway and a pair of bright headlights shone through the window. The roar of the motor ceased, and presently they heard boots stamping off snow on the granite sill. Cousin Sid shoved open the door, his frostbitten lips cracking in a stiff smile. "Zeb saved the day," he announced. "He's got us all plowed out."

Zeb Towle clumped into the cabin behind him and took a drink that Cousin Sid poured for him. "Allus glad to be accommodatin'," he said.

The members gazed at their rescuer in glum silence. "Don't you think it's kind of risky, driving home through a blizzard?" Judge Parker protested feebly.

"Oh, the snow's stopped," Cousin Sid told him. He glanced at the battered alarm clock on the mantel. "It's only a little after ten. We can still make the dance before midnight if we hurry."

Mister MacNab shifted uncomfortably in his chair. "I'm afraid I couldna get the hair-r-rse started in this cold."

"We can hitch it to the rear of the tractor," Cousin Sid said, "and Zeb will tow us." The others made no move to rise. "Come on, we'd better get going."

Uncle Perk reached quickly for the jug of Old Stump Blower. "Better have another li'l drink before ye leave, Zeb," he urged, filling his glass again. "After all, it's New Year's Eve . . ."

The hands of the alarm clock stood at five of twelve, the empty jug lay on the floor beside the hearth, and the celebrants were sprawled in somnolent postures around the sweltering cabin. Uncle Perk yanked the cork from a fresh jug, but Zeb shook his head. "No more f'r me," he said thickly. "Gotta plow the rest of that highway, if I c'n find it." He stumbled to the door. "You fellers comin'?"

"I'm 'fraid it's too late now," Doc Hall said with an elaborate sigh of regret, "but we 'preciate it jus' the same."

"You might call our wives when you get to a phone," Judge Parker added, "and tell 'em we'll be home soon's we can find a show snuvel." He corrected himself. "I mean a slow shover." He gave it up. "Jus' tell 'em we'll be home t'morrow."

"Allus glad t'be 'commodatin'," said Zeb, striding through the door and sprawling face forward in a drift. He rose, blowing snow crystals from his mustache, and climbed into the tractor. "Hap' New Year!" he shouted, and stepped on the starter.

The members waved cordially as the tractor turned in a wide circle around the driveway, knocking down a stack of firewood and demolishing Cousin Sid's privy, then set out in a zigzag course toward the highway. Its roar was drowned by the sudden clanging of the alarm clock on the mantel.

"Midnight," Uncle Perk said, refilling the tin cups all around.

The members of the Lower Forty placed their arms around one another's shoulders in a cheerful circle. "An' here's a hand, my tr-r-rusty frien'," Mister MacNab began, leading the chorus, "and gie's a hand o' thine . . ."

The rumble of the tractor receded in the distance, punctuated by a sharp rattling sound as Zeb scraped along a length of picket fence beside the highway. The tractor crossed a snow-covered lawn, took off one wing of a summer cottage, and started toward the hill, mowing down trees and shrubs. The members chuckled and moved back to the jug.

"We'll tak a cup o' kindness yet," the Club sang, their heads bent close together, "and drink to auld lang syne!"

They clanked their tin cups and emptied them in unison. Through the window they could see the headlights of the tractor, wandering back and forth over the hillside in an erratic figure-eight. Doc Hall's arm was around Cousin Sid, and he beamed contentedly. "Bes' Noor's Eve we ev'r had," he said, "thangs to good ole Sidney's brigh' idear."

PART II

YOU CAN
ALWAYS TELL
A FISHERMAN

They say you don't really have to be crazy to be a fisherman, but it helps. Well, a dyed-in-the-wool dry-fly addict is somebody that even *fishermen* think is crazy. He belongs to an exclusive clique in the angling fraternity, a sort of circle within the circle. He's the purest of the purists. He's also the world's worst snob. He looks down his nose at plug fishermen, he snubs spinning fishermen, he regards bait fishermen with icy contempt. The difference is that all the others fish for fish. He fishes for fun.

The object of a dry fly, its advocates will tell you, is to simulate a natural insect on the water, in order to hoodwink a trout. Don't you believe them. In the first place, no trout in his right mind would confuse this feathered imitation with any known species of edible bug. Experts who have spent a lot of time lying around the bottoms of pools, looking at things from the fish's point of view, report that a dry fly floating downstream is so magnified by the water that it resembles a Catalina flying boat coming in for a landing. The leader is approximately the size of an eight-inch hawser; and clearly visible behind it, if the trout pauses long enough to look, are two enormous hobnailed brogans and a pair of ballooning waders, past which the stream foams and gurgles warningly. To make the deception even more apparent, the face of the fisherman himself is mirrored upside down in the water, his expression distorted by the current into a Frankenstein leer. My theory is that the whole spectacle strikes the trout so funny that he laughs until the tears come to his eyes, thus blinding him, and he inadvertently inhales the fly while gasping for breath.

The real object of a dry fly is not to please the fish, but to please the fisherman. He selects a particular pattern from his flybox because it happens to appeal to his mood of the moment. Maybe it has some sentimental association, maybe it just matches his shirt. His satisfaction lies in dropping it cocked at the head of a run, and watching it ride back down the swift current, bobbing lightly over a riffle, gliding around a boulder, reversing its course, and halting poised for an instant in a back eddy under the bank. If a trout happens to share his enthusiasm for the fly, well and good. The angler plays his adversary on a taut line until the fish is exhausted, and leads it carefully to shore. Then he kneels beside it and grips it firmly around the body — first wetting his hands so he will not damage its protective oily coating — and removes the barb from its upper lip. He holds the trout facing upstream a moment longer, until its gills begin to move regularly, and then he spreads his hand and watches it dart back into the current with a farewell flick of its tail.

At least, he never comes home empty-handed. His creel may be barren at the end of the day, but he brings back other things: the sound of running water and smell of wet rocks, the memory of a grouse drumming on a log, a beaver's V-shaped wake as it crossed the pool, the sudden skirl of a kingfisher like a winding reel. They will last longer than a fish curling in a pan.

Dry-fly enthusiasts have long since given up trying to defend this position to non-fly fishermen. When a minnow fisherman suggests with a condescending smile that the angler could get his limit much quicker if he used a live shiner instead of a bunch of feathers, he does not argue. He simply hits the skeptic over the head with his own minnow bucket, and goes on fly-fishing in sullen silence. A friend of mine, an ardent purist, was challenged once by a golfing acquaintance as he turned loose a large trout he had just netted. "Why go to all that trouble to catch a fish," the exasperated golfer demanded, "if you don't want to eat it?"

"Do you eat golf balls?" my friend inquired.

The answer, of course, is that fly fishing is a sport, just as golf is a sport, with its own self-imposed rules. Granted that the angler could take more fish if he used nightcrawlers or, for that matter, dynamite. By the same token, the golfer could achieve a hole in one if he picked up the ball and carried it across the green and dropped it in the hole with his fingers. The bigger the handicap, the better the contest. A purist uses a split-bamboo rod that weighs only a couple of ounces; he ties his fly to a leader as fine as a cobweb; he even files the barb off the hook to lengthen the odds against himself. I suppose the trout think he's crazy, too.

It is because they're so generally misunderstood that fly fishermen tend to be antisocial, and stick by themselves in small groups at social gatherings. There's nothing like the joy of a devout angler when he finds a dinner companion who shares his hobby. A couple of antique collectors are delighted to discover a mutual interest in pewter snuffboxes; a pair of camera bugs will talk each other's ear off; but when two dry-fly fanatics get together, the rest of the guests might as well go home. Long after the party is over, they'll still be huddled in a corner, discussing the technique of the roll cast or debating the comparative merits of the fan wing versus the spent wing, while their wives drum their fingers on the arms of their chairs and the hostess glances significantly at the clock on the mantel. This is why fly fishermen don't get asked out to dinner much.

It's a language all its own. Don't call the purist's rod a pole, for instance, or refer to his reel as a pulley, or his line a string. Don't say he *caught* a trout; he *takes* trout, and *kills* salmon. Above all, don't ask him why on earth he has to buy another rod when his closet is bulging with them already. No matter how much equipment an angler has, he always needs more. Hunting tigers with elephants may represent a large initial outlay as a sport, but once you've acquired a string of pachyderms your investment is largely over. Not the fisherman. He may possess a thousand feathered lures, stuffed into aluminum cases or empty tobacco tins or old typewriter ribbon containers, but he can't pass a tackle store on his way home without adding a half-dozen new ones to his collection. Every evening, when supper is over, he dumps them all out on the dining-room table like a miser hoarding his coins, fluffing and primping and combing out their hackles, and putting them back in individual compartments with their names on the covers: Royal Coachman and Gordon Quill and Whirling Blue Dun, Wickham's Fancy and Pink Lady, Hare's Ear and Cow Dung. He never fishes with them, of course. When the time comes, he'll tie on the same matted fly with its body unwound and both wings gone that he's been using day after day for the past ten years.

Every angler has his favorite pattern. Some like light flies, others prefer dark, one fisherman may go in for large White Millers, another may swear by miniscule Black Gnats, still another may favor a full-bodied tie to suggest a female insect ovipositing on the water. Personally I have a pet fly called the Corey Ford, which was tied by Walt Dette of the Beaverkill and which has heavy gray hackle and a cream-colored body. My own hackle is rather sparse, particularly on top, and my body is more or less the conventional pink, but otherwise it is a good resemblance. I haven't taken a trout on it yet, but I like the looks of it in the band of my hat.

It's a year-round disease. Dry-fly fever terminates sometime late in December, when the angler gets the last of his tackle put away, and starts again early in January when he hauls it all out to get ready for next season. The first symptoms show up early in the spring. The victim becomes increasingly irrational around the office, and is given to sitting behind his desk and staring out the window for long stretches of time, drawing fish doodles on his blotter or winding his pencil sharpener with a preoccupied frown. He grows more and more erratic and absent-minded as the season draws closer, and when he meets his wife on the street he tips his hat politely and walks past her with a faintly puzzled glance. He ignores his family, and lets his business go to pot. Night after night he sits in his living room in moody silence, thumbing through a fishing catalogue or gazing dreamily at the stuffed trout over the fireplace.

His tension mounts to a peak as the long-awaited moment arrives. On the eve of opening day, the house echoes to the slamming of bureau drawers upstairs, the thump of tossed boots, and an occasional bellowed inquiry from the second-floor landing: "Has anybody seen my wading socks, the ones with the red tops?" Everything is a shambles. His bedroom floor is littered with freshly dressed flies, and looks like the aftermath of a pillow fight. His waders are hanging inside the shower stall, turned inside out and filled with water to see if they leak. His greased line zigzags back and forth in a cat's cradle down the staircase. Varnished rod sections dangle from the living-room chandelier. His leaders are soaking in the kitchen sink. The entire contents of the coat closet have been tossed into the front hall in a frenzied search for his canvas fishing jacket. The children have restrung his landing net for a badminton racket. His wife has given away his old hat to the Salvation Army. Along about midnight he decides to grab a little sleep, and finish packing in the morning.

He has set his alarm clock for 4:00 a.m. in order to get to the stream ahead of the other fishermen, who have all set their alarms for the same reason. Unfortunately he sleeps right through the bell, and is awakened by the insistent beeping of his partner's horn in the driveway. He dresses in frantic haste, while his wife makes some sandwiches and puts them in his jacket, where they will be discovered when he goes through his pockets after the fishing season is over. He gallops downstairs two steps at a time, pulling on his waders as he runs, and bolts out the front door, returning almost immediately because his suspenders are looped around the newel post. He is halfway to the stream before he remembers that he left his pipe on the hall table.

It is long after dark when he staggers home. He collapses into a chair in the living room, extends a foot wearily so that one of his offspring can pull off his wading boot, and accepts a highball from his wife with a deep sigh. The bridge of his nose is sunburned a lobster red. His lips are puffed and cracked. One eye is swollen shut where a black fly nailed him, and he has rubbed some insect repellant into the other. He has worn a blister on his heel, because a pebble got down inside his sock, and he skinned both knees when he climbed a tree to retrieve his fly. His arms ache, his knuckles are raw, he stuck a fishhook in his thumb, and he's caught a severe cold from falling in. He hasn't seen a sign of a trout all day, but that doesn't matter.

He'll be right out there on the stream again tomorrow . . .

A DIALOGUE
FOR AUTUMN

Time: Late October. Call it Halloween. The height of the fall
color is already past; on the hillsides the birch thickets are bare,
and the leaves are off the alders in the swamps. You can see to
shoot now. This afternoon the sun was warm, but walking back
to the jeep at dusk it felt good to put your hands in your pockets.
When you bit into an apple, the juice was cold and hurt your
teeth. Probably there'll be a frost tonight, and the woodcock will
be moving with the full moon.

Place: A hunting camp. Actually it is Sid Hayward's camp, on
the shore of Pleasant Lake. But it could be any hunting camp.
A couple of shotguns are standing in the corner with cleaning rags
and oil, and two empty gamebags are hanging on the wall, and
two pairs of hunting boots are drying before the fire. The portable radio is turned on; the six o'clock news should tell how
Dartmouth made out this afternoon against Harvard. A pan of
water is heating on the stove, and the room smells of wood smoke
and nitro-solvent and pipe tobacco and boot-dubbing and wet
dogs — the smell of any hunting camp anywhere.

Characters: Two bird hunters and two bird dogs. The dogs are
big rangy English setters, sired by the same father, old Duke de
Coverly, the great New England grouse dog. The hunters call

each other Cousin Corey and Cousin Sid because their dogs are brothers. Corey's dog is called Cider, because he works in the fall, and Sid's is called John Buchan, after a favorite author, Bucky for short. As the curtain rises, both dogs are lying in front of the fire with their eyes shut, occasionally sighing luxuriously and spreading the pads of their forefeet to the blaze. Sid is peeling some potatoes for supper, and Corey is sipping a Scotch highball.

COREY (*Without moving*): Sure I can't help you with these potatoes, Cousin Sidney?

SID: It's okay, Cousin Corey. You just relax. That last hour was pretty rugged.

COREY: I'd sure like to know where those dogs were all afternoon. I bet I walked ten miles looking for Cider. I shouted till I was hoarse.

SID: Usually Bucky comes right to me when I call. He's very well disciplined.

COREY (*quickly*): I almost never have to shout at Cider. Just wave my hand is all.

SID: They must have been over in the next county somewhere. I couldn't even hear the sound of their bells. You don't suppose Cider got on a rabbit, do you?

COREY (*indignantly*): Cider never chases rabbits. Maybe Bucky jumped a deer.

SID (*bristling*): Buck doesn't run deer.

(*As their voices rise Cider stirs and opens his eyes. Bucky's muzzle is resting across Cider's flank; he lifts his head and looks up questioningly at the hunters.*)

SID: Best cover of the day, too. All those deserted farms and old apple orchards. That's why I'd been saving it for last. (*He *shakes his head.)* And then they had to run away and spoil it.

COREY (*sadly*): It takes a lot of patience, handling a dog. I wish I knew what went on in Cider's mind sometimes.

SID: Look at Bucky now, lying there so innocent and all, looking at me. Did you ever see anybody look at you like that? I wonder what he's thinking . . .

(Cider *yawns, stretches, and sits up. He speaks to* Bucky *in the same tone of voice the hunters use. The only difference is that when the dogs are speaking you can hear all the other sounds that people never hear: the silent pad of furred feet, the beat of unseen wings overhead, the thin shrill of night insects too high for the human ear.*)

CIDER (*to* Bucky): Brother, am I hungry! I could eat a horse.

BUCKY (*rolling over onto his back and exposing his damp belly to the heat*): That's what you'll get, too. I saw the boss put a package of horsemeat in the icebox this morning.

CIDER: I wish they'd quit talking and start supper. (*Hopefully.*) Look, my old man's getting up now.

BUCKY: He's just going over to pour himself another drink. I don't like to mention it, Cider, but isn't he hitting it up pretty hard lately? He seemed to be panting quite a bit coming up that last hill.

CIDER (*quickly*): Matter of fact, I never thought your old man would make the first hour this morning, coming through those alders.

BUCKY (*indignantly*): I noticed your old man had to sit down on a stump a couple of times to get his wind.

CIDER (*bristling*): He was just waiting for your old man to catch up with him . . .

(*Both dogs are sitting up now, glaring at each other and making rumbling noises in their throats. The hunters look at them in surprise.*)

[313]

COREY (*to* Cider): Charge, Cider! What's the matter with you?

SID (*to* Bucky): You ought to be ashamed of yourself, Bucky. Your own brother!

COREY: I guess they must be tired, after that long tour they took. It's still a mystery to me what got into them today.

SID: It's funny how they'll act. Sometimes they won't do anything right. Like for instance that cover we worked this morning on the Wilmot Road; usually there's a lot of birds in there, but Bucky wouldn't hunt it the way I wanted. I figured we'd work downhill and come out where we left the jeep, but Bucky kept circling around and getting out in front. I couldn't keep him in.

COREY: Cider did the same thing. Ran right down through the middle of it, without so much as casting either side. Wouldn't pay any attention to me at all.

SID: Sometimes they seem to understand you, and other times they're — I don't know — stubborn.

COREY: If they could only talk. If we could just *explain* to them . . .

(Bucky *is curled in a tight knot with his head on his hind legs.* Cider *has discovered a cocklebur in the fur on his chest and is tugging at it with his teeth.*)

CIDER: You know, Buck, I was just wondering.

BUCKY (*sleepily*): What?

CIDER: Do you suppose they really have a sense of smell?

BUCKY: Who?

CIDER: People (*He spits out the bur.*) Take my old man; sometimes I don't think he's got any nose at all.

BUCKY: My old man's the same way. All he uses his nose for is to keep his glasses on.

CIDER: Like for instance that cover we worked this morning;

[314]

that place was simply *loaded* with birds. I never smelt anything like it. I got so excited I started shivering all over. There were five grouse running ahead of us under those apple trees—

BUCKY: Six. I smelt where another one had been over by the stone wall. It went out before we got to it.

CIDER: That's what I mean. If they had any sense of smell at all, they'd never have worked that cover the way they did. They'd have started us down at the bottom of the hill and worked us back up through it against the wind—

BUCKY: Instead of yelling at us and calling us back, and making us work downwind so we couldn't smell a grouse until we were right on it.

CIDER: And then they complain about the birds getting up way ahead.

BUCKY: If we could only tell them! If we could only make them understand . . .

(Sid *sets down the pot of potatoes and fills his pipe.* Corey *settles back deeper into his easy chair and sips his highball reflectively.*)

COREY: Have you noticed how much wilder the birds are this year? They keep getting up way ahead.

SID: It seems to me they fly faster these days, too. I was reading a study the other day; it said their speed is in ratio to the increased hunting pressure. I think that's what it said.

COREY: That must be it. Our timing hasn't kept up with the pressure curve.

SID: Or maybe it has something to do with atmospheric conditions. That might be the explanation.

COREY: There must be some reason why we didn't get any birds. Maybe the dogs were a little off today. I had a grouse this morning that got up out of some juniper where Cider was pointing, an easy going-away shot. I know I was right on it with both barrels, but Cider couldn't seem to find it. I don't know what was wrong with him.

SID: It's funny how a dog will refuse to hunt dead. I had the same thing happen with a woodcock. It came up out of the alders and I nailed it right at the top of the spin, a perfect shot, but do you think Bucky could locate it? Never even smelt where it fell. I hate to lose a dead bird like that . . .

(Corey *and* Sid *shake their heads sadly.* Cider *discovers another bur in his fur, yanks it out, and spits it on the floor.*)

CIDER (*to* Bucky): Maybe they can't smell, but they make up for it in other ways.

BUCKY (*trying to sleep*): What ways?

CIDER: Well, they can do things we can't do. For instance, they can shoot.

BUCKY: Who says they can shoot? I suppose that grouse that got up out of the juniper in front of your old man this morning — an easy going-away shot if I ever saw one — I suppose you call *that* shooting. Missed it with both barrels.

CIDER (*reacting*): I wouldn't say your old man was exactly hot on that woodcock you were pointing in the alders. I had to laugh — making you hunt dead, and I could still see it flying. He never touched a feather.

BUCKY (*bristling*): Listen, bub, my old man could shoot rings around your old man—

CIDER (*growling*): My old man could wipe your old man's eye—

(*Both dogs have risen and are facing each other stiff-legged, the hackles standing up on their shoulders.*)

COREY and SID (*simultaneously*): Cider! Bucky! SHUT UP!

COREY (*frowning*): What's got into those two dogs tonight?

SID: They're restless. Maybe they want to go out. (*He opens the door. Both dogs exit hurriedly.*)

SID (*continuing*): While I'm up I might as well get supper started.

COREY (*without moving*): Sure I can't give you a hand with those steaks, Cousin Sid?

SID: It's okay, Cousin Corey. No trouble at all. Just mix yourself another drink and relax.

COREY (*sweetening his highball*): Come to think of it, you know, it must be hard on a dog, not understanding what people are saying. Take posted land, for instance. How can you explain to a dog that you can't hunt in a certain field where you know there are birds, because a printed sign says you mustn't? I guess it's pretty confusing at times.

SID: Or closed seasons. How can a dog understand why we suddenly start shooting on the first of October, and suddenly stop again on the first of December?

COREY: If we could only tell them a few things, think how much easier it would be.

SID: Or would it?

COREY: How do you mean?

SID: Did you ever stop to think what they might tell us? The birds we put up wild, the shots we miss. (*He lowers his voice.*) Take that woodcock this morning, for instance. If Bucky could talk, I might find out I never hit it at all.

COREY (*sheepishly*): Now you mention it, I might have missed that grouse.

(*Outside, in the moonlight, the two dogs are completing their evening rounds.*)

BUCKY (*to* Cider): Those two farm collies have been around here again this afternoon.

CIDER: I'll check behind the woodshed. (*Sniffing.*) Two squirrels, some stinkbirds, a rabbit or something, and a skunk.

BUCKY: Listen, the woodcock are moving. I heard one go over.

CIDER (*excitedly*): Wait till I tell the old man!

BUCKY: How are you going to tell him? You can't make him understand you.

CIDER: That's right. I forgot. (*He writes his name dejectedly on the corner of the woodpile, under* Bucky's.) It's too bad we can't tell them a few things, isn't it?

BUCKY: Such as?

CIDER: Well, this afternoon, for instance. That last cover we hunted. There we were, locked up tight on those four birds, standing shoulder to shoulder. Not a tinkle from our bells. You had a pair in front of you and I had a pair, and they were really sitting for us. I can see them now, looking back at us and scolding a little and running off a few steps and then freezing again. The drool was running right down my jaws.

BUCKY: I know. I bet we held those birds for half an hour. And all the time I could hear your old man and mine, yelling their heads off and blowing their whistles and calling us. They walked within a hundred yards of us, but they never saw us. What a shot it would have been!

CIDER: That's what I mean. If we could have told them they'd have had a perfect chance for a double apiece.

BUCKY: Did you ever think, though — suppose we could tell them? Suppose every time they went out everything was perfect. What would happen then? They'd get their limit the first hour, and the hunt would be over. It would be too perfect. It wouldn't be fun anymore.

COREY and SID (*their voices calling offstage*): Come, Cider! Here, Bucky, Bucky!

CIDER (*to* Bucky): They're calling us. Maybe it's supper.

BUCKY (*moodily*): Horsemeat.

CIDER: That's one thing I wish we could tell them. I wish we could make them understand about horsmeat.

(Corey *holds open the door and the two dogs enter, wagging their tails expectantly. The room smells of fresh-broiled steak and melted butter and coffee perking on the stove.*)

SID (*abruptly*): Darn! I forgot to take their horsemeat out to thaw.

COREY (*after a moment's hesitation*): You know, Sid, there's actually more steak here than I can eat.

SID: It's a pretty big portion for me, too.

COREY: I mean, they've been working hard and all, and I was just thinking . . .

SID (*dividing his steak*): I was just thinking the same thing.

(Bucky *gulps down half of* Sid's *steak, and grins at* Cider.)

BUCKY (*to* Cider): What was it we wanted to tell them just now?

(Cider *swallows half of Corey's steak, and grins back.*)

CIDER (*to* Bucky): I guess we understand each other well enough.

(*The two dogs crawl up into the easy chairs and settle themselves comfortably.* Corey *and* Sid *hesitate in front of the chairs, look at each other and shrug. They sit on the floor beside the dogs.*)

JUST A DOG

Ray P. Holland
Editor of *Field & Stream*
New York, NY

Dear Ray:

I know this is a kind of unusual request; but I'd like to borrow some space in your columns to write an open letter to a man I do not know. He may read it if it is in your columns; or some of his friends may notice his name and ask him to read it. You see, it has to do with sport — a certain kind of sport.

The man's name is Sherwood G. Coggins. That was the name on his hunting license. He lives at 1096 Lawrence Street, in Lowell. He says he is in the real estate and insurance business in Lowell.

This weekend, Mr. Coggins, you drove up into New Hampshire with some friends to go deer hunting. You went hunting on my property here in Freedom. You didn't ask my permission; but that was all right. I let people hunt on my land. Only, while you were hunting, you shot and killed my bird dog.

Oh, it was an accident, of course. You said so yourself. You said that you saw a flick of something in the bushes, and you shot it. All you saw was the flash of something moving, and you brought up your rifle and fired. It might have been another hunter. It might have been a child running through the woods. As it turned out, it was just a dog.

Just a dog, Mr. Coggins. Just a little English setter I have hunted with for quite a few years. Just a little female setter who was very proud and staunch on point, and who always held her head high, and whose eyes had the brown of October in them. We had hunted a lot of alder thickets and apple orchards together, the little setter and I. She knew me, and I knew her, and we liked to hunt together. We had hunted woodcock together this fall, and grouse, and in another week we were planning to go down to Carolina together and look for quail. But yesterday morning she ran down in the fields in front of my house, and you saw a flick in the bushes, and you shot her.

You shot her through the back, you said, and broke her spine. She crawled out of the bushes and across the field toward you, dragging her hind legs. She was coming to you to help her. She was a gentle pup, and nobody had ever hurt her, and she could

[322]

not understand. She began hauling herself toward you, and looking at you with her brown eyes, and you put a second bullet through her head. You were sportsman enough for that.

I know you didn't mean it, Mr. Coggins. You felt very sorry afterward. You told me that it really spoiled your deer hunting the rest of the day. It spoiled my bird hunting the rest of a lifetime.

At least, I hope one thing, Mr. Coggins. That is why I am writing you. I hope that you will remember how she looked. I hope that the next time you raise a rifle to your shoulder you will see her over the sights, dragging herself toward you across the field, with blood running from her mouth and down her white chest. I hope you will see her eyes.

I hope you will always see her eyes, Mr. Coggins, whenever there is a flick in the bushes and you bring your rifle to your shoulder before you know what is there.

Corey Ford

FOREWORD FROM . . .

HAS ANYBODY
SEEN ME LATELY?

A couple of years ago, while I was walking upstairs, it struck me a trifle breathlessly that the steps were steeper than they used to be. What's more, I reflected as I climbed, they seemed to be using finer print in telephone directories lately, and my shoelaces were farther away when I reached down to tie them. So I decided to sit down on the landing and record some of these changes that were taking place around me in an essay entitled "How to Guess Your Age."

People who read the piece when it was published evidently felt that it applied to them. It seemed so personal, in fact, that they made typewritten copies of my little essay and mailed them to their friends. Whereupon their friends were so pleased that they made carbon copies and mailed them to other friends, and all these friends in turn made mimeographed copies and sent them along to all *their* friends. I began to feel like the composer of the original chain letter. I was well on my way to becoming the most widely quoted author in America.

The only trouble was that I was also the most anonymous.

Somehow, in the course of copying the piece, my name invariably got lost. People would leave off the by-line, or substitute their own instead, and forward it with a little card reading, "Compliments of the J.S. Printwhistle Rutabaga Co., Inc." Executives sent it out as their personal Christmas card. Fraternal organizations distributed it gratis at their weekly luncheons. I received quite a few copies myself, usually with a sneering comment on the margin such as, "why don't you write something funny like this for a change?" Several hopeful authors submitted it to the *Reader's Digest*, and I had some difficulty establishing ownership when the *Digest* reprinted the piece. Before Doubleday & Company could bring it out in book form, Mr. Ken McCormick had received five other copies in his mail — under five other names. I barely got under the wire with my own book.

To make matters worse, the thing began popping up everywhere in business house organs and advertising pamphlets. It was published in such varied media as the Juneau (Alaska) *Empire*; the Automobile Old-Timers Club of Gary, Indiana; the Bodine Automatic Tapping, Drilling and Screw-Inserting Machinery Corporation; the Harvard Class of '17; the Ordnance Department of the Frankford Arsenal; the *Journal of the American Medical Association* (I think they called it "How to Guess Your Ague"); and the Pardeeville-Wyocema *Times*. Keeping track of the piece was like chasing a toupee in a wind tunnel. A veteran in a Walla Walla hospital submitted it in a national contest and won first prize. I found a copy of it one day in my mailbox at the New York hotel where I was staying, printed up in an attractive gift booklet with the compliments of the management.

Still the thing kept snowballing. Columnists reprinted it all over the country, under their own signatures. The Hallmark people borrowed chunks of it for a commercial birthday greeting card. I put the matter in the hands of my lawyers, and before I knew it I had more suits than Adolphe Menjou. At one time, I remember, I was plagiarized simultaneously by seven life insurance companies (life insurance people have a morbid interest in getting old); the *State*, a weekly survey of North Carolina; a large chain store (which ran my essay with a modest admission of authorship by the president, together with his photograph); a plumbing supplies company; the U.S. Army; and Arthur Godfrey.

Mr. Frank Sullivan took up what he would doubtless call the cudgels in my defense in his review of the book in the New York *Herald Tribune*. "The whole affair," wrote Mr. Sullivan, "is an amusing commentary on the casual contempt with which most Americans regard the Profession of Writing. They would not steal a writer's watch (if he had one, which is unlikely), but they think no more of stealing his brains than they would of stashing a souvenir ashtray from the Stork Club. They do not feel that a piece of writing constitutes a property, since they do not think any effort or talent is required to write. They could write as well as Ernest Hemingway themselves if they weren't so tired when they got home from the office or filling station . . . Corey Ford, like Queen Victoria, to whom he is not related, was not amused at this blithe kleptomania, and he sued a horde or two of the pirates who had lifted his handiwork. That is why, to this reviewer, one of the most comical lines in the book (and their number is legion) is the one on the first page which says: 'All rights reserved.' "

The strangest part of it was that the people who stole my piece were highly indignant when I objected. I just tossed it off for a laugh, didn't I? Where was my sense of humor, anyway? A manufacturer in Middletown, Connecticut, who had been handing out hundreds of copies to customers, was outraged when I suggested that some token remuneration might be in order. "Why, that piece about getting old was delivered last June in New Haven as the Alumni Day address by a member of the Yale class of 1900," he snorted, "and I took it down word for word." A textile firm in Georgia, which had reprinted it in an illustrated brochure at considerable expense, threatened countersuit. When Mr. Godfrey used it on the air, without credit, of course, my lawyers suggested that he might acknowledge my authorship on a subsequent program. Mr. Godfrey's lawyers replied brusquely that the U.S. copyright laws were written in 1913, before the invention of radio, and consequently Mr. Godfrey had the legal right to steal anything he wanted. As far as I know, he still does.

After the publication of the book the wholesale pilfering of the piece began to fall off (though only last week I spotted it again in a signed column in the Washington *Post*), but my troubles were not over. Requests for permission to reprint it began to pour in. Anthologists wanted to include it in collections of humor they were putting together. I had to hire an extra secretary to handle appeals from high school graduating classes, animal hospitals, and private charities who offered credit but not cash. One night I was awakened at 3:00 a.m. by a collect telegram, and after I'd paid for it ($3.76) I discovered it was from the National Pear Growers Association, inquiring whether it would be okay to hand out my essay free with each box of pears. I wired back that people should be able to guess the age of a pear without help from me. Yes, I sent it collect.

I have no idea how many anthologies and encyclopedias and

treasuries are using the piece today; but I've made up my mind about one thing. It's time I got in on the act, too. If other people can make a living by picking my brains, I'm going to pick them, too. That is why I've collected myself in a book under my own name for a change.

I can always sue myself later.

HOW TO GUESS YOUR AGE

It seems to me that they are building staircases steeper than they used to. The risers are higher, or there are more of them, or something. Maybe this is because it is so much farther today from the first floor to the second floor, but I've noticed it is getting harder to make two steps at a time anymore. Nowadays it is all I can do to make one step at a time.

Another thing I've noticed is the small print they're using lately. Newspapers are getting farther and farther away when I hold them, and I have to squint to make them out. The other day I had to back halfway out of a telephone booth in order to read the number on the coin box. It is obviously ridiculous to suggest that a person my age needs glasses, but the only other way I can find out what's going on is to have somebody read aloud to me, and that's not too satisfactory because people speak in such low voices these days that I can't hear them very well.

Everything is farther than it used to be. It's twice the distance from my house to the station now, and they've added a fair-sized hill that I never noticed before. The trains leave sooner, too. I've given up running for them, because they start faster these days when I try to catch them. You can't depend on timetables anymore, and it's no use asking the conductor. I ask him a dozen times a trip if the next station is where I get off, and he always says it isn't. How can you trust a conductor like that? Usually I gather up my bundles and put on my hat and coat and stand in the aisle a couple of stops away, just to make sure I don't go past my destination. Sometimes I make double sure by getting off at the station ahead.

A lot of other things are different lately. Barbers no longer hold up a mirror behind me when they've finished, so I can see the back of my head, and my wife has been taking care of the tickets lately when we go to the theater.

They don't use the same material in clothes anymore, either. I've noticed that all my suits have a tendency to shrink, especially in certain places, such as around the waist or in the seat of the pants, and the laces they put in shoes nowadays are harder to reach.

Revolving doors revolve much faster than they used to. I have to let a couple of openings go past me before I jump in, and by the time I get up nerve enough to jump out again I'm right back in the street where I started. It's the same with golf. I'm giving it up because these modern golf balls they sell are so hard to pick up when I stoop over. I've had to quit driving, too; the restrooms lately in filling stations are getting farther and farther apart. Usually I just stay home at night and read the papers, particularly the obituary columns. It's funny how much more interesting the obituary columns have been getting lately.

Even the weather is changing. It's colder in winter, and the summers are hotter than they used to be. I'd go away, if it wasn't so far. Snow is heavier when I try to shovel it, and I have to put on rubbers whenever I go out, because rain today is wetter than the rain we used to get. Drafts are more severe, too. It must be the way they build windows now.

People are changing, too. For one thing, they're younger than they used to be when I was their age. I went back recently to an alumni reunion at the college I graduated from in 1943 — that is, 1933 — I mean, 1923 — and I was shocked to see the mere tots they're admitting as students these days. The average age of the freshman class couldn't have been more than seven. They seem to be more polite than in my time, though; several under-graduates called me "Sir," and one of them asked me if he could help me across the street.

On the other hand, people my own age are so much older than I am. I realize that my generation is approaching middle age (I define middle age roughly as the period between twenty-one and 110), but there is no excuse for my classmates tottering into a state of advanced senility. I ran into my old roommate at the bar, and he'd changed so much that he didn't recognize me. "You've put on a little weight, George," I said.

"It's this modern food," George said. "It seems to be more fattening."

"How about another martini?" I said. "Have you noticed how much weaker the martinis are these days?"

"Everything is different," said George. "Even the food you get. It's more fattening."

"How long since I've seen you, George?" I said. "It must be several years."

"I think the last time was right after the election," said George.

"What election was that?"

George thought for a moment. "Harding."

I ordered a couple more martinis. "Have you noticed these martinis are weaker than they used to be?" I said.

"It isn't like the good old days," George said. "Remember when we'd go down to the speak, and order some orange blossoms, and maybe pick up a couple of flappers. Boy, could they neck! Hot diggety!"

"You used to be quite a cake-eater, George," I said. "Do you still do the Black Bottom?"

"I put on too much weight," said George. "This food nowadays seems to be more fattening."

"I know," I said, "you mentioned that just a minute ago."

"Did I?" said George.

"How about another martini?" I said. "Have you noticed the martinis aren't as strong as they used to be?"

"Yes," said George, "you said that twice before."

"Oh," I said . . .

I got to thinking about poor old George while I was shaving this morning, and I stopped for a moment and looked at my own reflection in the mirror.

They don't seem to use the same kind of glass in mirrors anymore.

THE TIME OF LAUGHTER

December 5, 1933, was as festive an occasion as New Year's Eve. Utah had become the thirty-sixth and final state needed to ratify the Twenty-first Amendment, the Prohibition law was revoked, and New York's speakeasies swung their doors open for the first time since 1920. No more basement bells, no more sliding panels, no more thirteen-year-old air. Drinks on the house, boys. Ring out the old era, ring in the new.

That night Jim Moriarty gave a mammoth cocktail party to celebrate repeal. He had moved recently from "109" to the Marlborough House at 15 East 61st Street, next door to Mrs. Payson's town residence. The fashionable address, the marble foyer and broad winding stairs, the crystal chandeliers and rich carpeting were no more elegant than Jim himself, tall and suave and impeccably dressed, mingling affably with his guests and dispensing champagne and caviar with the prodigality of a real-life Gatsby.

All the old Moriarty crowd was on hand. Frank Sullivan and Russel Crouse and Alison Smith. Heywood Broun and Harold Ross. Alva Johnston, a cigarette twitching and occasionally leaping from his long nervous fingers. F.P.A. downing his martini in a single gulp as if it were medicine. Prince Mike Romanoff, still just a jump ahead of the law. (The immigration officers had tracked him to Marlborough House once, but friends lowered him to safety in the dumbwaiter.) Deems Taylor. Marc Connelly. Edna Ferber and George and Beatrice Kaufman. Don Stewart and Mr. Benchley at a table with Mrs. Parker, demure as a kitten, her claws sheathed.

A gala gathering; but somehow the merriment seemed a little forced, the clink of glasses had a hollow ring. Perhaps we sensed, that night of repeal, that more than Prohibition had died, that a whole way of life was gone forever. Within a few months Marlborough House, like most of the taverns of the twenties, would be shuttered and silent, deserted by former patrons who would flock instead to gaudy new nightclubs and hotel cocktail lounges. The Golden Age of Humor, uninhibited and irreverent, had drawn to a close; the party was over. Later that evening John Held, Jr. strolled over to join our table. He had set the pattern for the Jazz Age, and it seemed fitting that he should be here to see it end . . .

Overnight the saxophones stilled, the Black Bottom halted in mid-swing, the laughter was stifled. The climate of the thirties was more serious, more responsible. The stock market crash, the Depression years, the bank closings had jolted the country out of its complacency. Hitler was already casting his long chill shadow across the decade, and there was an increasing sense of tension, of foreboding.

As the national mood sobered, the demand for humor declined. The comic magazines had ridden out the Wall Street typhoon, but now they foundered one by one: *College Humor*, then *Vanity Fair*, scuttled by Condé Nast; then *Life*, taken over for salvage by the Luce empire; then *Judge*; then, after a brief meteoric career, Norman Anthony's *Ballyhoo*. Only *The New Yorker* remained, but its high standard of excellence discouraged young writers, and the lengthy articles and stories and departments left little space for experimenting with unknowns, as Ross had done in the days when White and Thurber and Gibbs were testing their wings. The comedy market was drying up. Back in the twenties, Don Marquis and F.P.A. had run contributions by unknowns, and their columns had served as a breeding ground for burgeoning talent; but they were gone, and no similar outlets had taken their place. Slowly but surely the production of humor dwindled, and so did the producers. Ross observed sadly, shortly before his death in 1951, "Not one genuine new humorist has emerged in this country since the middle thirties."

Frank Sullivan, writing in *The New York Times Book Review*, wondered whether the dearth of new fun-makers might be due to what he called "the Moola factor," by which promising young humorists, along with other kinds of promising young writers, are lured into writing for radio, television, or Hollywood by the promise of vast sums of moola, bigger messes of pottage, more imposing gastric ulcers, and anxiety neuroses designed to astound psychoanalysts at a distance of thirty couches . . . No wonder young writers trembling on the verge of becoming humorists think twice and then take a job at $500 a week writing gags for Uncle Milty or Bob Hope. You cannot blame them for trying to collect the maximum dividends on their talents. In the world we live in, they owe it to themselves to earn enough to provide their wives and kiddies with the best bomb shelters money can buy."

There is another reason, Sullivan suggested. Humorists are edgy about seeming frivolous in these troubled times. Their fun-making might be considered trivial and in bad taste, a sort of fiddling while Rome burns; and they try to avoid public reproach by packing a message of Social Significance into their comedy — a worthy ambition, but disastrous to humor. Their feeling of inferiority is understandable, for we tend to regard our comedians with contempt. "The world . . . decorates its serious artists with laurel," as E.B. White wrote, "and its wags with Brussels sprouts." And Bennett Cerf adds, "We've never given any of our serious prizes to a humorist — the Pulitzer Prize, the National Book Award, the great international Nobel Prize. Somehow the honors never go to the people who make other people laugh."

Whatever the reason, I miss the comedy of the twenties, and the great comedians whom I knew and loved. F.P.A.'s gruff and pithy comments. Mr. Benchley's generous laugh. The solemn clowning of Ring Lardner, the sweet sad humor of Don Marquis, W.C. Fields's snarling asides (I wonder if any modern producer would have the courage to film that defiant and larcenous old rogue), the pantomime of Buster Keaton. Most of all I miss the incisive satire and parody that used to level its lance against contemporary targets, pricking pretensions, deflating stuffed shirts. I've tried my own hand at parody over the years, but I think it is done best by younger writers. Where are they? When will a new generaiton of comedians grab the torch from the gnarled hands of yesterday's funnymen as they toddle off to what Frank Sullivan calls the Petroleum V. Nasby Home for Aged and Infirm Humorists?

For we need humor today, as we have never needed it before. I mean the warm and clean and graceful fun of the Golden Decade, the sense of nonsense which would give this careening world of ours some sanity and balance. Now, if ever, is a time for laughter.

PART III

THE ROAD TO TINKHAMTOWN

It was a long way, but he knew where he was going. He would follow the road through the woods and over the crest of a hill and down the hill to the stream, and cross the sagging timbers of the bridge, and on the other side would be the place called Tinkhamtown. He was going back to Tinkhamtown.

He walked slowly at first, his legs dragging with each step. He had not walked for almost a year, and his flanks had shriveled and wasted away from lying in bed so long; he could fit his fingers around his thigh. Doc Towle had said he would never walk again, but that was Doc for you, always on the pessimistic side. Why, now he was walking quite easily, once he had started. The strength was coming back into his legs, and he did not have to stop for breath so often. He tried jogging a few steps, just to show he could, but he slowed again because he had a long way to go.

It was hard to make out the old road, choked with alders and covered by matted leaves, and he shut his eyes so he could see it better. He could always see it when he shut his eyes. "Yes, here was the beaver dam on the right, just as he remembered it, and the flooded stretch where he had picked his way from hummock to hummock while the dog splashed unconcernedly in front of him. The water had been over his boot tops in one place,

[343]

and sure enough, as he waded it now his left boot filled with water again, the same warm squidgy feeling. Everything was the way it had been that afternoon, nothing had changed in ten years. Here was the blowdown across the road that he had clambered over, and here on a knoll was the clump of thornapples where a grouse had flushed as they passed. Shad had wanted to look for it, but he had whistled him back. They were looking for Tinkhamtown.

He had come across the name on a map in the town library. He used to study the old maps and survey charts of the state; sometimes they showed where a farming community had flourished a century ago, and around the abandoned pastures and in the orchards grown up to pine the birds would be feeding undisturbed. Some of his best grouse covers had been located that way. The map had been rolled up in a cardboard cylinder; it crackled with age as he spread it out. The date was 1857. It was the sector between Cardigan and Kearsarge Mountains, a wasteland of slash and second-growth timber without habitation today, but evidently it had supported a number of families before the Civil War. A road was marked on the map, dotted with X's for homesteads, and the names of the owners were lettered beside them: Nason, J. Tinkham, Allard, R. Tinkham. Half the names were Tinkham. In the center of the map — the paper was so yellow that he could barely make it out — was the word "Tinkhamtown."

He had drawn a rough sketch on the back of an envelope, noting where the road left the highway and ran north to a fork and then turned east and crossed a stream that was not even named; and the next morning he and Shad had set out together to find the place. They could not drive very far in the jeep, because washouts had gutted the roadbed and laid bare the ledges and boulders. He had stuffed the sketch in his hunting-coat pocket, and hung his shotgun over his forearm and started walking, the setter trotting ahead with the bell on his collar tinkling. It was an old-fashioned sleighbell, and it had a thin silvery note that echoed through the woods like peepers in the spring. He could follow the sound in the thickest cover, and when it stopped he would go to where he heard it last and Shad would be on point. After Shad's death, he had put the bell away. He'd never had another dog.

It was silent in the woods without the bell, and the way was longer than he remembered. He should have come to the big hill by now. Maybe he'd taken the wrong turn back at the fork. He thrust a hand into his hunting coat; the envelope with the sketch was still in the pocket. He sat down on a flat rock to get his bearings, and then he realized, with a surge of excitement, that he had stopped on this very rock for lunch ten years ago. Here was the waxed paper from his sandwich, tucked in a crevice, and here was the hollow in the leaves where Shad had stretched out beside him, the dog's soft muzzle flattened on his thigh. He looked up, and through the trees he could see the hill.

He rose and started walking again, carrying his shotgun. He had left the gun standing in its rack in the kitchen when he had been taken to the state hospital, but now it was hooked over his arm by the trigger guard; he could feel the solid heft of it. The woods grew more dense as he climbed, but here and there a shaft of sunlight slanted through the trees. "And there were forests ancient as the hills," he thought, "enfolding sunny spots of greenery." Funny that should come back to him now; he hadn't read it since he was a boy. Other things were coming back to him, the smell of dank leaves and sweetfern and frosted apples, the sharp contrast of sun and cool shade, the November stillness before snow. He walked faster, feeling the excitement swell within him.

He paused on the crest of the hill, straining his ears for the faint mutter of the stream below him, but he could not hear it because of the voices. He wished they would stop talking, so he could hear the stream. Someone was saying his name over and over, "Frank, Frank," and he opened his eyes reluctantly and looked up at his sister. Her face was worried, and there was nothing to worry about. He tried to tell her where he was going, but when he moved his lips the words would not form. "What did you say, Frank?" she asked, bending her head lower. "I don't understand." He couldn't make the words any clearer, and she straightened and said to Doc Towle: "It sounded like Tinkhamtown."

"Tinkhamtown?" Doc shook his head. "Never heard him mention any place by that name."

He smiled to himself. Of course he'd never mentioned it to Doc. Things like a secret grouse cover you didn't mention to anyone, not even to as close a friend as Doc was. No, he and Shad were the only ones who knew. They had found it together, that long ago afternoon, and it was their secret.

They had come to the stream — he shut his eyes so he could see it again — and Shad had trotted across the bridge. He had followed more cautiously, avoiding the loose planks and walking along a beam with his shotgun held out to balance himself. On the other side of the stream the road mounted steeply to a clearing in the woods, and he halted before the split-stone foundations of a house, the first of the series of farms shown on the map.

It must have been a long time since the building had fallen in; the cottonwoods growing in the cellar hole were twenty, maybe thirty years old. His boot overturned a rusted ax blade and the handle of a china cup in the grass; that was all. Beside the doorstep was a lilac bush, almost as tall as the cottonwoods. He thought of the wife who had set it out, a little shrub then, and the husband who had chided her for wasting time on such frivolous things with all the farm work to be done. But the work had come to nothing, and still the lilac bloomed each spring, the one thing that had survived.

Shad's bell was moving along the stone wall at the edge of the clearing, and he strolled after him, not hunting, wondering about the people who had gone away and left their walls to crumble and their buildings to collapse under the winter snows. Had they ever come back to Tinkhamtown? Were they here now, watching him unseen? His toe stubbed against a block of hewn granite hidden by briars, part of the sill of the old barn. Once it had been a tight barn, warm with cattle steaming in their stalls, rich with the blend of hay and manure and harness leather. He liked to think of it the way it was; it was more real than this bare rectangle of blocks and the emptiness inside. He's always felt that way about the past. Doc used to argue that what's over is over, but he would insist Doc was wrong. Everything is the way it was, he'd tell Doc. The past never changes. You leave it and go on to the present, but it is still there, waiting for you to come back to it.

He had been so wrapped in his thoughts that he had not realized Shad's bell had stopped. He hurried across the clearing, holding his gun ready. In a corner of the stone wall an ancient apple tree had littered the ground with fallen fruit, and beneath it Shad was standing motionless. The white fan of his tail was lifted a little and his backline was level, the neck craned forward, one foreleg cocked. His flanks were trembling with the nearness of grouse, and a thin skein of drool hung from his jowls. The dog did not move as he approached, but the brown eyes rolled back until their whites showed, looking for him. "Steady, boy," he called. His throat was tight, the way it always got when Shad was on point, and he had to swallow hard. "Steady, I'm coming."

"I think his lips moved just now," his sister's voice said. He did not open his eyes, because he was waiting for the grouse to get up in front of Shad, but he knew Doc Towle was looking at him. "He's sleeping," Doc said after a moment. "Maybe you better get some sleep yourself, Mrs. Duncombe." He heard Doc's heavy footsteps cross the room. "Call me if there's any change," Doc said, and closed the door, and in the silence he could hear his sister's chair creaking beside him, her silk dress rustling regularly as she breathed.

What was she doing here, he wondered. Why had she come all the way from California to see him? It was the first time they had seen each other since she had married and moved out West. She was his only relative, but they had never been very close; they had nothing in common, really. He heard from her now and then, but it was always the same letter: Why didn't he sell the old place, it was too big for him now that the folks had passed on, why didn't he take a small apartment in town where he wouldn't be alone? But he liked the big house, and he wasn't alone, not with Shad. He had closed off all the other rooms and moved into the kitchen so everything would be handy. His sister didn't approve of his bachelor ways, but it was very comfortable with his cot by the stove and Shad curled on the floor near him at night, whinnying and scratching the linoleum with his claws as he chased a bird in a dream. He wasn't alone when he heard that.

He had never married. He had looked after the folks as long as they lived; maybe that was why. Shad was his family. They were always together — Shad was short for Shadow — and there was a closeness between them that he did not feel for anyone else, not his sister or Doc even. He and Shad used to talk without words, each knowing what the other was thinking, and they could always find one another in the woods. He still remembered the little things about him: the possessive thrust of his jaw, the way he false-yawned when he was vexed, the setter stubbornness sometimes, the clownish grin when they were going hunting, the kind eyes. That was it: Shad was the kindest person he had ever known.

They had not hunted again after Tinkhamtown. The old dog had stumbled several times, walking back to the jeep, and he had to carry him in his arms the last hundred yards. It was hard to realize he was gone. He liked to think of him the way he was; it was like the barn, it was more real than the emptiness. Sometimes at night, lying awake with the pain in his legs, he would hear the scratch of claws on the linoleum, and he would turn on the light and the hospital room would be empty. But when he turned the light off he would hear the scratching again, and he would be content and drop off to sleep, or what passed for sleep in these days and nights that ran together without dusk or dawn.

Once he asked Doc point-blank if he would ever get well. Doc was giving him something for the pain, and he hesitated a moment and finished what he was doing and cleaned the needle and then looked at him and said: "I'm afraid not, Frank." They had grown up in town together, and Doc knew him too well to lie. "I'm afraid there's nothing to do." Nothing to do but lie here and wait till it was over. "Tell me, Doc," he whispered, for his voice wasn't very strong, "what happens when it's over?" And Doc fumbled with the catch of his black bag and closed it and said well he supposed you went on to someplace else called the Hereafter. But he shook his head; he always argued with Doc. "No, it isn't someplace else," he told him. "It's someplace you've been where you want to be again." Doc didn't understand, and he couldn't explain it any better. He knew what he meant, but the shot was taking effect and he was tired.

He was tired now, and his legs ached a little as he started down the hill, trying to find the stream. It was too dark under the trees to see the sketch he had drawn, and he could not tell direction by the moss on the north side of the trunks. The moss grew all around them, swelling them out of size, and huge blowdowns blocked his way. Their upended roots were black and misshapen, and now instead of excitement he felt a surge of panic. He floundered through a pile of slash, his legs throbbing with pain as the sharp points stabbed him, but he did not have the strength to get to the other side and he had to back out again and circle. He did not know where he was going. It was getting late, and he had lost the way.

There was no sound in the woods, nothing to guide him, nothing but his sister's chair creaking and her breath catching now and then in a dry sob. She wanted him to turn back, and Doc wanted him to, they all wanted him to turn back. He thought of the big house; if he left it alone it would fall in with the winter snows and cottonwoods would grow in the cellar hole. And there were all the other doubts, but most of all there was the fear. He was afraid of the darkness, and being alone, and not knowing where he was going. It would be better to turn around and go back. He knew the way back.

And then he heard it, echoing through the woods like peepers in the spring, the thin silvery tinkle of a sleighbell. He started running toward it, following the sound down the hill. His legs were strong again, and he hurdled the blowdowns, he leapt over fallen logs, he put one fingertip on a pile of slash and sailed over it like a grouse skimming. He was getting nearer and the sound filled his ears, louder than a thousand church bells ringing, louder than all the choirs in the sky, as loud as the pounding of his heart. The fear was gone; he was not lost. He had the bell to guide him now.

He came to the stream, and paused for a moment at the bridge. He wanted to tell them he was happy, if they only knew how happy he was, but when he opened his eyes he could not see them anymore. Everything else was bright, but the room was dark.

The bell had stopped, and he looked across the stream. The other side was bathed in sunshine, and he could see the road mounting steeply, and the clearing in the woods, and the apple tree in a corner of the stone wall. Shad was standing, motionless beneath it, the white fan of his tail lifted, his neck craned forward and one foreleg cocked. The whites of his eyes showed as he looked back, waiting for him.

"Steady," he called, "steady, boy." He started across the bridge. "I'm coming."